"Jean Rabe is a helluva story...

Gallant-Stallion has found his charge, a young girl by the name of Kalantha, whose brother is soon to be king and the pawn of a deceitful and murderous bishop who covets the royal power and has allied himself with creatures of the dark arts. The Finest has successfully removed her from his influence but now must contend with the other temptations of the world—the lure of power, the mystery of learning and knowledge, and the intrigue and freedom of adventure and independence.

Kalantha is still young and bitter over her lot in life, betrayed, envious, and scared, and her mentor, Gallant-Stallion, is unsure of how to lead her, as is his duty as her Finest.

On *The Finest Creation*

"Rabe's fun, galloping romp of a story launches a new fantasy series. . . . Rabe (*Redemption* and other titles in the Dragonlance series) deftly puts some beguiling twists on the guardian-angel theme. The rearing steed on the jacket will signal young horse lovers that this is a book for them."

—*Publishers Weekly*

"The author of several novels set in Wizards of the Coast's 'Forgotten Realms' setting has created her own world and populated it with vibrant characters both human and animal."

—*Library Journal*

LOGAN-HOCKING
COUNTY DISTRICT LIBRARY
230 E. MAIN STREET
LOGAN, OHIO 43138

TOR BOOKS BY JEAN RABE

The Finest Creation
The Finest Choice

The Finest Choice

JEAN RABE

A Tom Doherty Associates Book New York

NOTE: If you purchased this book without a cover, you should be aware that this book is stolen property. It was reported as "unsold and destroyed" to the publisher, and neither the author nor the publisher has received any payment for this "stripped book."

This is a work of fiction. All the characters and events portrayed in this book are either products of the author's imagination or are used fictitiously.

THE FINEST CHOICE

Copyright © 2005 by Jean Rabe

All rights reserved, including the right to reproduce this book, or portions thereof, in any form.

Edited by Brian Thomsen

A Tor Book
Published by Tom Doherty Associates, LLC
175 Fifth Avenue
New York, NY 10010

www.tor.com

Tor® is a registered trademark of Tom Doherty Associates, LLC.

ISBN-13: 978-0-765-34728-2
ISBN-10: 0-765-34728-8

First edition: September 2005
First mass market edition: September 2006

Printed in the United States of America

0 9 8 7 6 5 4 3 2 1

FOR BRUCE,

my finest choice

Acknowledgments

Several people helped make *The Finest Choice*—and me—look good. Thanks to Tom Doherty, for taking a chance on my horses; to Natasha Panza, for being so pleasant to deal with on proofs and galleys; to Madeleine George, my excellent copy editor, for catching things my eyes aren't able to notice; and to Brian Thomsen, editor and friend, for making me a better writer.

The Finest Choice

Prologue

When first you look, the people of Paard-Peran appear as varied and beautiful as the flowers in a well-tended garden. The colors are remarkable, and each one catches and holds the eye. But if you study that garden closely, with the keen senses of a Finest, you'll discover that amid the glorious blooms, there are thriving, deep-rooted weeds.

~The Old Mare, from the chronicles of her first visit

Meven stood in front of a full-length beveled mirror, shoulders back and chin tipped slightly up, eyes narrowing as he scrutinized every inch of himself.

There were scratches on his face and hands—from getting caught last night in the middle of a flock of malicious, deadly birds. Several minutes ago a maid had applied a creamy powder that covered up most of the marks. There were the faintest cracks in the powder, but Meven suspected no one would get close enough today to notice.

"Do you think I look kingly?"

"Indeed, Sire Montoll. Most kingly—and handsome!"

"Well, I don't think so. I think I look . . . blue." Meven's normally honeyed voice was laced with brittle annoyance. "This outfit is simply too bright . . . Gerald, is it?"

A nod from the attendant.

"Gerald, I asked for something in grays or black. Maybe I

asked for something brown. Maybe. I certainly would not have said blue. And I certainly would not have requested something quite so . . . fancy. By all the gods, I look like a peacock, not a man about to be crowned King of Galmier."

One more glance in the mirror, then he sadly shook his head and stood to the mirror's side so he could no longer see himself. "A peacock, I say!"

Meven's doublet was fashioned of quilted linen that had been stuffed with the finest cotton, effusively embroidered with swirling vines and heart-shaped leaves, and then dyed a brilliant cerulean. It had a white neckline rimmed in pearls that was high and stiff and newly fashionable—"Scratchy and wholly uncomfortable," Meven had pronounced it.

Padded shoulders helped his thin frame appear more substantial. Sleeves extending to just below his elbows were trimmed with more pearls and with thick, shiny ribbons he thought unduly feminine. With this he wore long, tight hose that were a few shades lighter than the doublet and perfectly matched the color of a voluminous cloak that draped to his ankles. The cloak was wool, welcome in this weather, and was lined with an imported ivory material that he'd been told the name of and had subsequently forgotten, and that made a soft and bothersome shushing sound every time he moved.

"Too bright, I say again! Not acceptable." He shook his head and made a hissing sound. "Kalantha would like this, though."

The attendant shifted nervously back and forth on the balls of his feet and raised an eyebrow in question.

"Kal . . . Kalantha is my sister. You've not met her, Gerald, and you won't meet her today. I doubt very much that she'll be at my coronation." *Because I frightened her away*, he added to himself. "She likes colorful clothes. Colorful bugs. Colorful anything. Ribbons. Yes, I'm sure she would like this . . .

dandy . . . outfit." Meven thrust two slender fingers inside the front of his collar and tugged, trying to stretch the fabric. All he succeeded in doing was pulling loose a few pearls that hit the marble floor with soft pings and sent the attendant scurrying after them. "All these ribbons and stitches. Ugh. Not acceptable. Not acceptable. Not acceptable!"

Gerald cupped the errant pearls in the palm of his hand, looking uncertain what to do with them and more uncertain what to do about the situation. Finally, he offered: "The garment fits someone of your high rank and young age, and the dyes are very expensive. The clothes are most valuable and extraordinary."

"My age. My *young* age." Meven's perturbed expression grew darker. "I'm fourteen, you know, Gerald. But I will be fifteen next week. I will be the youngest King of Galmier. The youngest king in all the world, I'd wager." Softer, he added: "And hopefully the best."

Meven was tall for his years, nearly six feet, with a face all angles and planes and with dark brown hair that had been expertly styled to rest at the tops of his ears, slanting down from there to settle at the base of his neck. His eyes were also dark brown, nearly black, and normally they seemed empty or unreadable. This morning, however, they flashed with ire.

"And the King of Galmier should be able to wear what he wants, don't you think, Gerald? Dark colors, I told them. I have plenty of dark things in my closets, and I'll find something in there before I wear this to my coronation. My gray velvet tunic perhaps. I don't believe I've worn that in public before."

The only new articles of clothing Meven seemed to approve of this morning were soft, black leather slippers and a leather belt, also black, that was studded with carved wooden beads for counting prayers and had been given to him by the Bishop. Doeskin gloves were tucked under the belt at his back where they couldn't be seen. He considered putting them on, as his hands were pink from the chill air blowing in through the window. It was the end of fall, and the air was crisp and carried with it the fusty scent of dead grass and rotting leaves and the welcome sound of the crowd forming outside on the palace grounds.

He reached for the gloves, then stopped himself. The gloves would cover up the rings he so admired, two on each hand. They were thick gold bands of exquisite workmanship, set with large sapphires, emeralds, and rubies. One was more impressive than the others, and this he wore on the first finger of his right hand. It had been his uncle's, reworked to fit him, and festooned at his request with two small pear-shaped diamonds.

"In memory of my uncle, the former King of Galmier, and his son Prince Edan," Meven had told the jeweler. "Those two little diamonds look like tears, don't you think? Like I'm mourning them. Showing my respect."

The jeweler had replied with a polite nod.

Meven wore other baubles. Three gold chains of varying lengths draped around his neck. A flashy brooch in the shape of a stag's head, the eyes perfect fire opals, served as a cloak clasp. There was an armband of hammered gold that was etched with the Montoll family crest and that had been made for Prince Edan, though he'd never had the opportunity to wear it.

"I like dark clothes," Meven repeated. "The tailor knows that." He made a huffing sound, and the attendant shivered nervously.

"Sire . . . I . . ."

"Black and grays. Like the Bishop wears. And the acolytes from the Temple of High Keep where I used to live. I miss that place, Gerald." A whisper: "And I miss Kal. I should not have scared her away, shouldn't have said she had to go to Dea Fortress." He sucked in a breath and raised his voice again. "Dark clothes, and for the most part, simple. People should pay attention to the man, not what he wears—I was taught that. Listen to him, not always be looking at him."

"I understand, Sire . . . ."

"Then help me change, Gerald. I won't be a peacock strutting on a stage when I'm crowned."

"Yes, Sire."

There was the sound of another man clearing his throat. "That won't be necessary, Gerald." The words were thin and melodious, and there was power behind them that made the attendant pause. "King Meven will wear that blue outfit. It was made just for his coronation."

Meven turned to see Bishop DeNogaret glide to the middle of the room. The elderly priest waggled his fingers to dismiss the attendant, and then smoothed at the folds of his ash-colored robe as he remained silent until Gerald's retreating footsteps faded to nothingness.

The Bishop locked eyes with Meven. "Those are my colors you wear today. The same as my guards wear on their surcoats and tabards, the same as is on the pennants that hang from the Nadir Temple and the High Keep Temple, the same as is on the silk cloths that drape the altars." The Bishop's skeletal fingers dropped to the sash at his waist, the blues on it precisely matching the shades in Meven's outfit. *"My colors."*

Meven's face instantly reddened and he tucked his chin to his neck. "My deepest apologies, Bishop DeNogaret. I—I—I paid no attention. I am deeply honored to wear your colors, ashamed that I didn't notice. By all the good gods of Paard-Peran, please forgive me." His face managed to redden even further, and his thumbs rubbed furiously at the wooden beads on his belt as if they were worry stones. "This outfit is beautiful, Bishop DeNogaret. I—I—I'm just not used to . . ."

"Bright colors. I know, Meven." The Bishop allowed a few moments of silence to slip between them. Then he stepped forward and rested a hand on Meven's shoulder. "But today is a day like no other. Today you will be formally crowned King of Galmier. Let the people see you sparkle like an ornament. You wear this outfit for them."

Meven nodded and slowly raised his head, his eyes fixed on the Bishop's narrow mouth this time, not wanting to meet what he feared might be an icy stare. "It truly had not dawned on me that these colors are yours." His fingers brushed the spot where he'd tugged the pearls free. "I am honored, Bishop DeNogaret," he repeated. "Blessed to wear them."

The Bishop seemed not to have heard the last bit from Meven, and was no longer looking at him. He was gazing beyond the youth and out the window, at a sky that had turned pale gray and was threatening rain. A few beams of light poked through gaps in the clouds, shining down like divine silvery beacons. The breeze grew colder still in the passing of a few heartbeats, and from somewhere out on the palace lawn came faint music, no doubt a minstrel entertaining the growing crowd. The threatening weather was not keeping the townsfolk at home. Coronations were rare and storied events and would likely bring out the entire populace—could bring out the entire city since this was taking place on the lawn and there was room for them.

"The people need you to look royal and important, Meven," the Bishop said after a few more moments had passed and the minstrel finished his tune and began another. "They just lost the man who led them for many, many years. Your uncle was beloved by these people, and they grieve for his passing. But you will give them cause to celebrate."

Meven's gaze remained fixed on the Bishop's mouth. "I want to be a good ruler, Bishop DeNogaret."

"Of course you do."

"Just and kind, wise and . . ."

"And I will help you, Meven."

"I could not do this without you, Bishop DeNogaret."

"I know." The Bishop nudged Meven to the window. The elderly priest seemed unaffected by the nippy air that raised goosebumps on Meven's hands and face. The Bishop gestured to the throng of people standing and sitting on the palace lawn, and to the line streaming in through the west gate. Bundled in coats and blankets, they had arrived early to garner the best spot to watch the festivities.

Meven had never seen so many people in one place.

"I would not *want* to do this without you, Bishop DeNogaret," Meven said. "With Kal gone, you're the only family I have left."

1 · Alone Together

The world was born perfect, my mother told me. But the people crawling across its rocky surface and navigating its seas are, for the most part, flawed~avaricious, needful, prideful, never satisfied. Still, there are some among them worthy of salvation, she claimed. And for these the Finest Creations are intended.

~Nimblegait, first foal of the Old Mare

The horse was the color of wet clay, with a slightly lighter blaze running from between his ears to just short of his black muzzle. He had a coarse mane and tail as dark as the mud puddles he was tromping through, and he had none of the attractive feathering around his legs that most of the horses from the north displayed. Called a suffolk-punch, or simply a punch, he was considered an "old breed," who traced his line back more than a thousand years and had been used primarily for farming and hauling timber.

His sturdy legs looked overly short for his massive body and powerful quarters. He had a large head with kind, expressive eyes; a thick, muscular neck; and a deep, broad chest that was crisscrossed with cuts from a flock of birds he'd fought off.

He was not a pretty horse, not compared to the magnificent mares and stallions that were warm and dry in the royal stables on the palace grounds in Nadir—where he'd been staying until yesterday. But he was a strong creature, and despite being terribly weary, he continued to plod through the marshy land many miles south of where Meven Montoll was about to be crowned King of Galmier.

Meven's sister sat astride the punch's wide back, leaning against his neck. Kalantha had fought sleep all of last night and this morning. It had only recently claimed her. She slept soundly now, despite the rain that fell gently, and so the punch chose what appeared to be the most level course, keeping his gait slow and regular now so she wouldn't be disturbed.

Though cold, the rain felt good against the punch's hide and gave him something to listen to. It *rat-a-tat-tatted* softly against the branches and oak leaves and downed logs he navigated around. It echoed faintly when it thrummed against puddles that dotted the ground as far as he could see. There were few paths to follow where the water didn't come up above his hooves. The horse gathered it had been raining on and off here for many days, the ground too saturated to soak up any more water.

The punch had been traveling with the girl since late the previous evening. At first he galloped, trying to get her far away from the palace as quickly as possible. He didn't slow until after well more than an hour, when his sides ached from the effort and when the woods thickened and knobby, exposed roots threatened to trip him and spill her.

A normal horse would have needed rest before now. But the punch wasn't truly a horse—though no person native to this land would see him as anything but. He was called a Finest creation, sculpted by the good powers of Paard-Peran. His kind was charged with secretly guiding and guarding the Fallen Favorites—the select few people who possessed some inner spark that would lead them, and thereby perhaps some of their fellows, to salvation.

"Rue?" The girl on his back stirred. "Where are we, Rue?"

She was the Fallen Favorite he was destined to protect. That this slight girl of twelve years could have any impact on the world seemed doubtful . . . but the Finest was not one to question his mission.

"The sky's awfully dark, Rue, for this time of the day. I think it's going to keep raining forever." She yawned and stuffed her hand against her mouth, shook her head and tipped her face up into the rain. The canopy was denser here, with tall pines, and with plenty of oaks that kept their leaves this late into the fall. And so the rain that made it to the forest floor seemed to bleed slowly from the sky. It grayed the air in front of her and the punch, making it look like they were passing through a veil of smoke.

As she glanced around, she saw a small hawk drop from a branch high overhead and dive on something hiding in a patch of stunted evergreens. Claws outstretched, beak open, its black eyes were as shiny as fresh ink and were fixed on whatever was making the needles of the spreading ground cover quiver. The hawk's movement and sudden cry startled a flock of bluebirds that flew from the cover of a nearby willow, scattering and throwing bits of color into Kalantha's view. She focused on one small bird in particular. It was puffed up and angry-looking, and had settled on a low branch directly ahead, scolding the hawk and Kalantha and the punch for disturbing it. A moment later it flew off, still scolding. The hawk climbed and disappeared in the canopy, a large ground squirrel skewered on its talons.

Kalantha shuddered. "Birds worry me, Rue."

Since she was awake, the punch picked up his pace, managing to find his way around submerged roots when the water deepened to his knees.

"Aren't you tired, Rue? You must be tired. We should stop so you can rest."

He came to a stretch of ground that felt comfortably spongy beneath his hooves, but for the most part was devoid of standing water. He galloped across it, mud and grass flying up behind him. Then he slowed when he reached thin clumps of birch trees at the edge of a large stand of black walnuts.

"Do you know where we are, Rue?" She twined her fingers in his mane and clamped her legs tighter when he vaulted over a fallen river birch and edged deeper into the thickening woods.

Safe, the punch told her finally. *We are safe, Kalantha. And we are thankfully away from the assassin-birds and your brother, Meven. He cannot reach you here. We are to the south in the forest, where the trees cut the cold and the rain. And we are near the river. I can smell it.*

"I can, too," she said, yawning again. "It smells good."

Yes it does, Kalantha.

"Maybe we should go to the river, Rue. I don't think we'd get lost if we followed the river."

I would like that.

The punch's Finest name was Gallant-Stallion. Like other Finest creations that traveled Paard-Peran, he was also given a human name. Meven named him Rue some time ago, referring to him as an ugly, rueful-looking horse. Gallant-Stallion hadn't liked the connotation then, but he didn't mind the name when Kalantha used it. "Rooooo," she pronounced it, the word sounding like a beautiful purr that reminded him of a songbird's sweet call.

Gallant-Stallion angled toward the river. The Sprawling River's tendrils spread like the outstretched fingers of a hand through Galmier and the country to the south. Gallant-Stallion considered the river the best feature of the country, shiny and musical, and following it south was as good as anything to do right now.

The river might keep him from becoming completely lost in these woods.

The sky was turning from gray to green with the onset of afternoon. It was the shade willow leaves take on toward the end of their lives before yellowing and dropping. And its hue hinted that the rains would worsen. A storm was definitely coming, the Finest knew, and the rain that had been falling on and off throughout the day had simply been a prelude.

Gallant-Stallion could smell the water thick in the swollen clouds, the scents of the river and wet tree bark, and sodden fallen leaves and mud and creatures that had drowned and were starting to rot. The river was the most favorable smell, so he brought it to the fore.

Soon he reached a bloated tributary. Small bushes were completely submerged along the banks, and the water was well up the trunks of hickories and maples. Something prickled at him as he watched a catfish circle around the base of a pin oak and then dive deeper out of sight. He set his ears forward.

What? he wondered. *What bothers me? Something I smell? Something I smell and cannot put a name to? It is nothing I hear.* There was the faint rustle of oak leaves, stirred by the falling rain and a slight breeze. The flutter of wings . . . this unnerved him for a moment, but then the sound ceased. It had been only one bird, and not an especially large one. There was the river, sloshing at its muddy banks, wearing away at the earth in an effort to grow wider still. Across the river he could see a road, precariously close to the far bank and looking like a glistening snake weaving amid the stark outlines of birches and honey locusts.

Kalantha slipped from his back and carefully edged toward the water, barely avoiding a tangle of holly. Branches caught at her tunic, and she roughly tugged it free. The clothes were worn and dirty and had belonged to a boy in Nadir's poor quarter. She stole them to replace worse ones she'd been wearing, and had felt bad for it. "But my other clothes were falling apart. I needed these," she'd told Gallant-Stallion yesterday, finding it necessary to justify her thievery to someone.

He watched her cup her hands to drink. Those threadbare clothes were not keeping her warm now, he was certain, and she shouldn't spend another cold, rainy night in them. That would mean finding people who might help her.

After several moments, Gallant-Stallion let the scent of the river fade to the back of his mind, and he tried to stop worrying about his charge. He thought that perhaps he indeed smelled something that was disquieting, something only vaguely familiar. But he still couldn't put a name or an image to it, and now the wind was shifting and he lost whatever it was. He knew it wasn't birds, he'd well committed their various scents to his memory. And so after several more moments he forced himself to relax a little. He stepped forward and dipped his head.

So thirsty. The water so good. He'd traveled so far without stopping.

"I want to go as far south as we can possibly go, Rue." Kalantha was staring across the river, eyes fixed on something far beyond the trees and the opposite bank. "All the way to the Namidir Ocean, I think. Someplace where my brother will never find me. Someplace where . . . oh, Rue, he's the only family I have."

She dropped to her knees and cried then, silently, her shoulders shaking slightly as if she didn't have the energy to grieve properly and forcefully. "My uncle the king, dead to some horrible sickness. My cousin the Prince, dead. Dead to those birds. Dead. Dead. Meven . . . Meven. I'm all alone, Rue," she sobbed. "There's no one left."

Gallant-Stallion watched her. He knew she was an orphan,

her parents having died when she was three. She'd been raised at the High Keep Temple, she and Meven wards of Bishop DeNogaret.

He'd met her and Meven and his Finest mentor, Steadfast, less than two years past when they all traveled with Prince Edan on the way to his royal wedding. It was to be a festive time, but Steadfast and the Prince and his entourage were slain by a band of avian assassins, and Gallant-Stallion was barely able to get Kalantha and Meven to safety.

"I shouldn't have gone to Nadir, Rue," Kalantha was saying. "I should've known my brother would agree with the Bishop, that he would send me to Dea Fortress. Maybe the Fortress is not so bad. And maybe I would've liked it, a religious life. But there are only strangers there. I want it to be my choice."

Bending over the edge of the engorged river, fingers stirring the water, there wasn't enough light to clearly see her reflection, just a shadowy distorted image. "He'll be all right, Meven will. He'll be the King of Galmier before sundown, Rue. I bet it will be a beautiful ceremony. And I bet there will be music and cakes. Lots of sweet treats. I wish I could have seen it." She stirred her image away. "He has soldiers, Rue, and he'll be safe. The birds won't be able to get him. He'll be royal and warm and full. And there'll be none of those wonderful things for me." She paused and rubbed at her eyes. "I don't have anyone."

Gallant-Stallion knew it wasn't like her to give up and wallow in pity. He'd seen her at her best—determined and stubborn and unwilling to give in or give up. Still, she was only twelve, and she was a child, he reminded himself. But she wasn't *childlike*. She was just tired now, worn out physically and emotionally. She was cold and drenched and filled with despair. Let her cry, he told himself.

And in spite of what she said, she wasn't alone. Gallant-Stallion was with her.

2 · Royal Beginnings

That people cannot tell us apart from common horses is understandable. Most of them cannot tell the difference between sweet birch and river birch and hornbeams. To them wrens and dusty finches are all the same little brown birds. Fortunate for us they see horses and not Finest creations. But unfortunate for them they haven't the eyes to truly see the details in all living things.

~Mara, guardian of Bitternut, in a report to the Finest Court

By early afternoon the last trace of the sun had vanished, and the sky looked like a charcoal rubbing. Rain spattered down slowly in cold, fat drops, seeming to blend the colors of the crowd that had gathered on the palace grounds. Someone in the crowd was laughing loud enough for Meven to hear high in his chambers. It was a deep belly laugh, something Meven hadn't experienced in . . . how long? Had he ever? Meven listened to the laugh climb into the dreary sky, and heard others laughing, though not so raucous as the first fellow. Meven wasn't much for humor, as he prided himself on being serious and studious. But he wished he knew what they thought so funny, and he found himself envying them just a little.

He stood by the window until the laughter died down, then he listened hard, trying to pick up bits and snatches of conversations. So many people were talking, their words sounding like the buzz of a swarm of insects. He couldn't discern a single word. He could, however, recognize the tune that the lone, strolling minstrel played. It was one he remembered his mother humming to him. That seemed like such a long, long time ago.

Minutes more, and the music of the minstrel was replaced by the louder strains of a chamber group positioned beneath a large canvas tent. The rain and the first few booms of thunder made the promenade piece they played sound dissonant.

"They're ready for you, Sire," Gerald announced.

Meven faintly hummed the minstrel's tune and tried unsuccessfully to picture his mother's face. Then he turned from the window and followed Gerald out into the hallway.

PERCHED ON THE ELABORATE PLATFORM, CLOTHES AS GRAY AS the clouds and face pale and heavily lined by the years, Bishop DeNogaret addressed the crowd. He expounded on glorious Nadir, capital of Galmier—greatest city and greatest kingdom in all of Paard-Peran, "veritable jewels in the crown of the world." His words rang as poetic as any skald's. There were other speakers, though not as impressive, these coming from the farthest away to attend the event: an ambassador from Uland, the Prince of Kande Digna from across the Esi Sea, the Lord Mayor of Dolour from the country of Vered. They'd all been in Nadir to visit the dying King, and had stayed on for the coronation of the new one.

Then the Bishop took over again.

He praised Galmier's rich history and legendary rulers, touted her fine people and the future, the latter made brighter and more promising by a young, intelligent King. Then, when his voice began to fail from speaking so long, he directed Meven to kneel before him, and he slowly lowered a crown on the young man's head.

The crown was not so ostentatious as the one the previous

monarch wore. While Meven seemed to enjoy jewelry, he was uncomfortable with the massive crown of his uncle. His was simpler, a band of hammered gold, edged in platinum and decorated with a dozen sapphires and diamonds. It was showy, but not extravagant, and he thought it suited him better.

"Meven Montoll," the Bishop intoned. It took effort for his voice to carry, barely cutting above the murmurs of those in the throng who'd become anxious and cold, and certainly not reaching to the back of the audience. "It is my honor to name you the thirty-first King of Galmier. May the gods of Paard-Peran bless your long and glorious reign!"

There was a bright flash of lightning, followed by a shock of thunder that was felt through the ground and the platform. The rain started falling harder.

"An omen, do you think? This loathsome weather?" A visiting Dea Fortress clergyman on the front bench spoke louder than he'd intended.

His fellows responded with head shakes and whispers.

Another flash of lightning.

"Rise, King Meven Montoll," the Bishop continued, seemingly oblivious to the worsening weather. "Rise and greet your people." Bishop DeNogaret turned to the crowd. "I present your liege. Bow before King Meven Montoll of Galmier!"

A cheer went up, starting with those in the front and catching on through the rest of the crowd, the volume surpassing the next boom of thunder. Bishop DeNogaret stepped back and closed his eyes. He listened to the cheers and whoops and applause, the rain pattering on the canvas roof of the platform, to the musicians—the best in Nadir. Barely discernible was the creak of the wood, Meven stepping to the edge of the platform where the rain could reach him.

King Meven offered a smile and raised his arms wide.

He nodded to the visiting clergy and to the Prince of Kande

Digna. He knew he would have to provide more than mere ges-
tures at the reception inside to come. He would have to appear
older than his years and make speeches and mingle and stuff
his face with delicacies he couldn't pronounce and only half of
which he'd likely find palatable. Hopefully he could change
into something dry and darker, something without so many
pearls and ribbons—if the Bishop would not be offended. The
Bishop certainly would not want him to become ill from remaining in drenched clothes.

The musicians began a grand recessional, as Meven continued to soak up the rain and praise and stand squarely before
the visiting dignitaries and the crowd of townsfolk, all of them
shielding their eyes against what was turning into a downpour.
Meven had considered being crowned in the Nadir Temple,
where everything would be dry and where the music would not
be competing with the wind. But Bishop DeNogaret said the
Temple could not hold so many people as would want to attend, and that this was as much a day for the people as it was
for Meven.

Meven hoped Kalantha might sneak onto the grounds to
watch him being crowned. So Meven tolerated the rain, and he
clenched and unclenched his hands in a futile effort to keep them
warm as he scanned the faces, fervently hoping to see his sister.

"Please, Kalantha," he mouthed. "I won't send you away
this time."

He didn't know that the Bishop, too, wanted someone to attend the festivities—a creature that could not do so were the
coronation held inside the Temple.

High on the palace wall to the side of the platform, shielded
beneath the wings of a stone gargoyle, perched a large owl. His
wide golden eyes took everything in, and he softly hooted his
approval of the coronation to a small flock of drenched blackbirds on the roof above him.

Below, the music persisted, still sounding inharmonious accompanied by the growing storm. Suddenly the wind whipped at the musicians' tent and nearly drowned out the strings. Sprigs of evergreen came loose and fluttered over the heads of visiting priests, ribbons ripped free, and the heavy fabric draping the coronation platform flapped like some ponderous bird trying unsuccessfully to take flight.

"An omen, this storm?" the visiting clergyman repeated.

Meven, too, now shielded his eyes with one hand and waved with the other as he continued to survey the people. His cloak twisted in the wind and nearly sent him off balance. He glanced past the luminaries in their expensive, sodden clothes and heavy jewelry, all of them bowing and nodding to him, water running off their hats, cloaks and coats straining to break free. He only recognized a handful of the onlookers. Among the townsfolk he noted a few familiar merchants whose shops he had visited, wealthy landowners whose homes he'd dined at and whose daughters had been introduced to him. His soldiers were stationed at intervals throughout, the rain bouncing off their mail and helmets. Some of the Bishop's men were scattered among the crowd too, the blues of their waving tabards indeed matching the colors in Meven's elaborate coronation outfit. The blues looked much darker now soaked.

The faces he saw were expectant and pleased. Despite the cold and the rain and the wind it seemed that most everyone was happy to be witnessing this royal and historic event. Only some of the children looked uncertain about it all, a few he could see markedly uninterested and uncomfortable, by the tugging on their parents' hands making it clear they wanted to be out of this foul weather.

Meven mused that he was little more than a child himself, and that he was becoming overly cold too, and also would like to be inside. Shivering, he'd wished he'd been crowned in the Nadir Temple after all. It felt like the heart of winter, not fall. And he swore bits of ice were now spitting down amid the raindrops and nipping at his face, threatening to wash off the powdering cream that hid the marks on his face. He wanted to be dry and sitting in front of a fire, reading one of the books Bishop DeNogaret had brought here from the High Keep Temple. He wanted to be dining on warm roast beef and drinking mulled cider . . . alone and away from all these people . . . or maybe with Kalantha.

Meven alternated between glancing to the southwest, where the sky looked as dark as evening, and skimming the faces in the crowd, hoping he might somehow—by some miracle—see her.

"Where is my sister?" Meven said too softly to be heard above the rain. Tears threatened the corners of his eyes. The most important day in his life, and his sister wasn't here to share it with him. "Where in all of this world has Kalantha gone? Why did I chase her away? Where is she?"

There was another bright flash of lightning, then another. The musicians stopped when the thunder made the ground shudder with a greater force this time. The storm grew in intensity, and people closest to the gate began to leave the palace grounds in a hurry.

Moving up to Meven's shoulder again, the Bishop continued to smile and politely gesture to the dignitaries, who were now looking wholly miserable in the deluge.

To the elderly priest there was nothing at all dismal about this day.

3 · The Hungry Woods

No creature is more blessed than a Finest. No creature can appreciate the perfect pastures of the Court and at the same time find beauty in the world of the Fallen Favorites.

~Patience, Finest Court Matriarch

Gallant-Stallion studied the trees on the far side of the river. Most of them had shed their leaves or needles. A scattering of pines, oaks, and a few sugar maples in the distance were the only exceptions. At first glance the branches looked hastily sketched against the canvas of a storm-threatening sky. But to the Finest's eyes, the scene was an intricately rendered piece of artwork, and he found the stark-looking trees every bit as interesting as if they were full with summer leaves.

The water was up so high on the trunks of a row of pitch pines and blackgums that the trees' lowest branches were submerged, waving gently in the current, enthralling and relaxing him, and lulling him toward sleep.

He thought the Sprawling River would be moving faster given all the recent rain, but he realized after watching it for a bit longer that it was an old river, certainly not in a hurry to go anywhere despite the power it obviously possessed. It moved at a deliberate pace, happily wearing at its widened banks and slowly swallowing bushes and seedlings that got in its way.

The Finest could tell by marks on nearby trunks that in years past the water had been higher still. In the pastures of the Finest Court the rivers and streams never threatened the trees that cordially shaded the banks. And there were no violent storms or severe weather—at least none that he could ever remember. Everything was idyllic and for the most part predictable. The weather here was far from either of those things.

There was great beauty and peace in the lands of the Finest Court, and Gallant-Stallion found himself missing them terribly. But these lands of Paard-Peran were . . . intriguing, he decided. The swings in temperature, though sometimes uncomfortable, were far from dull. And he was especially enjoying watching the Sprawling River. It continued to calm him, and the mud that oozed around his hooves felt wonderful and added to his growing lethargy. He was so tired, had been awake so long, moving through these woods for hours to get Kalantha farther from the palace in Nadir.

He closed his eyes and listened to the water and the gentle rustling of oak leaves from somewhere above and behind him. Would it hurt to sleep for just a little while?

"I want to find someplace where they've never heard of the Montoll family."

Kalantha had been talking to herself for some time, and the Finest had been so distracted with thoughts of the river, the coming storm, and just simply resting that he'd not been paying attention to her. He'd missed some of what she'd said and scolded himself.

"I don't want people to know that the King of Galmier is my brother. I don't want anyone to know that I'm part of a royal family. I just want to lose myself, Rue."

He slowly opened his eyes again and had to crane his neck

around to see her. She was standing away from the bank now, rubbing her tunic against the rough blue-gray bark of a hornbeam. She was trying to get a smudge of dirt off, but was only wearing the fabric thinner and finally putting a noticeable hole in it.

"I guess I'm not really part of the royal family after all, Rue. If I was . . ." She shook her head. "We'll have to find something to eat soon. I'm so hungry. I bet you're hungry, too. Probably hungrier than I am. My head hurts, and I know it's 'cause I'm so hungry. Maybe we can find a beech tree. My friend Morgan taught me that beechnuts stay well into fall . . . if the birds haven't got them all. Too cold to fish. Too tired to fish. I'm so tired. And I've ruined this." She shook her head again, upset that she'd worn such a large hole in her tunic. "Rue, are you hungry?"

Kalantha looked to the punch, but he was no longer looking at her. He was fixated on the other side of the river, finding something amid the pitch pines and blackgums. It was a gray shape, low to the ground and keeping to the shadows, moving only slightly. Not large, but somehow discomfiting. Gallant-Stallion stared harder, and he flared his nostrils hoping to catch a trace of the animal. The wind changed in that instant, as if to accommodate him, bringing the strong scent of the beast. It was the same scent that had bothered him earlier and that he couldn't place. But he put a name to it now, as the shape edged close to the water and locked its dull yellow eyes with Gallant-Stallion's.

"Aren't you hungry? Tired? Rue . . ."

Wolf, the Finest replied. *There is a wolf across the river.*

Kalantha stepped to his side and stretched a hand up to comb through his mane. "I see it," she said. "It's just one wolf." There was no worry in her voice, only fatigue. "A skinny one, Rue. Hungry like us. Nothing to worry about. He's too far away, and he wouldn't bother us anyway, and certainly wouldn't cross the cold river. But we might want to move on. Just in case. And, besides, there aren't any beech trees here. Aren't you hungry, Rue?"

The wolf chose that moment to throw back its head. It let out a howl, low at first and soft, then growing louder and higher in pitch. It howled again and again, and Gallant-Stallion snapped his head around when he heard the muted crunch of wet, fallen branches behind him.

He cursed himself for being so distracted. For being hypnotized by the river, for dropping his guard, for thinking they were far from the palace and so they were reasonably safe.

"More wolves," Kalantha supplied. She frantically grabbed handfuls of Rue's mane, jumped and pulled herself onto his back.

The Finest snorted loudly and pawed at the wet ground. His breath puffed away from his muzzle in the cool air and added to the grayness of the place, but it did nothing to intimidate the wolves that had crept up behind them.

There were nine in the pack that Gallant-Stallion could see, all in a line like soldiers, lips bared back to reveal yellow-white teeth, all snarling and with heads slightly lowered. Ridges of hair stood up on their backs, and their yellow-gray eyes practically glowed.

Most of them were the color of fog or ashes, with dark patches in the centers of their backs and on the tips of their ears, their noses shiny black. Two were shades of brown, with cream-colored patches on their chests and on their feet, making it look like they were wearing boots. The largest was also the darkest, his coat iron-colored, tipped in black, and with a tail that was oddly the color of snow. His ribs stood out so much that Gallant-Stallion pitied him. But the Finest wasn't about to provide the pack with an easy meal.

"They're all hungry," Kalantha said. There was a touch of panic in her voice now.

Yes, very hungry, the Finest replied.

He could see the hunger in their eyes, evidence that all the recent rains had hurt their hunting. He heard a splash from the river and without looking knew it was the wolf on the other side swimming across. Some of them starving, Gallant-Stallion guessed, else the wolf behind them wouldn't be braving the cold, widened river, and his fellows would not consider a big punch a meal. There was another splash, and a heartbeat later another. More wolves had been on the other side of the river and were swimming across.

Leave us be, Gallant-Stallion told the wolves. Like all Finest, he knew the languages of the beasts of this world. *Let us pass. I do not want to hurt any of you.*

The thinnest wolf, one with bones protruding so pronouncedly it looked painful, snarled and stamped at the mud. His snout was white, and the fur around his eyes was gray, making it look like he wore a mask. *What manner of thing are you? You can speak to us, but you do not wear our skin.*

Others in the pack growled softly.

What are you? an old wolf echoed. This one had a gray stripe down its nose and a mask of white. His sharply pointed ears were edged in black, as if they'd been painted. *A horse you look to be, but not a horse from the smell of you. What are you? Horses do not speak to us.*

One with a left ear ragged from a recent fight edged closer and sniffed. *Smells near to being a horse, my brothers. Smells like a child on his back. Smells like food. Sweet, warm food.*

I am a horse, Gallant-Stallion told them. Not even the creatures of this world were to know about the Finest. *A most powerful horse. I do not want to harm you. And I can so very, very easily harm you.*

"Rue, are you talking to them?" Kalantha was clutching his mane so tightly her fingers were turning white. "Can you tell them to go away?"

He is a thing I have not smelled before in these woods, this big talking horse. This came from a young wolf that seemed not so starved as his fellows. He was the lightest gray of the pack, and there were patches of brown on his face. His eyes were more milky blue than yellow. *He is a curious thing to speak with us. I would talk longer to him were I not so hungry. He will taste good.*

I want only to pass through your woods with this girl, Gallant-Stallion told them. Kalantha was nudging his sides with her heels.

"Rue, get moving."

I want no trouble, Gallant-Stallion continued. He took a few slow steps forward. *I am a visitor here, and I want only . . .*

I want food, said the one with the ragged ear. *My belly burns with hunger.*

Food, repeated the youngest wolf. *My belly burns, too. Burns badly. You would fill it, talking horse. You would fill all our bellies and make glad the carrion that would pick your bones.*

The one that had first spoken moved forward now, still stamping at the ground, tail lowered and twitching. *What manner of thing are you, I ask for the last time? Why should we not feast on you, horse-that-is-not-a-horse? How can you know our tongue?*

Gallant-Stallion realized this bony wolf was likely the eldest in the pack, perhaps the leader. He directed his reply to this one. *I am exactly what you see, a horse. I simply know the tongues of all beasts,* Gallant-Stallion told him. *And, wolf brothers, you are among the most noble beasts in this forest.*

The bony wolf straightened its back in pride.

You are the rulers of these woods, Gallant-Stallion continued. *And I look for your blessings as my companion and I travel south. I am sorry your hunting has been poor. But it will improve. It is the cycle of nature. Again I say that I do not want to hurt any of you.*

And were it spring or summer, I would not want to hurt you, the bony wolf answered. *As you say, hunting is poor and winter comes. One hare today was caught. Only one. Not enough for all of us. The deer are scarce, moving south to the dark woods or falling to the men in the village. Our bellies are so empty they burn, and you give us no reason not to eat you. I am sorry, great horse, but you would fill all of our bellies.* He sprang forward, jaws snapping and regret in his yellowed eyes.

Gallant-Stallion reared back and Kalantha threw her arms around his neck. She clamped her legs tight when his front hooves slammed against the earth and mud and dead moss flew up. Then he bolted forward, straight at the wolves that were running toward him.

Within a heartbeat he was past the pack, and he thought he was running free of all of them. He angled for a game trail, where it would be easier going and where the branches would not be so close and would not grab at him and Kalantha. But there were more wolves racing at him, coming from the north, a half dozen he could see, maybe two or three more than that judging by the thrashing in the brush. The pack was bigger than he'd first thought, and they'd initially hid their numbers.

He paused, and paid the price. The wolves behind him were catching up—at least some of them. One was leaping at the Finest, slathering jaws nipping at his rear legs and claws tearing at his haunches. He felt the flesh of his haunch rip, a more painful sensation than the slashing talons of the black birds he'd fought last night. Blood was running down his back leg, the warm sensation contrasting with the damp, chill air.

From the beginning the Finest had considered the wolves a threat, but not a serious one, and he felt certain that he could talk his way free. He was large and powerful, and they were smaller and weak with hunger and should fear or respect him. But their growing numbers were making them formidable, and one fast and persistent one on his heels leapt at him again and again and finally sank its teeth deep into a rear leg.

"Rue! Hurry!" Kalantha thumped her heels into his side. She was barefoot, her sandals must have slipped off somewhere, or she'd left them by the river. "More wolves! Look there!" Holding on to his mane with her left hand, she was gesturing wildly with her right.

Gallant-Stallion saw them, smaller gray wolves charging from the northwest, cutting past a clump of willow birches and trying to cut him off. The damp ground and wet branches had let them approach almost noiselessly. More than two dozen wolves altogether, he guessed, an especially large pack for these temperate woodlands. Some of the wolves were little more than big pups, probably born this past spring. One was coal black with tiny patches of gray on its face, looking silvery. It was an especially handsome wolf, and one that on another occasion Gallant-Stallion would have stopped to admire and converse with. But it was also a young, fast wolf, thicker and healthier than many of its fellows, and so it presented a greater menace.

The Finest sped on, pushing off a muddy swath of ground and hurdling a fallen cedar, putting some distance between himself and the wolves behind him. He could keep ahead of the first nine, he was certain, and the ones that had come across the river. A Finest, he was faster than a common horse and could sustain a gallop for quite some time—despite his weariness. However, the wolves running from the north and the northwest were closing and were going to catch up.

"Rue!" Kalantha kicked out at the young black that was leaping for the Finest's side. Her foot connected and pushed him back, but she was nearly unseated in the process. "Faster, Rue!" She kicked out again at another one, then clamped her legs tighter as the Finest struck the game trail and galloped across the mud.

Some of the wolves looked just like the shepherd dogs that the Finest noticed around the grounds of the High Keep Temple and on farms around Nadir. Perhaps they were indeed dogs, ones that went feral and joined the pack. Or perhaps they were half-breeds. A scrawny one cut in front of him, gaunt-looking in spite of all its fur.

You will stop the fire in my belly! You will warm my throat, the wolf growled.

Gallant-Stallion reared back and came down hard, feeling the wolf's bones break beneath his front hooves and feeling sick deep down. It let out a cry, like an injured dog, then the Finest ran forward, back hooves digging into it and killing it. The Finest's throat went dry and his stomach churned as he flailed with his hooves at another. This one he didn't kill, not outright, but he snapped its back leg and knew that was a death sentence.

Kalantha screamed as a young wolf darted in and leapt, claws raking her leg before she managed to kick it away. It leapt again, but Gallant-Stallion swerved off the trail and into the woods, deciding that the trail had proved as much to the wolves' advantage as to his.

Branches clawed at his neck and tangled in his mane, and he was certain they were battering Kalantha, too. But there was no time to study the land in front of them and pick a kinder path. Instead, he raced forward blindly, twisting between the walnut trees and scratching his sides on their rough bark.

Kalantha whimpered when he banged into a thick oak, and she leaned against his neck. At the same time, she kicked out, trying to keep the wolves from getting close. But she couldn't keep them away from Gallant-Stallion's hindquarters.

An achingly thin wolf managed to jump onto the Finest's rump, teeth clamping down on his back and claws digging in. But Gallant-Stallion reared up and sent the wolf crashing to the forest floor, where his fellows raced over him in their attempt to catch their prize.

We hunger! growled a wolf trying to keep pace with the Finest.

Catch him! howled another. *Bring him down.*

End the burning!

Let us feast!

No! Gallant-Stallion shouted to them. *You'll not stop me!* He reached deep inside himself, to some secret place that held a spark of energy. He called it up and coaxed it brighter as his hooves pounded ever faster across the muddy forest floor. He vaulted a fallen pine, then leapt over what looked like the remains of a stone wall. He heard the wolves behind him, but their voices were softer now.

He ran faster still to increase his lead. Mud and dead moss flew up all around him, and the leafless branches continued to scratch at him, as if they were trying to grab him and hold him in place for the famished wolves.

I am a Finest! he admonished himself. *They cannot catch me!* They should not be as fast and they should not be as strong, he knew. He pictured his lead growing, but instead the howls were getting louder. They were catching up again.

Desperation was giving the wolves speed, and several were matching him now. One that looked like a shepherd dog was suddenly at his side, racing through the tangle of moss patches and low bushes, leaping up to snap at his front legs.

I do not want to harm you, Gallant-Stallion tried one last time. He was sickened by the thought he'd killed the young black and had effectively slain the one with the broken leg. *Find food elsewhere.*

You will fill our bellies this day, the shepherd-wolf snarled. *Your blood will warm us!*

Gallant-Stallion spun and rose, brought his front hooves down on the back of the shepherd-wolf, then plunged forward into a grove of river birch. Again came the dryness in his throat for killing a creature that was not evil. There was nothing malicious in the wolf attack—unlike the attack of the assassin flock. There was only the desire to survive.

His hooves struck another and another, leaving these seriously wounded as he raced deeper into the woods. Water sprayed up from his hooves now, as he was crossing a clearing that was filled with puddles. He nearly tripped when his front hooves sunk deep into a muddy patch, but he managed to pull them free—just as another wolf closed and raked his side.

"Rue! You're hurt!" Kalantha batted the air with a fist. "Stay away from Rue!" she shouted at the wolves. "Leave us be!"

Gallant-Stallion's sides ached—from the exertion, from the cuts the assassin-birds' talons had made the previous night, from the gouges left by the wolves. It would be easy to give up, he knew, let the wolves catch him and then let his soul drift with those of the Finest Creations who went before him. With Steadfast, his mentor who was slain nearly two years past.

But there was Kalantha to consider. She was important to Galmier and perhaps to all of Paard-Peran . . . if Steadfast's spirit was to be believed. And Gallant-Stallion had no reason to think otherwise. If he gave up, the wolves would get her, too. So he searched deep again and nurtured the spark that would invigorate him, then he hurtled headlong into a tangle of young trees and then into a tributary of the Sprawling River.

The cold water was both a relief and a curse. It quelled the heat from his wounds, but its icy embrace struck him as hard as if he'd run into a wall. He threw back his head and gasped for air as he churned his legs to take him away from the bank and toward the other side.

He heard splashes behind him, the frantic wolves following. He heard their cries of "catch the horse," "we feed," and "bring them down" becoming a little fainter. He was finally putting more distance between himself and them. But how long could he keep it up? How much distance could he gain? Gallant-Stallion worried that he might actually tire before they did, and that he would have to stop soon or fall from exhaustion. His burst of strength was gone, and he was fading.

If he somehow managed to get away on the other side of the river, would they track him? Could he lose them?

There were no such predators in the pastures of the Finest Court, Gallant-Stallion knew. Unfortunate that he could not whisk himself and Kalantha there to escape the hungry pack.

Do not let the horse be away! This was a familiar wolf voice. Gallant-Stallion pictured the head of the wolf with a black stripe down its nose. *He leaves the river! Fast on him!*

The Finest felt mud beneath his hooves again and felt his legs brush submerged bushes. Then he was up on the opposite side of the swollen bank, sides heaving and foam flecking at his lips.

"They're following us, Rue!" Kalantha's voice was strained, and her breath was coming ragged. "Don't let them catch us!"

The Finest didn't answer her, he just started running again, clearing the fallen limb of a river birch and hurtling over the remains of another stone wall. Then he was on a game trail, this one wider and muddier than the last. It turned and widened still, and he followed it, galloping along and praying that Kalantha would continue to hold tight.

To his left and right he spied other traces of homes, so beaten down that the Finest guessed they had been abandoned decades ago. It looked as if the forest had grown up around the village, strangling it and tugging down all the buildings. Perhaps the rising river long ago drove the people off.

His heart was pounding in time with his pounding hooves as he vaulted another fallen limb, then a puddle that looked so murky he feared it deep. He only slowed when the trail became slick and water flowed across it from a stream that spread beyond its banks.

Ahead was more water—a lake, from the looks of it—and Gallant-Stallion's stomach knotted. He could swim it, but not at the pace he'd used when he crossed the river. His legs were on fire, he'd been pushing himself so hard, and his hindquarters and right side bled from where the wolves' claws raked him. He darted to the west of the lake and began to circle it. He wondered how badly Kalantha had been scratched. Had any wolves bitten her?

Lost, Kalantha, he said. *I do not know where we are.*

A howl cut through the air, mournful and frenzied. There was another, lower and more distant. He risked a glance behind him and saw three wolves about a hundred yards behind him. There could be more, judging by the chorus of howls that had just erupted, but the air was thick and gray and he couldn't see farther.

"You're hurt bad, Rue." Kalantha was holding tight to his mane with her left hand and reaching around behind her. "Bleeding, Rue! There's lots of blood. And those mean wolves, they're . . ."

Not mean, Gallant-Stallion corrected. *Not at all mean. Desperate, they are. Just hungry. And they cannot catch us. I will not let them.* To emphasize his point he somehow managed a little faster pace. The trail widened once again when he passed by a massive black willow, and there were faint indentations, indicating that wagons had come this way before all the recent rains. Wagons meant people.

The Finest thrust the pain to the back of his mind and concentrated his senses on the land ahead. He could smell blood—his and Kalantha's, blood from the wolves on his front hooves. He could smell the water from the river and from puddles scattered as far as he could see, rotting wood, the richness of the thick mud . . . and smoke. The hint of a favorite scent intruded, and he shook his head as if to chase away the phantasm. But the scent grew stronger.

Bread baking, Gallant-Stallion said.

"What?"

I smell bread baking, Kalantha.

"Where? I don't . . ."

Then the howls of the pack cut her off, and the Finest threw an impossible last measure of strength into putting more distance between them and the wolves. Eyes focused on the forest ahead, he charged along the road, which was leading straight toward another swollen branch of the river. He separated the shades of brown and gray and peered through the rain still bleeding from the sky. Something rose from the river.

A house? He blinked furiously. Trees and homes? The image seemed to come at him from a dream, but it spurred him on.

Hold tight, Kalantha, he urged. *And do not look behind us.*

Homes! At the edge of his vision he saw two thick tree trunks rising from the water. And stretched across their tops was a thatched-roof cabin. Smoke drifted from a chimney and melded with the gray air. Beyond that cabin were others, all of them perched on wide tree trunks. There was a man on a porch, dangling a fishing line down into the river below.

"Help!" Kalantha called, screaming as loud as she could to be heard over the pounding of Gallant-Stallion's hooves. "Wolves are after us! Help us!"

The man looked up as the Finest galloped closer. He hollered and waved his arms, dropped his fishing line and ran into his cabin. He returned a heartbeat later with a club and started clambering down a ladder.

Almost there, Gallant-Stallion thought. Despite his admonition to Kalantha, he risked a glance back. Three wolves still pursued him. But they were only fifty yards behind him now.

Hungry! the wolves growled in chorus. *End the burning!*
Feast on the horse!
Feast on the child!

The Finest plowed into the shallows of the river, his legs getting tangled in the branches of a submerged bush, tripping him and tugging him under. His head plunged into the river, the water filling his nose and throat and sending motes of light dancing in his eyes. He thrashed about, sensing Kalantha had fallen off his back. And after what seemed like an interminably long time, he managed to break free of the submerged branches and regain his footing on the muddy bottom. He pushed off and raised his head above the water and sucked in great gulps of air.

"Help us!" Kalantha swam to his side, reaching up for his mane and pulling, treading water and pointing to the homes built on tree trunks and the men climbing down ladders. The men were armed with clubs—real and improvised ones. An especially burly fellow clutched a thick iron skillet.

"Please, help us!" she called to them.

Swim to the men! Gallant-Stallion shouted to Kalantha. *Go, now!*

The girl shook her head defiantly and struggled forward, still tugging on the Finest's mane and looking back and forth between the approaching men to the south and the wolves to the north.

"I'm not going to leave you, Rue."

The three wolves that had been fast behind them were hesitating at the water's edge, caught between their fierce hunger and fear of the men.

The big horse is away, one large wolf snarled. It let out a whimper and pawed at the mud. *And men come.*

Hungry, another said. *I hurt with hunger. I do not fear the men.*

The third took a step into the water, saliva dripping from its jaws. It stopped as the men waded farther out into the water.

"Graybacks!" shouted the man with the skillet. He raised the skillet above his head and swung it menacingly, as he went in deeper. The water swirled around his chest when he reached the middle. With his free hand he quickly motioned to Kalantha. "C'mon girl, we'll protect you. Graybacks know not to bother us here."

He gestured with his head toward the far bank. More than a dozen men and women lined it, another dozen men were starting across the river, weapons held high. One man brandished an old sword with a curved blade.

"Get you back, wolves!" the man with the skillet hissed. "Go on! Away now! Graybacks, go!"

The wolf in the water was the first to retreat, snarling and snapping as he went. The other two waited a moment more, until they were certain the men would come to their side of the river. Then they followed their brother, howling their anger and hunger and defeat as they went.

"I've got you, girl!" This came from a tall, reed-thin man, who dropped his makeshift club and pulled Kalantha to him. She released the Finest's mane. "They hurt you bad, didn't they, girl?" He was looking at the numerous cuts on her skin, not aware that some of the wounds were from the assassin-birds that attacked the night before. "Girl shouldn't be out in the woods alone. Good thing you found us."

"You got her?" the man with the skillet called.

"I got her. I'll take her to my house. Becca'll tend to her."

"See you there, then. Trandal and I'll make sure the gray-backs are gone."

The thin man walked Kalantha across the river. By its depth and the submerged bushes, she realized it was a small branch, perhaps no more than a creek that had been made large and bold by all the rain. The man was strong, and Kalantha rested her head on his shoulder. So tired and sore, she struggled to keep her eyes open.

"My wife Becca will take good care of you," he told her. "Dry you off, make you warm, get you something to eat. Then we'll find a way to get you back to your parents."

"I'm all alone," Kalantha whispered. After a moment, she added: "No . . . I have Rue." She squirmed in his arms to look to the center of the river, where she'd been tugged away from the Finest. "My horse!"

Kalantha struggled and looked all around, and the man nearly dropped her. "Rue! Where are you, Rue?"

"Easy, easy," the man said. "That big horse of yours? He was there a moment ago. Don't see him now. Must've run off or drowned."

Kalantha stared at the water. There were only the men, tromping back to the village side of the bank. There was no sign of the punch anywhere.

4 · The Shimmering Paddocks

> In the lands of the Finest Court I will run the remainder of my days. I will drink cool, perfect water from ice-blue streams. I will relish the feel of long willow leaves caressing my back. I will share great stories of Paard-Peran with my brothers and sisters. And I will praise the powers for giving me four strong legs with which I will dance across the endless, rolling pastures.
>
> *~The Old Mare*

The dale pony was large and heavily built at roughly fourteen hands high. His coat and mane were a rich dark brown, the shade of melted chocolate, and the tip of his near-black tail disappeared into the grass. He had delicate light brown featherings around his steely blue hooves, and he had one white patch, this being a narrow blaze that began between his eyes and extended to just above his upper lip.

At the pony's side was a halflinger, slightly smaller, considerably thinner, and contrasting sharply because of her pale chestnut coat and bushy off-white mane and tail. The halflinger snorted loudly, the air from her big nostrils fluttering the hair that hung down her forehead and revealing large, expressive eyes that were filled with concern.

"Welcome home, Gallant-Stallion," the halflinger said. Her voice was melodic and low, and Gallant-Stallion enjoyed listening to it. "This pasture is richer for your presence, and we are gladdened by your company. But we are sad at your appearance. What has Paard-Peran done to you?"

"Yes, what indeed?" the dale pony asked. "You bleed! You bleed all over!" His nostrils flared, taking in the scent of Gallant-Stallion's wounds. It was as if the cosseted pony hadn't seen an injured Finest before. "What did the people of Paard-Peran do to you? So far indeed they have fallen!"

Gallant-Stallion silently regarded the pair. The halflinger reminded him of some of the mountain ponies he once ran with west of High Keep on Paard-Peran. But this one hadn't a single burr in her mane, and there wasn't a speck of dirt on her legs or belly. The dale was likewise flawless. Their muscular forms were free of scars, their manes and tails looking as if they were newly groomed.

Gallant-Stallion, however, carried with him plenty of mud from the banks of the Sprawling River, and his legs and sides were crisscrossed with welts from the assassin-birds and gouges from the wolves. His mane and tail were tangled and peppered with twigs, and he smelled strongly of sweat and the decaying vegetation of late fall. He imagined that he must reek to this pair.

"No man or woman did this to me," Gallant-Stallion finally replied. He quickly recounted the tales of the attacks by the assassin-birds and the starving wolves, though in his haste he left out many of the details. He gave them just enough to satisfy their curiosity. And he knew they would spread the stories to the other Finest creations they came across.

"And so you left your charge behind," the halflinger observed.

Gallant-Stallion gave a nod, tossing his mane and inadvertently spattering a little mud on her pale chestnut coat. She seemed not to notice. "Yes, I left Paard-Peran when I knew she was safe in the arms of good-hearted and brave villagers. But I have not abandoned her. She is still my charge. I am only away for a brief time."

The dale cocked his head, asking him to continue.

"She needed tending and rest," Gallant-Stallion explained, letting out a great sigh to show that he was tired of talking with them and really had no need to explain himself. "Her name is Kalantha, and she suffered wounds, too. And I could not risk her telling the villagers about her 'magic' horse. I could not risk prying eyes and discovery. Not today. Not as tired as I am."

The halflinger bowed her head and made a wuffling sound, indicating the worst of the Finest's injuries—four parallel gashes from a wolf's claw that ran from his withers and down the length of his side.

"Not to be discovered? I would say that wolves indeed discovered you, Gallant-Stallion," the halflinger said. "Discovered and tried to kill you." Her eyes were still flooded with concern.

"*Noticed* me," Gallant-Stallion corrected. "To the wolves and the birds, and to all the creatures of Paard-Peran, I am nothing more than a strong, fast horse."

"Your wounds will heal quickly here," the dale said. "No doubt that is why you retreated to the Court lands and left your charge. You need to mend. You must be whole to shepherd her."

Gallant-Stallion didn't reply to that. He simply continued to regard the ponies. A slight breeze plucked at their manes, the halflinger's off-white hair swimming in the air and sparkling like spun gold. The wind eased the pain in Gallant-Stallion's sides and somehow took some of the sting out of the more serious wounds. He closed his eyes and relished the sensation. The ache in his sides melted in the passing of a few heartbeats.

It was early morning here, while where he left Kalantha it must be heading toward sunset. Time passed differently in the Court lands.

"Tell us more of your charge, Gallant-Stallion." The halflinger broke the silence. "I have not yet been chosen to shepherd a Fallen Favorite, and so I am curious. What is she like, this person of yours? Is it difficult living a life in shadows? How old is she? What does she look like? What country do you wander across? Tell us about all of the people."

Gallant-Stallion instantly remembered back to the mountains of Galmier, where well more than a year ago he met a Finest pony named Arièg. She'd lost her charge decades before because her inquisitive nature got the best of her, and she was relegated to helping travelers as penance. Perhaps all Finest ponies harbored a pernicious curiosity. He shook his head, wishing that when he'd arrived in the Finest Court lands minutes ago and spotted these two in the distance he would have galloped the other way. But he needed information and thought they could be helpful, and so he'd come closer. He had not known they would be so young and talkative.

Maybe they could be helpful still if they would stop asking questions.

"Brother and sister," Gallant-Stallion said. His voice carried a measure of force now. "As I said, I cannot stay long in our lands, and I have no more time to talk about the world of the Fallen Favorites. I will not leave my charge for longer than necessary. I am here to speak to the Court."

The ponies reluctantly bobbed their heads in understanding.

"Do you know where the Court meets this day?"

The halflinger snorted "no," but the dale tipped his head up and to his right. "I believe, brother, that they gather in the Shimmering Paddocks."

"By the Twisting River," the halflinger added. "The paddocks is where the river bends back upon itself and . . ."

"I know where the Shimmering Paddocks is." Gallon-Stallion nickered his thanks and galloped beyond the ponies, across a meadow dusted with sweet-smelling clover. The ground felt cushioned beneath his hooves, the air comfortably warm and so unlike the chill and rainy fall of the Galmier woods. The breeze that teased his nostrils carried the scents of honeysuckle, lilacs,.and a dozen other flowers that grew near copses of sweet gums and honey locusts. He couldn't pull enough of the fragrances into his lungs. It forced out the last trace of the fetid fall woods.

The grass was always a brilliant green in the lands of the Finest Court, always long enough to tickle his shanks, and never would a stickle-weed dare grow in it. There were never clumps of dead grass or briars, like Gallant-Stallion noted in the fields near the High Keep Temple in Paard-Peran. The ground was even, and it was easy to run here, the slight wind combing his mane, no worry of tripping, just level ground to endlessly charge across. The fatigue he'd felt from galloping so long with Kalantha on his back vanished, and he managed an even faster gait. There was joy in the simple act of running. There were no knobby roots in his path, and no surprises hidden by the grass. So he pulled the air ever deeper into his chest and stretched his legs as if he was hurdling fallen logs in the sodden forest.

He pushed his worries away as he continued to race, listening to the drumming of his hooves against the comfortable earth and hearing, in the distance, the song of a fast-moving stream. There were no insects to bite at him, not even a single dreaded fly. He abhorred all the flies of Paard-Peran, biting at him in the spring and summer. An endless supply of them!

But neither were there any birds—no rabbits, foxes, or other small creatures—to be admired here. None of the variety of animals that crawled, hopped, ran, and flew. There were only Finest. They were taught about all the creatures of Paard-Peran, however, and so knew every form and every language.

They saw images in reflecting pools—it was like looking through a window into the realm of the Fallen Favorites.

Gallant-Stallion didn't know the extent of the Court lands. It wasn't like Paard-Peran, drawn out on a map with visible, finite boundaries. This was a mystical place, and so there seemed to be no end to it. Also unlike Paard-Peran, it had no seas to serve as barriers. There were lakes, of course, and rivers and streams, all of them blue and musical, made for wading and drinking, and none of them too deep.

It was . . . perfection, Gallant-Stallion decided, as he ran faster still. By the gods, he'd missed this place, even though he'd been absent less than two years! How could the other Finest shepherds stay so long away? How could his mentor Steadfast have shepherded one Fallen Favorite after another after another . . . decades after decades . . . with only brief visits here?

He felt the wounds on his flank and brisket closing, as was the deep bite healing on his rump. The scratches on his withers and back had already mended. Within several minutes all trace of pain was gone. There was no more weariness, and he was no longer hungry—though the grass looked inviting and he intended to graze on some after he met with the Court.

Thirsty? He was that. The Twisting River was not far, and he would drink deep there. In fact, the river was too close as far as he was concerned, his journey too short. He embraced the sheer joy of running and sadly knew he would have to stop before too long. He would be at the river, where he could clean the mud from his legs and belly, and then he would be at the Shimmering Paddocks.

But first he could run for just a little while longer.

THE SHIMMERING PADDOCKS GENTLY SLOPED AWAY FROM THE river and were rimmed with delicate-looking trees that resembled Paard-Peran's pink-flowered bunchberries. But these trees never lost their flowers or their leaves, and the ambrosial scent was stronger. A mist hung low to the ground, twinkling in the sunlight like liquid diamonds and lending the name to the Shimmering Paddocks. The mist would burn off at midday, and then the wildflowers that dotted the ground would glimmer with dew until evening set in. This was a favorite spot of many Finest.

As Gallant-Stallion came closer, he took in the herd gathered there. Three dozen, he counted, including eight members of the Court that he saw. He galloped toward the latter.

They were larger than their brothers and sisters, the most beautiful and purest of the Finest creations. Half of them were barbs, with long profiles and sloping quarters, their tails low set, and their manes short. Their legs were slender, and their hooves narrow. Two were pale gray, slightly darker than the mist that hung above the grass, and two were bay. Gallant-Stallion knew the three stallions as Blackeyes Longmane, Pureheart, and Stoutspirit, and the mare as Firemane Stormwithers.

Two other mares were dalusians, with white coats that carried a hint of a mulberry shade and wheat-colored manes and tails that were slightly curly. The luxuriant hair hung over their eyes, though they could well see through it. Their elegant heads looked a little hawklike in profile. These were Tadewi Sadgaze and Meara Swiftgait. Their color marked them as the oldest in the Court. It was known to all in the Court lands that when the powers painted the Finest, the first fourteen were snow white, absent of color, perfect and pure. The next fourteen after that carried a hint of other shades—and Tadewi Sadgaze and Meara Swiftgate were of that second ancient group. The powers believed that all these pale Finest stood out too starkly in Paard-Peran, and so those created later were painted the shades of earth and fog and rocks. Gallant-Stallion knew that, though it was not spoken about, Tadewi and Meara were centuries upon centuries old.

The most impressive Court member was a shagya stallion, his coat, mane, and tail as dark gray as a Paard-Peran storm cloud. The only things that weren't gray about him were his unreadable coal black eyes, and a patch on his muzzle that was the shade of a ripe peach. He had curled ears, the tips of which touched above the center of his forehead, and which he swiveled now in Gallant-Stallion's direction. He was called Gray Hawthorn, and he was the Finest Court Patriarch.

At his side softly nickered the Matriarch, an akhal-teke, one far more remarkable than the breed found on Paard-Peran. She was dun colored, but her fine coat gleamed gold in the sunlight. Her mane and tail looked like silk, and she had a long, thin neck that was set quite high to her body. Her big eyes and wide nostrils were accented by an interrupted white stripe that ran the length of her head and that matched the color of the stocking on her right front leg. This was Patience, named personally by the powers because she exuded that trait. Of all the Finest, she had the most forbearance and inner strength, and though she and Gray Hawthorn were considered equals, he often looked to her for counsel.

Gallant-Stallion felt a mixture of excitement and awe as he closed the distance. He had hoped more of the Court would be present—there were fourteen of them in all, the number settled upon because that was the initial number of Finest the powers created. It was unusual for all of them to be in one place at a given time. That only happened when they assembled to discuss matters of grave importance or during religious convocations.

When Gallant-Stallion had been named a secret shepherd one morning in the Misty Pasturage, there had been only seven members of the Court in attendance, but among them were Patience and Gray Hawthorn.

"Matriarch," Gallant-Stallion began. He bowed deep and waited a few heartbeats before he raised his head and looked into her golden eyes. "And Patriarch." This time he bowed to Gray Hawthorn.

Patience stepped forward, wuffling and nostrils flaring. "Child of the Great Grassland," she addressed him. "Gallant-Stallion."

He bowed again.

"You come from Paard-Peran because?"

Words tumbled from him as he looked between Patience and Gray Hawthorn. The remaining members of the Court formed a semicircle behind the Matriarch and Patriarch. The other Finest who had been grazing in the Shimmering Paddocks kept a polite distance, but wandered just near enough to overhear.

Gallant-Stallion regaled them with the story of the assassin-birds. It was a tale he was getting tired of repeating. But this time he left out none of the details, as Patience and Gray Hawthorn seemed especially interested.

"They clearly wanted to kill Kalantha, and her brother Meven. We are taught in the lands of the Court that the creatures of Paard-Peran are not malicious . . . unlike the Fallen Favorites can be. The wolves that attacked me were not evil, just hungry. Starving. But the birds . . . they were indeed vile."

Gray Hawthorn snorted loudly and looked to Patience. His eyes opened wide, and he waited for her.

The melody of the river cut through the paddocks, along with the gentle nickerings of the Finest who were politely eavesdropping. It was several moments before Patience spoke.

"Gallant-Stallion, just as the good powers of this world created us, their evil brothers birthed something, too. They dipped it in darkness, and they gave it a heart as twisted as their own. The two evil brothers created an animal with a mind bent on malevolence. They gave it perfect feathers, keen senses, and a lust for blood. They wanted it to fly above the world the good powers made."

"So we are not alone in being blessed," Gallant-Stallion said.

Patience nodded. "We never were."

"They hunt your charge still?" This from Blackeyes Long-mane. "The birds?"

Gallant-Stallion cocked his head, as if to say he wasn't sure. "And it is not all the birds, my brother. Not all of the birds of Paard-Peran are a threat."

"Who is your charge that the dark ones would have an interest in her?" This came from Tadewi.

Gallant-Stallion pawed at the ground. "When first I went to Paard-Peran, less than two years past, Steadfast was to introduce me to my charge." He met Patience's stare. "But we were attacked by the assassin-birds, and Steadfast was killed. I managed to save the royal cousins of Galmier. And I thought Meven Montoll my charge, as he was now the Prince . . . now the King. I knew my charge would be important. Steadfast had told me that much."

Tadewi interrupted him. "But your charge was not Meven Montoll?"

"No. My charge is his sister, only twelve years old. Steadfast's spirit told me she was vital to the country and . . ."

"And his spirit spoke true," Patience said. "Much rides with you and the young one, Child of the Great Grassland. The one you call Kalantha is a Fallen Favorite who . . ." Her voice trailed off and her eyes took on a distant look. "Life is a mystery, Gallant-Stallion, and it is not proper to know all the answers. None but the powers know everything, and perhaps they have their own puzzles. Simply understand that she is worthy enough to have a secret shepherd, and understand that you are fortunate enough to be paired with her."

Gray Hawthorn tossed his head, his mane catching in the

wind and for a moment looking like a swirling piece of fog. "Perhaps Steadfast did not know which of the royal cousins was meant for you, Gallant-Stallion. Perhaps fate made the choice. Or perhaps you did."

Gallant-Stallion had intended to ask the Court members dozens of questions . . . why, precisely, his charge was important, how such a young girl could make a difference, whether the assassin-birds would come back, where was he to take her, how he could safeguard her, what the future held for them. But he instantly knew the answers wouldn't be coming. The Finest Court either wouldn't tell him . . . or couldn't. It was possible even the members of the Finest Court didn't hold the solutions to his wonderings.

So instead he told them that Meven was formally crowned the Prince of Galmier before the cold, cold winds came, and that this very day he was crowned King. He explained that Meven essentially sent Kalantha away by demanding she go north to a place called Dea Fortress. And so instead they were traveling south and hadn't yet settled on a destination. Maybe they were meant to wander, he speculated.

"Maybe so," Patience said. "Maybe the two of you will find your destiny . . . and your real destination . . . along the way."

"If he can keep his charge safe." The whispered words came from Tadewi, as Gallant-Stallion let himself fade from the Court. "If he can survive the land of the Fallen Favorites."

GALLANT-STALLION PICTURED THE WOODS HE'D LEFT AND THE branch of the Sprawling River he'd been slogging across, and he felt himself drifting there. The Shimmering Paddocks became insubstantial, and Gray Hawthorn, Patience, Tadewi, Firemane Stormwithers, and all the others became an ephemeral haze.

The scents of lilacs, honeysuckle, roses, and jasmine became faint, and the fusty odor of the Sprawling River and of dead and rotting vegetation took over. The sun that had warmed his back vanished, and the early-evening cold of late fall wrapped tight around him. The rain was falling hard in the Galmier woods, *rat-a-tat-tatting* against his hide and leaving small concentric circles on the river. He was thankful his visit to the Court lands had healed him. He felt refreshed. He was only sorry that he hadn't tarried to taste the sweet grass.

There were only a few yards of earth ahead of him before the land dropped away and a great marshy pond stretched to the south. Rising from that marsh were the homes built on tree trunks. Gallant-Stallion counted thirty homes, a reasonably large village considering it sat in the middle of the woods . . . and was built on shorn-off trees. The homes glowed with fires and candlelight, and the rain drummed against the woven bark roofs.

Kalantha was in one of those homes, Gallant-Stallion sensed. He would wait at the edge of the village for her, hidden amid the pines that rose from the cold marsh. And when she felt well and rested, she would find him and they would leave this place for . . . where?

The night sky above the village was suddenly lit by a stroke of lightning, and then another. Thunder raced through the ground and the wind picked up. As Gallant-Stallion stood there, the rain came down harder, looking like a wall of water in front of him and hammering into him so hard it was almost hurtful. Within the passing of a few more minutes the wind became fierce, and the branches of trees surrounding the village were whipped around maniacally.

The storm that Gallant-Stallion had earlier smelled approaching had arrived in full force.

Already he was missing the Court lands.

5 · A Town Above the Ground

> I believe the cities of Paard-Peran challenge the Fallen Favorites. Certainly it must be a difficult matter for them to establish a government, build all the dwellings, sculpt the myriad statues and fountains, and pave the streets with smoothed cobblestones so that they cannot feel the soft carpet of grass beneath their feet.
>
> ~Meara Swiftgait of the Finest Court

She's got a fever, Becca. And chills." Trandal carefully placed Kalantha on the bed.

"And she's filthy!" Becca waved a pale hand in front of her face. "Whew! She's got quite a stink about her, Tran."

Her husband instantly reddened and looked at the quilt, muddy now. "M'sorry, Becca, wasn't thinkin'. You're right. All this dirt." He made a move to pick up Kalantha, but his wife stopped him.

"Leave her be, Tran. Let me tend to her." The woman bent over Kalantha and placed the back of her hand against the girl's forehead. Her hands moved quickly, gently prodding and poking, looking like fluttering white birds. "Where did you find her?"

"Hedge saw her. Comin' across the stream on a big horse. Graybacks were chasin' them. Deaver drove them off, though, wavin' that big skillet of his like usual. I brought her here. Hedge'll be over to check on her soon most likely."

Becca made a clucking sound. "What about her parents, Tran? She's just a child. Shouldn't be out in the woods alone. Her parents have to be nearby. Wonder where she came from?"

He ran a big hand through his thinning hair and shook his head. "Said she was all alone, she did. I asked her. But I didn't think to ask her name, or what village she came from. She was on a horse, so you wouldn't think she was poor. But look at her. Those clothes! We should . . ."

"Not be asking her any questions for a little while. And don't you hover so close. The girl should sleep. And while she does, I'll clean her up." Becca dipped a cloth in water and began smoothing at Kalantha's face. "My, my, Tran. Look at this scar she has."

Becca brushed the hair away from Kalantha's neck, revealing a thick ropy scar. "Wonder how she got this? And look at all these scratches on her arms. She's been through more than a bit of a tussle. Wolves didn't do all of this."

"She's a mystery, all right. Eh, Becca?"

"GOOD MORNING, CHILD!" BECCA SLIPPED A HAND BENEATH Kalantha's back and helped prop her up.

Kalantha blinked furiously, rubbed at her eyes, and stared.

Becca was stocky and filled Kalantha's vision. The woman had once been pretty, her mannerisms and bearing delicate and poised, her shoulders squared and back straight. But her doughy flesh and the years had taken their toll, and no doubt the rough life in the village contributed. Her hair was mostly brown, with strands of gray along her temples, hanging in loose curls below her shoulders. Her eyes were dark, looking like buttons against her pasty face, and her hands were incongruously small, pale and always moving.

A shudder passed down Kalantha's spine. She'd dreamt of fluttering white birds.

"I'm Becca. So glad you're awake. Have you a name, girl?"

"Where am I?" Kalantha managed.

Becca smiled warmly. "Tran? Tran! She's doing well. Come see!" Then Becca stood and backed away from the bed. "You're in Stilton, girl. My husband brought you here last night, Trandal did. Found you in the river, the wolves after you. Praise Peran-Morab, you're going to be all right. Worried all night over you, I did."

Kalantha returned the smile and swung her legs over the edge of the bed. She looked at her feet—no trace of mud. Her mouth dropped open in surprise. "I'm clean!" Then she studied her arms and hands and felt her face. She was wearing clean clothes, too. A shirt she figured was Becca's, as it fit her like a dress. It was brown and tied at the waist with a cord, and the sleeves were rolled up and tied, too.

Becca was nodding, her hands still fluttering. "You were a sight, girl. All dirty and tattered you were, burning hot like a summer day and smelling like that horrible river. Cleaned you up. Your clothes weren't worth saving. Not even fit as rags. We'll find you something else to wear. Smaller. Gretchen has a girl, or Marta a boy about your size." She shook her head, the curls bouncing. "Get you something more suitable. Then we'll find your folks."

Kalantha scowled. "My parents are dead. Years and years ago."

"By Peran-Morab's eyes!"

"I've been on my own for some time."

"But someone has to have been minding you! Who? Do you have a name, girl?"

Kalantha didn't say anything at first. And so Becca edged closer and bent over until their noses practically touched.

"There has to be someone for you," the woman insisted.

"Not anymore," Kalantha said finally. "After my parents died, a gardener took me in. But I'm on my own now."

"And your name?"

"Kal. My name is Kal Morgan." It was as she'd told Gallant-Stallion when they rode from Nadir. She had no intention of letting anyone know she was part of Galmier's royal family. And she didn't think that her friend Morgan the gardener would mind that she borrow his name. "I have a horse, though, called Rue. He kept me from the wolves, but I lost track of him in the river."

Becca made a clucking sound. "Well, I'm sure he's all right, Kal Morgan." Her eyes were lying, though. It was clear the matronly woman thought the wolves had got the girl's horse.

Kalantha's heart sank. She was worrying the same thing.

LESS THAN AN HOUR LATER, THE SMALL HOME WAS FILLED with people. It would have been drafty, had there not been a fire in the hearth, heating cauldrons of pigeon soup and almond milk—Kalantha had found both reasonably tasty.

And it would have been cold had there not been a crowd.

More than two dozen people were bunched into the home, and Kalantha worried that the floor might give out under their weight and send them all into the water below.

A hunchbacked woman with a pinched face introduced herself as Senya. "Word has stretched to every treetop in Stilton about you, young woman." She grinned, revealing yellowed, but even, teeth. "Said you nearly got caught by the graybacks. Good thing you made it over the river."

"The graybacks don't like Stilton much." This came from

the man who'd waded into the river, skillet raised over his head. He'd seemed the bravest of the lot to Kalantha, and certainly not afraid of the wolves.

The big man was shaped like a shed, blocky and with wide shoulders that sloped. His face was craggy-looking, and his white hair, slicked against the sides of his head from the rain, was white and looked like strands of thick string. He'd changed clothes from what he'd had on when he was yelling at the "graybacks." He was wearing gray trousers, the knees of which were so thin they were shiny like satin. His shirt hung on him, despite his size, but the sleeves were too short for his long arms and drew attention to his hands, which were large and callused, fingertips cracked from labor, dirt so embedded in the grooves as to be a permanent part of him.

The big man stretched a hand forward and tapped her shoulder. "Name's Hedge, short for Deaver Hedgeworth. So you're Kal Morgan, huh? Is Kal short for something?"

Kalantha shook her head. "Thank you for rescuing me," she told the assembly. She dropped her gaze to the woodplank floor, just to make sure it wasn't bowing under all the weight.

"Put some excitement into our day," Hedge continued. "Haven't pulled anyone from the river in . . . oh . . . three or four years, I'd wager. And that was in the summer, when it wasn't so deep and . . ."

"Says she's got no family," Becca cut in. "Says she's on her own."

Hedge shook his head sadly, a gesture echoed by most everyone in the room.

"She's welcome to stay here." This came from a man Kalantha had not seen before. He introduced himself as Alden. He had a careworn face, and the fingers on his left hand were crooked. "Marta and I can take her in if no one else has a mind to. Set up another bed and . . ."

Senya the pinched woman waggled a finger at him. "You've four children, you and Marta. And another on the way. Someone else can help her. Someone like Becca and Trandal. Their child is grown and gone."

Becca gave a disapproving look, but said nothing.

Kalantha sat on the edge of the bed and shook her head. She'd felt bad enough that Becca and Tran had taken her in last night and gave her their bed.

The villagers stayed for a few hours, some leaving and others taking their places. Though most of the questions were directed at Kalantha, she was able to glean a little bit from her hosts.

Stilton was an old village, originally called Stilt Town. People had moved here from the north after repeated floods and after fires caused by lightning destroyed enough homes that they gave up on those locations. Kalantha guessed they might have been talking about the ruined buildings she and Rue had picked their way through earlier.

"Our great-grandparents, and the ones before them, realized they couldn't defeat the river," Hedge explained. "So the woodsmen among them started cutting down trees. Right here. Oh, they didn't cut them off at the roots, they cut them off six, eight feet up, the one closest to the river ten—though that wasn't at all necessary. Used the trunks as stilts for the homes, and used the wood they'd cut for building places to live and for boats."

Nearly every home had some sort of boat tied to its ladder. Most were rafts, but a few were long and wide enough to fit a large family. Not all of the village was so high above the ground as those homes near Becca and Trandal's. The farther away from the river Stilton stretched, the shorter were the "stilts." At the most southern point, homes rose only two or three feet above the surface of the swollen river, and beyond them rose an earthen rise the villagers had built up. There were pens of cows, goats, pigs, and a few sheep. There were also two sway-backed horses, a mule, and a pair of donkeys. In big cages hanging from thick tree limbs they kept chicken, geese, and ducks. In the summer when the river shrank, the villagers farmed and stored as much as they could for the "wet months."

Kalantha was given a tour of it all in the late afternoon, after she'd been given a pair of breeches and a woolen tunic from one of Marta's boys, and after Hedge gave her a cape made of wolf skins.

She was comfortable, warm, and terribly sad and uneasy because there was no sign of Rue.

She was amazed at Stilton, and that helped a little to keep her mind off the big punch. It had stopped raining, and a thick beam of sunlight cut through the canopy and made the water the village rose from sparkle like a plate full of glass beads. Color was everywhere—from painted shutters and window boxes to curtains and pennants, to ribbons that fluttered from little girls' braids. There was a slight breeze, and it sent branches playfully clacking against each other and caused the wind chimes that hung from many of the homes to compete for Kalantha's attention. There wasn't a trace of yesterday's dreariness.

Two hundred people lived in the village. Most of the men were trappers, but there were also fishermen and bow-hunters, the latter responsible for cutting down the deer and boar populations particularly in the fall and winter and making it hard on the wolves. There were a few furrier shops, and a shoemaker, barber, butcher, chandler, baker, weaver, tailor, and a hatmaker. Like in Nadir and in the villages around High Keep, all the businesses were run by men, and women were relegated to keeping homes and taking care of children . . . though she was told a woman named Marguer Butler was responsible for the bakery, having inherited the business when her husband died. That piece of news seemed almost scandalous.

That night Kalantha, Becca, and Trandal were invited to the home of Rungus Kinwin, a successful bull-necked trapper who had the largest home—and the largest family—in the village. There, all the attention was once again on her, and the dozen or so people feasted on cholent, a delicious stew of spiced meat and vegetables, while listening to every word she had to say.

With everyone so friendly and good to her, Kalantha let some of her defenses down. She didn't mention her brother Meven, but she talked about the malevolent birds that had attacked her and that were responsible for the thick scar on her neck and so many of the scratches on her arms.

"They weren't like normal creatures," she told them. "I've never seen so evil a thing as the big black hawk that led them. I think he would have killed me, but my horse Rue killed him first." She sucked in her lower lip and kept herself from crying. She missed the horse terribly, and was downhearted that it was clear the villagers didn't believe her bird story.

When she climbed down the ladder and got into Becca and Trandal's boat, she heard Rungus tell his wife: "That girl has quite the imagination, doesn't she, I'm thinking. She's probably a runaway, making up all the stories. Lies come easy to little ones."

IN THE MORNING, KALANTHA WAS VISITED BY A GAWKY-looking man named Ergoth Thistlebrook. He was twice her age and reminded her of Meven because of his thinness, but he had tiny scars around his dark eyes, and a crooked nose that hinted he'd been in plenty of fights. He walked with a pronounced limp, practically dragging his left leg and making Kalantha wonder if that infirmity was also acquired in a brawl.

They talked on Becca and Tran's porch, both bundled in wolfskin cloaks.

"I believe you, Kal Morgan, about the birds."

She was startled by his comment—because of his admonition and because he had not been at the trapper's last night. Gossip must flow through the village faster than the river travels, she thought.

She didn't reply, just sat there and looked across Stilton, fixing her gaze on a long set of wind chimes dangling from Hedge's porch.

"I've read about such things, malicious birds. When I was a child. It was in an old book. The book wasn't about birds. I think it mentioned someone in my family, and was about priests and such. I don't recall the title. Sorry. Anyway, the book didn't say where the birds flew, Kal Morgan. Just that . . ."

She shook her head. "Where did you read about them? Where was the book?"

He was staring now, at two girls peering out Hedge's window. It looked like they were laughing, and one of them was pointing his way.

"Where . . . Ergoth?"

He glanced away from the girls and met Kal's gaze. His eyes were dark and bright and looked like they held secrets. "At Vershan Monastery. I remember now. I read the book quite a while ago, as I said. I was a child. I read it in the library tower."

"A monastery."

Ergoth nodded. "I studied there when I was younger, younger than you. And I was so impressed with the religious people there . . . my brother and I were both impressed . . . that we entered the priesthood."

Kalantha's eyes narrowed and she regarded him suspiciously. She instantly thought of Bishop DeNogaret from High Keep Temple. The elderly priest had been her mentor, essentially a parent, and with Meven being named King of Galmier the Bishop had decided she would be sent to Dea Fortress. Priests were not to be trusted as far as she was concerned—they only wanted to tell you what to do.

"You're a priest?"

"Yes, that's right. I'm a priest. I might not look like one, though. No fancy robes and such, Kal Morgan. In fact . . ."

"I'm not sure I like priests." She said this softly, not wanting Becca and Trandal to hear. She figured they were just inside the door, listening and waiting to spread more gossip through Stilton. "They think they can tell you what to do all the time. They paint the future for you."

Ergoth grinned broadly. "Well . . . I've seen a few of those priests in my time at the monastery, and . . ."

"And that's why you're here?" Kalantha chastised herself for interrupting him again. "You got tired of the priests at the monastery?"

He laughed, a merry sound that brought a smile to her face.

"No. No. I enjoyed my time at the Vershan Monastery very much, and I thoroughly relished the company of the priests and the acolytes there, and all of the hardworking villagers who lived nearby. Everyone so friendly. I just . . ."

"So why?"

"Why do you always intrude when I talk?"

She shrugged, deciding not to apologize. "So why did you leave?"

"I felt that to better do the gods' work, I should lend my talents to a place where there were no priests. So I guess my calling was to leave the monastery."

"A place like Stilton? Go to a village like this?"

A nod. "Stilton had no priest when I moved here three years past."

"And you thought they needed one?"

Another nod.

"Well, did they need one?"

Ergoth didn't answer that question, at least not directly. "Kal, there are dark places in the world, and dark places in people's hearts. Hate, corruption, mistrust, those are the bad seeds planted. I'm here to make sure those seeds don't take root here in Stilton."

"You sound like a gardener more than a priest." I like gardeners, she thought. Especially one named Morgan who lives at the High Keep Temple.

"So you have no parents, Kal Morgan?"

"Just call me Kal, all right? And, no, I've no parents. Not since I was very, very young. I've no one . . . no one except my horse, Rue. I'd like to think he's just lost somewhere in the woods."

I'm not lost, Kalantha.

Her eyes grew wide and she sucked in a deep breath. Ergoth was talking to her again, but she pushed his words aside and peered down into the woods beyond the river. She saw a shape there, large and dark and hidden by the shadows of the thick trees.

Do you intend to stay long in this village, Kal?

"I'm not going to stay here." Kalantha had raised her voice so Rue could better hear her. Ergoth thought she was talking to him.

"Where do you want to go?" the priest asked her.

"We're going to the Vershan Monastery," she told Rue. "There's a library with books about evil birds."

"*We're* going?" Ergoth raised his voice, too.

Kalantha gave him a stern look. "Not me and you, Ergoth. Me and my horse, Rue."

"I'll take you to Vershan," the priest volunteered. "We can leave first thing in the morning. My brother's at the monastery, and it's been a few years since I've seen him. I'd like to catch up with him again."

Kalantha headed toward the door, smelling pandemayn bread baking inside. "What about keeping the bad seeds from sprouting in this village?"

"I think Stilton can get along without their gardener for a little while."

It was after dinner, the sun just setting, when Kalantha climbed down the ladder. She told Becca and Trandal that she wanted to take the raft to Marta's home and see if the woman might have another tunic she could borrow.

But Kal didn't take the raft. She quietly waded into the branch of the river, where it was narrow and not too deep. The Finest crossed it slowly to meet her in the middle, careful to make no sound, and he bent his head so she could pat his muzzle.

"I was so worried about you!" Kalantha hushed. "I was afraid something horrible had happened. That you'd drowned or that the wolves got you."

They treated you well, Gallant-Stallion observed. *You are healing. You should stay a few days longer, Kalantha. The village has been good for you.*

"We're leaving for Vershan Monastery tonight," she said, grabbing at his mane and giving a gentle tug.

6 · War Games

Men think their minds wonderful and complex because of their glorious inventions, works of art, and intricate, conniving political plays. Some minds are indeed god-touched, I believe, allowing a few to rise above the rest and attract the attention and protection of the Finest Court. But most men have bland and simple minds, and while they talk of inventions, government, and art, and while they design impressive buildings and amass well-trained armies, they are actually thinking only about wealth and power. Their minds are pitifully narrow, not wonderful at all.

~Dunlegs of the Misty Pasture, once shepherd to a Dolour King

Paard-Peran was embroidered on a large tapestry that took up almost the entire east wall of Meven's principal study. Galmier was rendered in silk threads so that it would stand out, and Nasim-Guri and the High Keep Temple were indicated with seed pearls, crystal beads, and gold wire.

Nearby, on a massive low table, there was another map—painted by the palace's resident artist, who was also working on a portrait of Meven and the Bishop. The map detailed Galmier and the lands to the south.

The Esi Sea, the Sprawling River, and a few lakes were not quite dry, the artist had explained to Meven only an hour ago. The entire map had been rendered in oils atop an especially heavy canvas stretched across mahogany beams. The blue glistened like real water struck by the sun because it was still wet, and the artist asked King Meven if he might wait until tomorrow or the day after to use the map, when it most certainly would be dry.

But King Meven said that would be too late and ordered the map brought here. It was at Bishop DeNogaret's request, actually. But Meven decided the artist didn't need to know that.

There were several villages indicated: Stilton, Cobston, Riverpoint and Saphren. And in the country to the south, Nasim-Guri, the capital of Duriam was rendered half the size of Nadir—though in truth the cities were close in population. There was also Ko's Point, Greenrush, Resan's Tower, Giaia, Salshad, and Rel-Suel and Suel. Vered, the country even farther south, and its capital of Dolour, made up the far south edge of the map. There were more villages scattered throughout all three countries, but they were "too small to worry about," Meven had told the artist.

The young King of Galmier was marveling over the map, his fingers dancing just above its surface, careful not to get too close to anything blue. The Galmier Mountains were raised above the surface, sculpted of flour, sugar and water, hardened and painted, the artist had explained. The Old Forest and the Gray Woods of Nasim-Guri, as well as scattered trees throughout Galmier and Vered, were made of evergreen sprigs, preserved somehow, and carefully affixed to stand upright. There were marshy areas, and these were a mix of paint and a sprinkling of moss.

"I wonder where Kal is in all of this?" Meven mused. He glanced at the world map hanging on the wall. He knew she wouldn't be to the north, as that would be the country of Uland, where the religious cloister of Dea Fortress rose. No, she would have traveled south. "That's where I would have fled," he said. "As far south as that ugly punch's legs would take me."

Meven shivered. He was wearing a black woolen tunic and

leggings this day, plain but exceptionally fine, and quite warm. He wondered if Kal was keeping herself warm somehow. And if she was still alive. This late fall is especially cold, he thought, thick frost on the ground this morning, sleeting last night. He shivered again at the thought of being out in it. She well could have frozen to death last night or the one before. And if she was dead, it was his fault.

"What did I do?" he breathed. "My sister! By all the gods . . ." He stopped when he heard soft footsteps. "Bishop DeNogaret?"

"I see the artist delivered the map." The Bishop glided to Meven's side and began looking over the work. "Adequate." He dropped a finger to touch the Galmier Mountains, then to brush at a clump of trees south of Nadir. "Ah, the Sprawling River . . ."

"Is still wet, Bishop," Meven quickly finished. He didn't want the priest to either ruin the map or get paint on his finger.

"Like it is still wet outside." The Bishop let out a sigh, the sound dry like sand blowing. "Everything is so wet outside."

"Once the sun comes up and melts the ice, it will be wetter," Meven added softly. "Cold outside." Again he thought of Kalantha, and he felt his chest grow tight. He wanted to talk to the Bishop about her, perhaps send soldiers looking for her, a woodsman who could expertly track . . . no, with all the rain even the most seasoned woodsman would be useless. But soldiers could stop at villages to the south and ask about her. Talk to trappers and merchants. Someone has to have seen her . . . if she's still alive.

"Bishop?" Meven decided to risk broaching the matter. "I've been thinking, wondering . . ."

Bishop DeNogaret waved a hand and cut him off. "Wondering what these maps are for, Meven? I should have explained before now." The Bishop retreated to a cherry wood box, as wide as his shoulders. It was so highly polished his reflection appeared ghostlike in the top of it. The sides were carved with the images of swords and shields, and there were two shiny blue ribbons tied around it—the Bishop's colors.

He stared at his reflection for several moments, only half-hearing something Meven was muttering about. A moment more and his skeletal fingers were carefully untying the ribbons, then opening the box.

"I had these made for you, Meven." The Bishop raised his voice so that it was the deep, mellifluous one he used during sermons. "I had them commissioned for you the day you returned to the High Keep Temple, just before you left for Nadir to become the Prince of Galmier."

He had Meven's attention, the boy shuffling over, looking at the box, and seeing his own ghostlike reflection next to Bishop DeNogaret's.

"For me, this box?"

The Bishop nodded. "More precisely, Meven. What's inside it."

"For me?"

"Consider it a birthday gift."

"In three days I will be fifteen."

"You are Galmier's youngest, brightest monarch, Meven. I am proud of you."

The worry creases on Meven's forehead vanished, and he gave a slight smile. Then his face clouded. "I wish Kal could see me. See all of this. Bishop DeNogaret, do you think . . ."

"I think you should open the box, Meven."

Smooth, thin fingers traced the shields and swords. "It is a beautiful box, Bishop DeNogaret." He held the sides of the lid and regarded his reflection, then he released a breath and gently tugged the top free.

"Beautiful!"

Meven placed the lid carefully next to the box, reached inside and pulled out a miniature soldier. It was no longer than his little finger. There were many more similar soldiers in the box, pale gray paint for the armor, blues for surcoats and pennants, rosy flesh for their faces. Even their eyes and lips were painted.

"Incredible," Meven said. "Beautiful. How could someone have painted something this small?"

"It's bone, that figure. All of the figures. Carved bone," the Bishop explained.

Meven raised an eyebrow. "What kind of bone?"

"Animal bone, Meven. I don't know what kind of animal."

"Incredible," he repeated. He instantly wished he had had these years ago, when he was of a mind to play with toys. And then he wished that Kalantha could see them . . . she was certain to be impressed, too.

He started taking them all out of the box, discovering that there was another layer beneath them. And another beneath that. The soldiers at the bottom had longbows, and tiny twigs were resting in quivers on their backs.

"I must meet the man who painted these tiny figures, Bishop DeNogaret! Can you arrange it?" Meven was holding an archer up to his eyes. "I wonder however he managed this?"

The Bishop picked up two soldiers and moved to the painted map. "You will meet him, Meven. He's painting more for you."

"More? Wonderful!"

"A different army. One with yellow and orange tabards."

"But I like the blues. They're your colors."

"Your colors, too, Meven."

"Yes, my colors. I think I'd rather have more soldiers in the blues."

The Bishop placed the two soldiers south of Nadir, on the bank of a branch of the Sprawling River. He returned to the box and got two more. "But yellow and orange belong to Nasim-Guri's King."

Meven watched the Bishop place all of the soldiers on the map. Most were south of Nadir, but others were lined up just south of a branch of the Sprawling River, at the border of Nasim-Guri. Meven's hands dropped to his belt, and his fingers began touching the beads. He started mouthing a prayer.

Bishop DeNogaret walked around the table, making slight adjustments to the soldiers, then stepping back and assessing their positions. "I think that will do well for a start, don't you think?"

Meven's eyes were closed, and the words to his silent prayer were coming faster.

Bishop DeNogaret shook his head and let out a deep breath. Then he waited patiently until Meven was done.

"Don't you think that will do, King Meven?"

Meven stared blankly at the array of miniature soldiers. "Do for what, Bishop DeNogaret?"

Another shake of his head. "Do for the start of your war, King Meven."

Meven took a step back from the table, eyes never leaving the miniatures. "War," he said softly.

The Bishop came to stand in front of him, and Meven looked up into the old priest's rheumy eyes. "The war we discussed earlier, King Meven."

"I'm sorry, Bishop DeNogaret. I'd forgotten." He scratched at his head and started to look away, but the Bishop put a finger on Meven's chin and steered it back. "I—I—I'm having trouble sometimes, remembering everything."

Suddenly the Bishop's eyes seemed very wide, not an old man's eyes any longer.

"Meven, listen carefully."

"Yes, Bishop DeNogaret."

Meven's eyes were unblinking, seeing only Bishop DeNogaret's shiny eyes, looming larger somehow, looking as wet as the blue paint on the map.

"You are going to war, King Meven."

"Yes, a war." Meven's voice had gone flat, and his face lost all expression. "A war is a good idea, isn't it Bishop DeNogaret?"

"Meven, this war you're planning is a very good idea. It will take many months to gather and train the soldiers. A year, I suspect."

"Against Uland to the north, this war. I remember now." Meven seemed to brighten for an instant. Then his face became a stoic mask again.

"No, not Uland. We discussed Uland before. It is small and has not much of an army."

"An easy mark, then," Meven said. "It shouldn't take a year to get enough men."

"But not our target. You've changed your mind, King Meven."

"I have?"

The Bishop leaned closer, his eyes very large to Meven now. "Don't you remember that you changed your mind?"

"Yes, Bishop DeNogaret. I remember now."

"Uland would be an obvious target, as it is a smaller country, and a weaker one."

"Yes, obvious. But I changed my mind."

"You want to attack Nasim-Guri to the south. The army is more formidable, but the King will be wholly unsuspecting. We'll gather our soldiers quietly."

"A year from now, this war." Meven's fingers dropped from the prayer beads.

"Meven, you want to attack Nasim-Guri because the King

has married his daughter to the Prince of Vered. They have formed an important political alliance, and those two countries together are larger than Galmier."

Meven drew his lips into a fine line, and the blush of ire scudded across his face. "No country should be larger than Galmier."

"Of course not, King Meven. And that is why you decided to attack Nasim-Guri. Assimilate that country into Galmier, and nothing could be larger."

"Nothing."

Meven remembered that his cousin, Prince Edan, was originally supposed to marry the Princess of Nasim-Guri. That was a little less than two years ago, and it ended tragically in the deaths of everyone in the wedding party—because a swarm of vile birds attacked, and everyone except Meven and Kalantha died, and that was because the ugly punch saved them. Meven pictured the field in his mind, the one where he saw the bodies of the soldiers and of Edan. So much blood, the ground couldn't drink it all in. He became the Prince that day.

"And so you decided to strike a secret alliance with the King of Uland. So he could support you against Nasim-Guri."

"A secret alliance," Meven repeated. He remembered seeing crows and blackbirds picking at the remains of Edan and the soldiers.

"The King's representative will be here this afternoon. Uland will supply what soldiers it can to aid our endeavor."

"Soldiers."

"Yes, from Uland's King. And next year, after Nasim-Guri has fallen and Galmier's borders are expanded, you can turn your attention to Vered."

"Go to war against Vered."

"Yes, another war. It is a good plan, King Meven. No, more than a good plan. It is a brilliant one. When Galmier has subsumed Nasim-Guri and Vered, you can turn your attention on Uland. It will crumple beneath your forces."

Meven tried to swallow, finding that his throat had gone dry. "I thought we were forging a secret alliance with Uland."

"And that is why Uland will be unprepared for your assault. Eventually, perhaps in two years or so, all of this great island continent will be yours."

"All of it mine."

"Yes, mine." The Bishop stepped away and looked at the map again, stretched out his bony fingers and adjusted another miniature soldier. "A brilliant plan you've devised, King Meven."

"Thank you, Bishop DeNogaret." Meven shook his head, as if trying to dislodge some cobwebs in his mind. A few moments passed. "Bishop . . . I've been meaning to talk to you about Kalantha."

"No doubt you miss your sister, Meven."

"Yes, and I . . ."

"Bishop DeNogaret?" The attendant Gerald was standing in the doorway, trying not to look at the maps and to focus on the elderly priest. "Bishop?"

The Bishop tried to square his shoulders, though he couldn't completely get rid of the stoop in his back. A last look at the miniatures arrayed near the Nasim-Guri border, then he turned toward the doorway.

"Yes, Gerald?"

"You have a visitor, Bishop. Willum Corkstead, Bishop. A wealthy merchant, from the looks of him. Said you invited him here."

The Bishop raised an eyebrow.

"He has an owl with him, Bishop. A big, beautiful owl I suspect he is trying to sell. Can't see where you would want . . ."

"Take me to him, Gerald."

"Yes, Bishop DeNogaret."

The elderly priest followed Gerald into the hallway, then down a sweeping staircase, his long gray robes swirling around his slippered feet.

Meven was staring at the map and the painted soldiers.

"A war," he said. "Starting a year from now, when all the soldiers are properly, quietly trained. A brilliant idea of mine."

He wasn't thinking about Kalantha anymore.

7 · Fellow Travelers

I don't know why the men and women of Paard-Peran cluster in buildings that block out the sun and the stars. The walls blunt the soft wind that would comb their hair, and the roofs keep the rain from showering them. In their tiny buildings they are cut off from the gifts of this world. Perhaps the winds should blow all the buildings down and make the Fallen children face the real beauty of Paard-Peran.

~Bold Boliver, shepherd to Prelate Wallis of Rel-Suel

We have to be quiet, Rue," Kalantha whispered so softly that even the Finest had trouble hearing her. "No one must know I'm leaving the village. They might try to stop me."

Gallant-Stallion was worried about the wolves, knowing they were more apt to hunt in this darkness—especially in greater numbers. While she'd stayed in the village, he listened to their distant howling and moved around constantly, keeping upwind of where he guessed the wolves might be.

He fretted why Kalantha insisted on leaving the stilt village in the heart of the night—she had to know the woods were more dangerous now. He thought about arguing with her, but he didn't consider it his place to tell her what to do. It was his task to guard and guide.

It was colder traveling at night, and both Kalantha's and the Finest's breath feathered away from their mouths. It was eerie, too, the only sound being his soft footfalls.

She led Gallant-Stallion around the eastern edge of the village and past the livestock pens on the hillock. A mule brayed its displeasure at being disturbed by their presence, and a goat softly bleated its curiosity at someone traveling during the "frightening, frightening dark." When they were past the pens, she found a stump to stand on so she could get on Gallant-Stallion's back without jumping. That was the only indication she was still sore from the ordeal with the wolves.

She nudged him farther south, and he kept his eyes trained on the ground until he was past a tangle of exposed hickory roots. The land was soaked here, and there seemed to be even more puddles stretching out in this direction. At least the rain was being kept at bay by a near-cloudless sky, and the moonlight that cut through the canopy made it easier to spot fallen limbs. The Finest caught sight of a glint of metal. He stared closely and discovered it was a jagged-toothed animal trap. A shudder passed down his back. He knew men hunted for food, but he hated the notion of an animal being caught in something like that and dying slowly. The trap had caught prey before, as he could faintly see dark stains on its jaws. Kalantha seemed not to notice the trap, her eyes not as keen and currently trained on the village behind her.

When the last of the stilt houses was out of view, she leaned forward and scratched at Gallant-Stallion's ears. She whispered to him.

"Those people were nice, Rue, awfully nice to me. But some of them were too curious. I didn't want them to know that my brother is the King of Galmier." She twirled the fingers of her right hand in Gallant-Stallion's mane. "I think I would have liked to see it, the coronation. I bet he was dressed so fancy he couldn't stand it. And I bet they had a big dinner with lots of desserts. And I bet he's warm in his palace in a big, soft bed with lots of pillows and covers. I would've liked to watch him made King. But if they'd found me, I wouldn't be here with you. I'd be at Dea Fortress, and they'd make me pray all day."

She grew silent for several minutes. Away from the village, the noises of the woods came to the fore. There was an owl hooting from somewhere overhead, answered by another quite a bit farther away. Something rustled the branches of a tree to the west, a squirrel from the quick sound of it. A creature with some weight to it was trundling slowly to the east, not being careful to be quiet and brushing the branches of low-growing bushes. A wolf, Gallant-Stallion worried, or perhaps a large boar or even a bear. The wind, slight as it was, came from the east, and so the trundling beast should not be alerted to them.

A few more miles passed, and there was no more evidence of the beast, but Gallant-Stallion relaxed only a little. He didn't know this territory, and neither did Kalantha. They didn't know where the next village was, where the trade roads stretched, and just what the dangers were. And at night, all of those concerns were magnified.

"Nice as the people were in that village . . . Stilton, they called it, because the houses were on stilts . . . the men still made all the rules. There was a woman who lived alone and ran a bakery, but that was only because her husband, who used to be the baker, was dead. And because none of the men in Stilton could bake as good as she could."

Kalantha let out a sigh, her breath a lacy fan that stirred the hairs in Gallant-Stallion's mane. "I wouldn't want to run a bakery, Rue. But I don't know what I want to do . . . other than finding the Vershan Monastery."

Gallant-Stallion was curious about this Vershan Monastery and why she wanted to go there. But he didn't ask about it. He figured she would tell him in good time.

She slept shortly before dawn, finding a reasonably dry spot beneath a black willow. Gallant-Stallion remained alert outside the veil of branches, still anxious about the wolves, as he'd noticed their spoor a few miles back. He watched the spindly branches stir in the breeze, the thinnest looking like strands of an old woman's hair tickled by the wind. Behind him was a tall oak, the leaves making a comforting hissing sound as they brushed together.

As the hours passed, the sky changed from a dark velvet blue to something paler, yet more vivid, and he could see it turning rosy at the bottom through gaps in the trunks. The emerging sun tinged clumps of dead grass golden. The smell of the mud all around and of wet bark filled his nostrils. Fainter was the scent of Kalantha, and fainter still was the scent of wolves that had passed this way some time ago. Above all of that was the odor of stagnant water from the puddles that still dotted the ground as far as he could see.

Steadfast, so much rain! Gallant-Stallion thought. *It is as if the powers cry on the land, mourning for the Fallen Favorites. Never have I seen so much rain or water, and yet I do not find it displeasing.*

You are learning to appreciate Paard-Peran, the spirit of Steadfast replied.

Gallant-Stallion's eyes grew wide. He hadn't heard from his mentor's spirit in what seemed a long time. *Steadfast, I am so unsure of myself.*

It is the nature of things, Gallant-Stallion.

This child . . . how can she be important? How can I protect her? There is so much danger in this world, why? Why would the powers create a land where . . . Gallant-Stallion stopped his questions. The breeze faded to nothing, and he knew the spirit of his mentor was gone.

He nudged Kalantha awake and nickered softly. She likely needed more sleep, but he thought the scent of wolves faintly stronger now. It could have been his nerves or his imagination, he admitted. But he wasn't about to take any chances with his charge.

SHORTLY BEFORE NOON, THEY PASSED ANOTHER VILLAGE. Kalantha considered stopping, as she told the Finest she was quite hungry.

"But I'm not starving," she said, looking wistfully at the smoke curling gently up from a stone chimney. "I'm not cold. And I've more important things to do right now than eat and sleep."

Still, she continued to look longingly at the smoke as they passed the village, staring over her shoulder until the pines obscured her view.

"How is it that you can talk to me, Rue?"

It was a question he feared she would have asked before now.

"At least, how can you talk to me when you're in the mood for it?"

He made his way past the stand of pines and began to follow another branch of the Sprawling River.

"Rue?"

He snorted, what would have amounted to a sigh for a man. *Perhaps it is not that I can talk to you, Kalantha, but that you can listen to me.* It wasn't a lie, as she could listen to him. Rue couldn't bring himself to lie, but neither could he tell her the whole truth. She must never know about the Finest creations. *You are listening to me now, are you not?*

She thought on that for a moment, then shook her head, the motion sending the hood from her cloak loose. "I don't think it's because I can listen, Rue. I think it's because you can talk. But you don't talk to anyone else, do you?"

Now it was his turn to ponder. He talked to other Finest, when presented the opportunity. He could talk to all the animals of this world. And he spoke to the spirit of Steadfast, though he knew that his once-mentor wasn't always present.

"Rue?" She impatiently thrummed her fingers against his neck.

How not to lie to her?

"Rue? Do you talk to others? People? Other horses? Can you?"

He made a wuffling sound. *I talked to the wolves, Kalantha, but they did not listen. They chased us to the village on stilts, Stilton you called the place. I talk to you . . .*

"When you've a mind to," she finished. She leaned back and tipped her face up, scowling to see a few dark clouds. "I think it might rain today."

Yes, he answered to both statements. The Finest smelled the water in the air. It seemed to rain oh-so-frequently in these woods.

THEY STOPPED AT SUNSET, AFTER NARROWLY AVOIDING A TRIO of hunters armed with bows and axes. It had rained on and off for the past few hours, gently, but was cold given the brisk wind that joined it. Kalantha retreated into the wolfskin cloak she had been given in Stilton and was glancing around for a piece of dry ground that she wasn't going to find.

"Rue, look." She pointed through a weave of river birch, where a faint red glow could have been mistaken for the last bit of sun—were it west and not south. "What is it?"

The Finest sniffed. "Fire," he told her. And something else. He picked up the scent of flowers, a mix of honeysuckle and violets, fresh when there shouldn't be such this late in the fall and this cold. He trained his ears forward, barely hearing the crackling of flames. "A small fire."

"A campfire," she provided, as she slipped from his back. She stretched and rubbed the back of her legs. "Out in the woods. Someone is cooking dinner maybe. We should avoid that, too."

The Finest could tell she was torn between investigating—he'd heard her stomach growl more than once this afternoon—and between keeping her distance. They'd skirted the last village and the hunters.

She took a step closer and pulled back the branches of a small evergreen tree. "Too far away to see it. Can you see?"

Gallant-Stallion snorted, his breath puffing away in the chill air. *No*, he admitted after a few moments. *Not without getting closer*, he added to himself. His curiosity tugged him a step, then another, careful not to brush against low limbs that might rattle together.

He wasn't hungry, he'd eaten his fill of dead grass and some tasteless moss hours ago. And he wasn't terribly cold—Finest creations were sturdier than common animals. But there was something in the scent of flowers that was tugging at him. How could there be flowers in the late, cold fall?

"Rue, stop."

He didn't. The Finest edged closer still, keeping behind a thick white pine, peeking through a gap in the branches, making out the shape of a rotund man, a colorful wagon, and a pair of horses that had been pulling it.

Well met, brother Finest, the larger of the horses said. *Share our fire and share your story.*

Gallant-Stallion looked over his shoulder at Kalantha. Her arms were crossed and her lower lip edged out. Clearly, she wanted to remain out of sight. Gallant-Stallion stared into the camp, watched the man back away from the fire and wring his hands, then retreat to the other side of the boxlike wagon.

Share our fire, the large horse repeated.

Without another thought, Gallant-Stallion flicked his tail and walked into the camp.

8 · Bartholomew and Ruined Plans

> That we wear the forms of horses and ponies to hide our presence in
> the world is a blessing. The horses and ponies of Paard-Peran are
> among the most noble and magnificent of creatures. Strong, loyal,
> good-natured, and needed~we Finest have those things in common
> with horses. Would that men and women shared those traits as well.
>
> ~*Able Ironhooves, mentor of Steadfast*

The Finest was a warmblood, a trakehner, Gallant-Stallion
had heard men in the stables call the breed. Dark brown,
she was sixteen hands high and had a long neck and well-
shaped shoulders. Her ears were small and alert, her head held
well and her eyes intense-looking. She had powerful quarters
and noticeably hard hooves, and her black mane and tail were
braided and festooned with small red ribbons.

Her companion horse was a beautiful palomino, a full hand
shorter and golden-colored, with a mane and tail so white they
looked like spun sugar, and similarly braided and festooned.
The palomino was an old horse, his teeth jutting out at a forward angle, short and blunted. There was a blaze running
down his head, turning pink on his muzzle and forming a
heart-shaped patch there. His eyes were wide and glazed with a
milky-blue film.

Gallant-Stallion considered the old horse one of the most

striking he'd ever seen . . . Finest or common animal. Truly beautiful.

Scuddles is pretty, isn't he? This came from the warmblood. *Thirty-two years old, he is. Venerable for a horse. You should have seen him a decade or more ago. His mane looked like molten silver, it did. Put the stars to shame.* The Finest altered her words to talk in the language of horses. *Sir Scuddles of Willum's Bay, meet . . .*

Gallant-Stallion, though my charge calls me Rue.

The one is a powerful Finest name, the warmblood continued, *the other a sad, sad name. Rue for rueful, is it?*

It is not a sad name when she says it. In fact, it sounds like music.

Sir Scuddles nickered a greeting and agreed the name Rue sounded pleasant.

She? the warmblood pressed. *Ah, your charge! She is the girl behind the white pine, is she? Will she join us?*

Her name is Kalantha. And you are . . .

Prudent-Flehmen.

He nodded a formal greeting. Gallant-Stallion knew that flehmen was a term for a horse's lip when it curled back in response to strong smells like lemons and garlic. He wondered how she came by the unusual name, but decided that was a question for another time.

Good evening to you, Prudent-Flehmen, and to you Sir Scuddles, Gallant-Stallion offered.

The palomino wuffled to Prudent-Flehmen, asking her to describe their deep-voiced visitor.

Gallant-Stallion hadn't realized the old horse was blind, and Prudent-Flehmen caught his surprise.

Scuddles gets along quite well, especially harnessed next to me. Told me he's seen enough of the world, and now gets by just smelling it, he does.

Your charge? Gallant-Stallion pressed.

I sometimes think Scuddles is my charge. He's been with us for twenty years, he has. In truth, I do shepherd this old horse, I do. But my official charge is the man on the other side of the wagon. Bartholomew Heiser Wembly the Second, he calls himself. There's a sign on the other side of the wagon. It spells out his name in all manner of garish colors, it does. Do you care to see it?

Gallant-Stallion gave a shake of his head and listened. Scuddles was softly nickering again, asking the warmblood for more information about the visitor and why he smelled so much of mud. Kalantha was softly stirring the needles of the white pine behind him, and the Finest wondered if she was able to eavesdrop on the secret conversation. On the other side of the wagon, he heard a series of clanks and clinks, then the shuffling of paper.

I will introduce you to Bartholomew, Prudent-Flehmen offered.

Not necessary, sister Finest, I . . .

Prudent-Flehmen ignored him and gave out a loud whinny, then stamped her hooves against the damp ground.

A moment later, a stoop-shouldered bear of a man came out from behind the wagon. He looked almost humorous to Gallant-Stallion, a testament to excesses. The man had the bulbous red-veined nose of one who drinks far too much, and a belly that hung over his belt, obscuring the front of the belt and any buckle that might be there. His shirt strained at the seams and wouldn't button toward the bottom, and his pants were worn at the knees and shiny with age. His hair was a yellowed white, straggly and unkempt—the Finest noted twigs caught in it. His beard was the only thing that had been groomed recently, as it was short and even. But even it was not clean, as there was a red stain just under his lip, indicating wine or a piece of fruit that had spilled. A short sword hung from the side of his waist, sticking out at an angle because it could not lie flat against his ample hips.

"Sir Scuddles, Brown-Girl, what have we here?" His voice seemed too soft and high-pitched for his size. He waddled over to the palomino, rubbing at something in his eye as he went. "A big horse is what we have here. A big, big horse with his legs and belly all spattered with mud. No saddle, out in the open. I'd say we have us a big, big horse to help you pull the wagon. Get some extra tack up in Bitternut and . . ."

"That's my horse." Kalantha burst into the clearing and rushed to Gallant-Stallion's side. She reached up and twisted her fingers in his mane. "Rue is my horse. He just got away from me for a moment is all."

The rotund man squinted and took a step toward Kalantha. "So we have us a big, big horse and a slip of a girl. Who are you, girl?"

She squared her shoulders and kept her hand on Gallant-Stallion. "My name's Kal Morgan." It was the same name she'd used in Stilton. "And this is my horse, Rue."

He shook his head, a piece of food flying from his beard. "Out in these woods all by yourself?"

She nodded, but he wagged a finger at her as if to say he didn't believe a word.

"Where are your parents?"

"Not here," she answered. She gave a tug on Rue's mane, and gestured with her head back the way they'd came. "And we have to be going now. We're in a hurry."

"Where then? Where are your parents?"

"Not here," she repeated. After a moment: "Dead."

"On your own, Kal Morgan?"

She drew her lips into a thin line, then shook her head defiantly. "I have Rue. I don't need anybody else."

"Strong-looking horse," he observed. "Big, big horse. My name's Bartholomew, Kal Morgan. I am pleased to make your and Rue's acquaintance." He offered his hand, but she didn't take it.

Bartholomew and Kal silently regarded each other. His eyes locked onto hers for a moment, then dropped to the ropy scar on her neck.

Prudent-Flehmen, your charge is . . . interesting looking, Gallant-Stallion said, finding no other word to describe the man of age and excess.

As is yours. I have been with Bartholomew a little more than twenty years. He is my third to shepherd. How long have you been with the child?

Two years, nearly. She is my first charge. Gallant-Stallion was pleased to realize that Kalantha could not hear him while he talked to the other Finest. So she could only hear him when he specifically talked to her. It was good to know, he decided.

Then you will grow close and grow together, Gallant-Stallion.

If she and I survive. Gallant-Stallion cocked his head to better study the man. The Finest could detect a trace of cherries about Bartholomew, and something strong and sour underneath, which he suspected was ale or mash. Too, the man smelled as if he could use a bath—a long one. What possibly could be redeeming about this wreck of a Fallen Favorite? Why would the Finest Court want someone such as he shepherded? Why would they possibly want this man saved? There was still the scent of flowers, which initially drew the Finest's attention. That was coming from the wagon. The Finest was still curious about that.

"You shouldn't be out here alone, girl," Bartholomew lectured Kalantha. He was still fixated on her scar. "There are lots of wolves in the woods. A bear or two passes through once in a while, though not lately. They don't bother us. They don't like our bright and noisy wagon, I suspect. Probably afraid of His Majesty." He proudly pointed to the blind palomino. "And probably afraid of me." He let out a laugh, his belly jiggling and threatening the rest of the buttons on his shirt. He finally looked away from Kalantha's scar. "Don't think I could scare anything, girl, truly."

She took a step back, again trying to tug Gallant-Stallion with her. But the Finest didn't budge.

"Except maybe you." He shook his head and waggled a thick finger again. "I'm nothing to be afraid of, Kal Morgan. Why don't you come sit by my fire and I'll fix us some dinner?"

She looked over her shoulder to the white pine she'd been hiding behind.

"Safer by the fire. Wolves don't like fire none."

She was hungry and thirsty, and the big man was waddling to the wagon and rolling up a tarp on this side. She could leave now, but . . . there were all manner of things displayed on shelves, tied down with strings and lengths of yarn so they wouldn't fall over when the wagon was moving. Everything looking interesting.

Kalantha and Gallant-Stallion were both captivated by the assortment. There was a foot-tall wooden statue of an old man leaning on a knobby cane, a toad perched on his head. Next to that were painted clay figurines of hummingbirds and parrots. On the bottom shelf were a dozen wooden masks with garishly painted eyebrows and mouths and with hooped rings hanging from their lips and ears. One had curvy black horns and looked evil. Another mask looked like the face of a striped cat with a lopsided grin.

There was a gargoyle's head, mouth open wide and made to hold fruit or vegetables from the look of it; crystal blue vases, some thin and elegant, others thick around the middle like

Bartholomew; books; walking canes with carved handles in the shapes of snakes, claws, and twisting vines; and small boxes filled with dried flowers.

So that was where the smell of flowers came from, Gallant-Stallion realized. Preserved, they somehow retained their wonderful scent. The Finest breathed deep, pulling as much of the aroma into his lungs as he could. It was far preferable to the smell of himself and the damp bark and earth that was everywhere.

Behind these objects were more shelves, and things hanging from slats against the roof of the wagon. It was difficult to make everything out, given the setting sun and growing shadows. The light from the campfire wasn't quite bright enough to help.

Still, Gallant-Stallion's keen eyes could sift through the layers of gray to make out a few more of the trinkets. There was a pillow embroidered with the design of a gold-colored horse, likely a rendition of Sir Scuddles. Another pillow was embroidered with peacocks and fantastical leaves and flowers. There was a ring of big brass keys; an elaborate oil lamp; a cast-iron left gauntlet that looked too large for any man to wear; painted eggs decorated with beads and yarn; preserved fish, posed with their mouths open wide and hanging from wires; folded pieces of black and white lace; an ivory-handled gardening spade; and various pots and pans, which Bartholomew was picking through.

He sells those things to people on the road and in all the towns we visit, Prudent-Flehmen explained. *Except for the pots and pans. He doesn't sell those. He cooks with them.*

A merchant.

Obviously, Gallant-Stallion. He always has been a merchant, from even the time before I met him. His father was a merchant, so he says, and his father's father, too. So very, very many things he sells—and buys—so he can sell more things elsewhere. We travel the country, north to south to north again, then follow the coast all the way around. We never stay in one spot too long. He says it wouldn't do to let any grass grow beneath his boot heels. And he never makes much profit. Ever. Ever. I fear he will always be materially poor.

Gallant-Stallion wanted to ask the warmblood why she was guiding and guarding a mere merchant, and what about the man made him worthy of a Finest's attention. But he stopped himself. The same could be asked of him. Why was he shepherding a girl who wanted no one to know she was sister to the King of Glamier? What was so important about her?

Who buys these . . . things? Gallant-Stallion asked instead.

People, I told you. Prudent-Flehmen shook her head, the bows spinning in her dark mane. *People who do not need them. No one needs these silly trinkets.*

Bartholomew managed to pull out a large pot without upsetting too many things on the shelves. He hung it on a spit over the fire, then went to the back of the wagon, where he dug around before bringing out a mesh bag filled with potatoes. He held this in his left hand, his right wrapped around a block covered with a waxed cloth.

He sat on a flat rock by the fire, gingerly removed the waxed cloth, and showed a square of white cheese to Kalantha. "Sharp and tasty and from about as far south as a horse and wagon can take you, a town in the Sunsummit foothills," he pronounced. "I'll cook us up some potatoes, and add this cheese. Makes an excellent thick soup. Sound good? I got some sweet onions from Ko's Point, too. But I don't care much for onions with cheese."

Kalantha nodded and cautiously joined him. "I'll help you peel the potatoes. And I don't like onions."

She ate two bowls and considered Bartholomew's potato

soup one of the most delicious things she'd ever tasted in her entire life. She followed it with mint candies the merchant said he'd acquired from a port due west of Duriam.

"Now what in the name of Peran-Morab are you doing out here, slip of a girl? I've shared my hospitality, you can share your tale."

She didn't mention her brother or Bishop DeNogaret or the High Keep Temple. She just explained that she came from the north, was last in Nadir, and that she was going south. Kalantha didn't lie to the merchant, she just didn't tell him everything.

"Hard for someone as young as you to make their way in the world. Harder still for a girl." Bartholomew collected the bowls and washed them with water from a barrel hooked to the back of the wagon. He returned several minutes later for the soup pot. "World's not at all a friendly place for youngsters on their own, Kal."

She smiled, remembering how her old friend Morgan the gardener called her Kal and how he kindly lectured her. This man had the same manner about him. She decided it would be easy to like Bartholomew.

"World's tough enough for a crusty old fellow like me. Could be cruel to someone like you, little Kal. In fact, I think you should . . ."

She cut him off with a frown. "I can take care of myself, sir, thank you. Been on my own before. I'm twelve now, and I'll be thirteen in a few months. I can . . ."

"Sir? Not many folks call me that." It was his turn to interrupt. "Little Kal, there are bandits on these roads. You might not have any gold about you, but that doesn't mean they'd leave you alone."

"I killed a bandit some months back. Killed him with a dagger." She sucked in her bottom lip, angry at herself for telling him more than she'd intended.

"Did you now?" Bartholomew gave her a skeptical look.

She nodded, her eyes unblinking.

The merchant's brow furrowed. "So you did, didn't you?" He rubbed his meaty hands on his pants. "I'd like to hear about it."

"I just told you. I killed a man, a bandit who would've killed me. And I don't want to talk about that anymore." Kalantha pretended to be interested in the fire. She poked it with a stick and watched the embers spark. "But I can take care of myself, I say."

"Apparently. You're welcome to come with me, though. Safer with His Majesty around. Not even a bear would . . ."

"I'm going to the Vershan Monastery."

Bartholomew let out a low whistle. "So you're choosing a religious life. An acolyte would be an apt calling for . . ."

"I'm not going to be an acolyte. But I'm going there to study. They have a big library."

"So I've heard."

"Lots and lots of books. Hundreds maybe."

"Thousands is more like it, little Kal. Vershan Monastery is supposed to be one of the greatest storehouses of written knowledge in all of . . . well, likely in all the world. No place has more books than that monastery, I've heard. Never had a call to visit it, though. So I can't say for absolute certain."

"Are we in Nasim-Guri, sir? That's where I've heard the monastery is. Somewhere south in Nasim-Guri."

"Bartholomew, please."

"Bartholomew."

"Nasim-Guri? Just about, I'd say. A few miles beyond that row of pines is the thickest branch of the Sprawling River. Past the bridge and a mile or two more and you're in Nasim-Guri. The Vershan Monastery is about as far south in Nasim-Guri as you can go, just inside the Gray Woods, I believe. As I said, I've never been there, figured the priests wouldn't be interested in my baubles. Not much profit to make with religious folk."

She gave a nod. "That's where Rue and I are going, Bartholomew. To study at the Vershan Monastery, but not to be an acolyte. I'll do as I please with my life."

He returned to scrubbing the soup kettle. "Admirable, little Kal, to be so headstrong. But difficult in this world."

"I know," she said softly. "Men make the rules and women embroider and cook and . . ."

"Hey, hey, young lady, don't you ever ever ever belittle the fine art of cooking! It takes considerable work to make something pleasing to the palate."

"I'm sorry. It was very good soup," she offered.

He continued to scrub the soup pot until it gleamed like new and the fire had died down to a warm glow. Kalantha curled up next to what was left of the fire and quickly fell asleep.

BREAKFAST CONSISTED OF APPLES, SHIRRED EGGS, AND HAM, all of which Bartholomew had somehow kept fresh in his wagon. Kalantha ate as much as she could handle, knowing that it could be some time before another warm meal. Then she helped him with the dishes and watched him store them in the wagon behind a shelf of vases. He fed the horses two apples each and let them eat from a bucket of oats.

"I'll not force you to stay with me, Kal Morgan." He brushed at a spot on his shirt, then met her gaze. "But I'll make the invitation again. Not that I'd expect it to be a long-term arrangement, as I'm quite the loner."

"No, Bartholomew. But thank you."

"Off to the storied Vershan Monastery, then, is it?"

She nodded and grabbed Gallant-Stallion's mane. Tugged on

it and jumped, then settled behind his neck. "I can take care of myself."

"So you've told me." He rummaged around in his wagon and pulled out a canvas sack. Then he went to the rear of the wagon and began filling it. "But make sure you also take care of that big, big horse. Not the prettiest animal I've seen . . . His Majesty Sir Scuddles would be that. But your punch looks sturdy and young. So you take care of him. I always say you can measure a man . . . or a girl . . . by the well-being of their horse."

"I'll take care of Rue." After a moment: "We take care of each other." She stroked Gallant-Stallion's neck. "We've been through a lot together, this punch and I. And I think he's quite pretty! I've got to go now, Bartholomew. Thank you for dinner last night, and the eggs this morning."

"Here." The merchant caught her just as she turned Gallant-Stallion to the south. He held out the canvas sack in one meaty hand. In the other was an ivory-handled short blade in a black leather sheath. "The weaponsmith in Dolour who made it called it a sax. Quite in demand there, doubles as a tool and a dagger. Quite sharp, Kal. Be careful."

She hesitated in accepting it.

"It's in case you run into any more bandits that need slaying. And I suppose you'll be needing a belt for that blade."

He returned to the wagon and fumbled around in the back. There was the clink of glass breaking and a muttered string of curse words. Kalantha sat the sax and the canvas bag in front of her and behind Gallant-Stallion's neck, and she quickly opened the bag and looked inside. There were a few apples and potatoes and two blocks of the delicious sharp cheese. A smaller net sack filled with shelled walnuts, and another with dried strips of beef. At the bottom were a dozen or more silver and brass figurines and two coral belt buckles, all of which she knew she could trade for food and other things she needed at towns and villages. And there was a small sprig of dried flowers that gave off the scent of lilacs.

She tied the bag tight and made sure it rested securely between her legs. Then she looked up as Bartholomew returned. He was carrying a thin brown leather belt, ornate because it was spotted with pearl-shaped pieces of silver. It tied, rather than buckled, and she put it around her waist, hooking the sax sheath through it.

"A little too long for a slip of a girl," he pronounced.

"The belt is beautiful. Thanks."

"You're welcome. Take care of yourself and that big, big horse, Kal Morgan."

Then she started south, looking over her shoulder once and waving. The merchant was busy with securing everything on the wagon and didn't return her wave.

It is why he is worth guiding and guarding, Prudent-Flehmen said to Gallant-Stallion. *His kindness overshadows all of his faults. He lends a hand to needy strangers. It is why he will never be rich.*

Materially rich, Gallant-Stallion said.

Yes. And it is why he is a Fallen Favorite worthy of my time and affection. Safe journey, Gallant-Stallion who is also called Rue.

Safe journey to you and Sir Scuddles as well.

The old palomino nickered good-bye.

THEY REACHED THE THICKEST PART OF THE SPRAWLING RIVER by early afternoon, making good time because the ground was firmer—evidence it hadn't rained here in a few days. But the clouds overhead were tinged with gray and reflected darkly on the surface of the swift moving water. The moisture was thick in the air. It could rain at any time.

There was a bridge a hundred or more yards to the east, but two armored men stood at the far side of it. Because the bridge rails obscured some of the details, Kalantha and Gallant-Stallion could only tell that the men's tabards were dark orange, striped with black and yellow, the colors of the King of Nasim-Guri. And they seemed to have on shirts of chain mail—the little bit of sun showing through the clouds made the sleeves glimmer.

"We could probably cross there," Kalantha said, nodding toward the bridge. "But they might ask questions. I'm tired of questions. Or they might turn us away. Or worse, I suppose."

Gallant-Stallion doubted the guards would keep her out of the country, especially if she came up with a credible story for traveling alone. The guards were probably stationed on the bridge to make sure no one was bringing something into the country that the King didn't want brought in, or to keep bandits and rough-looking people out.

Still, the Finest respected Kalantha's concerns, so he followed the river to the west, crossing it when he felt they were a safe distance from the guards and likely wouldn't be noticed. The current was strong and fast, and Gallant-Stallion's hooves couldn't touch the bottom. Kalantha kept only one hand fastened in his mane, with the other she held the bag of food against her chest and above the water.

"You swim well, Rue," she said.

The water was cold, but smelled sweet, and Gallant-Stallion committed to memory the feel of it against his hide and the sensation of swimming. He didn't think there were lakes or ponds deep enough for swimming in the land of the Finest Court.

He swam as quickly as he could without jeopardizing Kalantha and the bag of food and trinkets. When he was on the opposite bank, the chill fall air stung his wet hide. He darted past a line of river birch and trotted briskly until he came to a clearing. The breeze was cut here by the trunks and weave of branches, and so he felt a little warmer.

"Bartholomew said we should follow a merchant's road. It should be a little that way." She waved an arm to the east. "It meets up with the bridge we saw, so it can't be far. He said follow it all the way through the country and past a couple of small villages. We'll have to ask someone along the way to make sure we're going the right direction. Funny . . . that priest in Stilton, Ergoth his name was. He said the Vershan Monastery was straight south of Stilton and a half a day's ride beyond the border. Bartholomew said it was farther away than that."

So one of them is wrong, Gallant-Stallion thought. Or perhaps both of them. Maybe neither knows where this monastery is. Or maybe neither is capable of giving good directions. Instead of voicing that to Kalantha, he said: *Why do you seek this Vershan Monastery?*

She covered her mouth with her free hand. "Oh, Rue, I thought I'd told you! I want to find out about those horrid birds that attacked me and Meven and you. Three times they attacked us. I told that priest—Ergoth—about the birds, and he believed me! He said the Vershan Monastery has lots of books, and he remembered reading something years ago about very smart birds. So I'm going to find that very same book and learn about the birds. And then maybe I can find out why someone wanted to kill me and my brother, and why they killed our cousin Prince Edan."

Gallant-Stallion admired her determination. But her notion of ferreting out information about the assassin-birds reminded him that she was a child. And seeking the Vershan Monastery to find one book in perhaps thousands was indeed a childish notion. If the book existed, it might discuss trained parrots or hunting hawks. And the book might not exist at all.

But there was no place else the girl or he needed to be. And going farther south would perhaps keep her safe from the birds and her single-minded brother. So visiting Vershan Monastery would do no harm. Too, it might be warmer.

I killed many of the assassin-birds, Kal, Gallant-Stallion said. *On the palace grounds in Nadir, and before that when you were with your cousin in the wedding party, then in the Galmier Mountains. Perhaps the birds no longer threaten you.*

"Maybe. I hope you're right, Rue. But I have to know about them. I have to."

THEY FOLLOWED THE MERCHANT TRAIL, THEN CUT INLAND, searching for signs pointing to Vershan Monastery or for fellow travelers who might provide better directions. They found neither, but they stumbled upon the place late into the evening, just as a cold, steady rain started to fall.

Illuminated by flashes of lightning and by the moon when it peeked through gaps in the ever-moving clouds, was a large wooden sign, cracked in the middle and lying in a growing puddle.

VERSHAN MONASTERY, it read. THE ACOLYTES OF PAARD-ZHUMD'S ABBEY WELCOME THEE AND THINE. There were more words, but they were obliterated by cracks and mud and age.

Several yards beyond the sign was part of a cobblestone walk. It looked like the walk used to form a circle, and that there used to be a garden in the middle of it. Some of the trees remained, and there were two headless statues and a shattered bench, and behind the circle rose a stone tower, also shattered.

It looked like a crooked finger, bent as if to scold the sky. Part of the crenellation around the top was missing, and there was a jagged gash in the stone along one side. Most of the ornate brickwork around the windows was either missing or had crumbled, and the two columns outside the main entrance looked as if they'd been sheared in two.

There had been several outbuildings, these were a mix of stone and wood. The remains of them stretched away from the tower and into the darkness. The rain pattered down on everything, soft against the wood but *rat-a-tat-tatting* against the stones.

Kalantha slid off Gallant-Stallion, taking the canvas bag with her, shoulders hunched around it and wolf-cloak keeping it reasonably dry.

"The merchant, the priest . . . neither of them told me this place was ruined." She shuffled toward the crooked tower. "They didn't say no one lived here anymore."

Indeed, there was no trace of even a single occupant, and all the Finest could smell was the rain, the mud, and the rotting wood.

"All my plans are ruined too," she said. Even in the darkness, the Finest could see her shoulders shake. She was trying to keep from crying.

"I don't know what to do now, Rue. What am I going to do?" Kalantha paused between the pillars and stared at the tower entrance. The door had fallen off the hinges a long time ago, and the opening beyond looked like the maw of some hungry, ancient beast.

9 · Eyeswide and the Bishop

There are pockets of darkness across the land of the Fallen Favorites. Nurtured by some unnameable and perhaps unknowable vileness, they hold men and women who give no thoughts of compassion and redemption. Though these pockets are small, some of them are very deep, and these hold the most corrupt, the men and women who have fallen the farthest and who have no desire, and no longer any ability, to climb toward the light.

~Nimblehoof Sundancer, shepherd to the Keeper of Resan's Tower

The room was paneled in polished walnut that glowed dark and warm in the light of a large, brass and crystal oil lamp. The wick was turned up high, and the lamp sat on the left-hand corner of a massive desk that was made of black-stained oak. Cherubs cavorting with fawns were carved into the panels on three sides, and the legs were made to resemble the clawed feet of some great cat.

The top of the desk was as polished as the walls, and it gleamed so intensely it looked as if it was wet. Its surface was for the most part empty, so Bishop DeNogaret could lean forward and see his reflection in it. But there were a few papers, orderly stacked, on the right-hand corner, and these pertained to a treaty with Uland he was toying with and that he intended Meven to sign the following morning.

The Bishop sat in a cushioned high-backed chair of the same black-stained wood, and drew his shoulders back as far as his age and infirmities would allow. He let out a deep breath between his teeth, sounding like a snake hissing a warning. Then he slowly leaned forward, just enough so he could see his face mirrored back at him, steepled his fingers, and raised his gaze to his visitor.

The owl was perched on the back of a chair across from Bishop DeNogaret's desk. His wide eyes narrowed in the lamplight.

"Too bright," the owl said.

After a moment, the Bishop leaned farther forward and turned down the wick. "Better, old friend?"

The owl let out a low, throaty hoot. He was a large owl, nearly two feet tall and thick. The feathers that covered his body were various shades of beige, ecru, and white, darker at his throat and lightest at his long, curved talons, which were digging into the chair back and leaving noticeable marks. He fluttered his wings, showing off rich shades of brown striped with snow white bands and threaded here and there with thin lines of black. The owl's head was his most stunning property, white around his sharp-looking beak and above his large sun yellow eyes. There was a reddish brown stripe that fitted around those eyes like a bandit's mask, and there was a darker shade of feathers at the top that looked like a monk's skullcap. The owl swiveled his head one way and then the other, practically spinning it all the way around before returning his gaze to Bishop DeNogaret.

"Yes, that is better. But no light would be best of all."

The Bishop chuckled, a rare sound that caused the owl to cock his head. "My old friend, were I to plunge my study into utter darkness, I could not see at all, and you would have all the advantage."

The owl let out a deep hoot and made a motion of ruffling his feathers. "I have no advantage but what you give me."

"Very political of you, Eyeswide."

"Very smart of me," the owl embellished. "Very careful of me."

"Indeed." Bishop DeNogaret rested against the back of his chair a moment, a silence settling heavy between him and the owl. When Eyeswide swiveled his head again, as if he was losing interest in the meeting and looking for something to occupy himself, the Bishop stood. He leaned against the desk, the oil from his hands smudging the polish and distorting the reflection. Then he pushed himself backward, moving the chair, which made an unsettling scratching noise against the slate floor. He reached for a cane behind the desk, gnarled black wood that looked like a serpent twisted around a branch.

Then he paced behind the desk, the lamp's faint light making his pale gray robes look charcoal. The light coming from beneath him cast shadows up his face and made it look as if his eyes were empty sockets. He stopped and faced the owl, and those sockets bore into Eyeswide.

"And you need to be smart and careful right now, don't you, Eyeswide? Despite your occasional, petty triumphs, such as killing Prince Edan and letting my puppet claim his title . . . my puppet who now is the King . . . you've displeasured me."

The owl straightened to his full height and put on an almost human expression of surprise and disbelief. "I have done as you bid me, Bishop DeNogaret. How is there no pleasure in that?"

The Bishop resumed his pacing, his free arm gesturing theatrically and his steps exaggerated so that the hem of his robe hushed against the stone and sounded like a serpent slithering across a patch of sand.

"You did not kill Meven when I dictated it."

"True," the owl was quick to reply. "But rather than leave the throne heirless and ceded by decree to you, Bishop, you decided to rule behind the boy. You safely and secretly rule from behind the throne, and you are therefore effectively cloaked by the hollow King of Galmier."

"I do rule this land," the Bishop admitted, still pacing. "The boy hasn't the guile, the stomach, or the mind for it. I, however, have all of those things—and more. I have a hunger for power and wealth, and I have a desire to sweep all of this land into one country under my divine aegis."

His course took him around the desk and behind the owl. Eyeswide swiveled his head so he was facing the Bishop again.

"You know, Eyeswide, dear friend, I have planned my ascension for many years. I am an old man, far older than I appear, and I still have a great many years left on this world. So many years, I must do something grand with them." He looked to the ceiling and worked a crick out of his neck. "I became a trusted confidant to Meven's parents and suggested they name me as guardian to their children—in the event anything untoward should happen to them. And when Meven and his sister Kalantha were very young, I had the 'untoward' happen. I had their parents killed. The children were offered to the King of Galmier, their beloved Uncle. But on my advice, and after reading the document that named me guardian, the King relented and gave them to me to look after. I raised them as if they were my own children, Meven especially. I made the boy dependent on me so he would trust me and never question my instructions. And when the time was right, I instructed Meven and Kalantha to travel with Prince Edan to his wedding. And I instructed you and your flock to kill the entire wedding party. There was not to be a single survivor. It was to look as if an army had swept in and murdered them all. Politics, certainly. Then I would implicate another country, and there would be a war. Ah, a glorious, bloody war."

Eyeswide opened his beak to offer a rebuttal, but a hissing sigh from the Bishop stopped the owl.

"You killed most of the wedding party, I'll give you that concession, old friend. But not Meven and Kalantha—mere children, and you could not defeat them! Then you failed to kill the children again in the Galmier Mountains. Oh, after that I concocted the plan to rule from the shadows, making wars and policies behind Meven—and letting all eyes and all manner of political foulness touch only him. It is an acceptable plan that perhaps has more merit than my initial bid. I will stay pure and clean, playing the mentor and advisor while making all the decisions in secret. I still want Kalantha dead, Eyeswide. And on the palace grounds days ago, you failed in that task. She is but a girl, a child, Eyeswide. Twelve years old and harmless and weak and you couldn't kill her!" Spittle flew from the Bishop's mouth, and his fist shook with fury. He pointed the cane at the owl. "A child! You could not best a child!"

"It was the big horse," the owl cut in, ignoring another hiss from the Bishop. "He protected her somehow, and he brought down dozens, more than a hundred, of my birds in the process. The best of my force! He killed my trusted lieutenant Fala. You are furious I did not slay the girl. I am furious that so many of my assassins fell to her ugly horse. That Fala died. Do you know how long it takes me to nurture my birds? To train them? To taint them with the darkness of the Old Forest and birth in them the desire to draw blood? They hunger to deal death by the time I am done with them. They fly in artful formations to hide their true nature, no easy skill to learn I assure you, Bishop. And so you are angry one girl still lives. I am angry so many, many, many of my birds do not."

A longer silence passed between the two, the light from the lantern growing dimmer and the shadows darker and longer. Bishop DeNogaret returned to his high-backed chair and steepled his fingers again. He leaned across his desk, but did not look down to see his smudged reflection.

"The loss of my birds is your loss as well, Bishop. Fewer puppets for you to manipulate." The owl closed his eyes and drew his head down closer to his body.

"The girl must die," the Bishop said. "I cannot afford to have her grow up and marry, have male offspring that might dare challenge my right to this kingdom because of their royal blood. She must be found and dealt with swiftly, finally. And when the time is right, I will deal with Meven . . . swiftly, finally. There will be no more Montolls, no more royal blood. And after Galmier . . . after all of this great island becomes Galmier . . . after whatever wars and however many years it takes . . . after all the threats and curses and attempts on King Meven's life are made . . . I will step in and wrest control. There will be no more Montolls. There will be only Bishop Therland DeNogaret, King of Galmier, Bishop of Nadir, and devout servant of the Dark Twins."

The oil lamp flickered in a breeze that rushed into the room, and the owl ruffled his feathers again and opened his eyes. "I will find the girl, Bishop, and I will take care of her. I will nurture my flock in honor of the Dark Twins."

"It is they, after all, who made you," Bishop DeNogaret purred.

"They made me, yes," Eyeswide said. "Gifted me with speech and an intelligence as great as any man's. But you gift me with purpose. And when I finish the girl, and when the time is right for you to take the crown, you will give all of the Old Forest to me." Soundlessly he left the chair and flew out the window, heavy dark curtains fluttering in his wake.

10 · Vershan Monastery

I paid close attention when my mentor passed on all her knowledge of the Fallen Favorites. I studied the words of the Finest sages about the men and women of Paard-Peran. And I made my own observations when I became a shepherd and was given a charge. Three Fallen Favorites did I watch over before I returned to the Finest Court to live the remainder of my days. One thing remained true through all the years~the more time I spent with the Fallen Favorites, the more I cherished and appreciated being a Finest. I thank the gods I was given this form and allowed to dwell in the Court lands. I am sorry for the Fallen Favorites, who have but two legs and flawed hearts. And I am grateful I am a Finest and not fated to live with the Fallen Favorites forever.

~Jorin Honeymane, from his life's chronicles

*S*teadfast, I had not expected her to find a book she sought. But I expected her to find the monastery. I just had not expected the monastery to be . . . destroyed. Gallant-Stallion stood between the two broken columns, listening to the thunder and watching as flashes of lightning illuminated the ruins of what once had been a magnificent structure. Up close, he noted that there had been four towers, not just the one that still stood. But the other three were mounds of rubble overgrown with scrub grass.

No matter how wise Kalantha seems at times, she is just a child. I fear she cannot take many more disappointments. It is as if the very world is against her, Steadfast.

The wind shifted slightly, catching the Finest's mane and holding it suspended in the air. It gusted warm for just a moment, and Gallant-Stallion felt Steadfast's spirit.

The lightning flashed again and again, and against the crumbling wall of the remaining tower, Gallant-Stallion briefly saw the shadow of two horses—one a punch with short legs and a large frame, and the other an impressive steed, Steadfast.

I met another Finest today, Steadfast, one called Prudent-Flehmen. She is shepherd to an old man who drinks and eats far more than he should, but who has an uncommon kindness about him.

None of the Fallen Favorites is perfect, Gallant-Stallion. If they were, they would not need us. And even we have our faults.

Gallant-Stallion gave a nod of his head. *I well know that, Steadfast. I met a mountain pony Finest with a curiosity so intense it caused her to lose her charge. Another in Bitternut is so fond of the entire village that she has taken it upon herself to watch over all the people there rather than return to the Court and be given one to guide on the path to perfection. I am far from faultless myself. I don't know how to guide this girl, Steadfast. I am keeping her safe, the best I can, but I don't know. . . .*

Thunder rocked the land and a thick stroke of lightning came to the ground, eerily lighting the crooked tower. There was only one shadow cast on the wall now, that of the punch. The ground shook again and the wind changed. The breeze was cold once more, and the presence of Steadfast had faded.

Where is it you go, Steadfast? Where do you come from? And where do you run when your spirit does not travel here on the breeze? Where is it that spirits dwell when their bodies fail them? Is it a place only for the Finest? Or can the Fallen Favorites, the best of them, go there too?

Gallant-Stallion closed his eyes and flared his nostrils and let the wind tell him what it knew. There was the scent of mud, something he'd been unable to lose since venturing from the palace grounds. And there was the scent of stone, old and clean from the rains. It was neither pleasant nor unpleasant, just something that settled strongly on his tongue. Rotting wood, of course, heavily tinged the air. Wood was strewn all over—broken doors, frames, furniture that through the years had turned to pulpy piles for the spring and summer insects to infest. It looked like someone might have tended a garden near the tower in the summer. But it was crude, and was more likely an artful assortment of weeds. Scraps of cloth trapped beneath stones smelled musty and moldy, so saturated with water and mud, grease from cookfires, and blood from injuries and sickness. There was a well, a thin rope and a battered bucket hanging from a crank. The water in its depths smelled sweet.

The wind brought him no news of wolves or people beyond Kalantha. Nor were there scents of birds or other creatures. It was as if the animals stayed away from the ruined Vershan Monastery.

Everything about this place was old, and Gallant-Stallion discovered he was disturbed that both this priest he hadn't met in Stilton—Ergoth, Kalantha called him—and the fat merchant who he had met, misled Kalantha about this Vershan Monastery. Hopefully the men truly did not know the place had decades ago fallen. But the merchant had spoke of thousands of books and thereby encouraged Kalantha. How could such a traveled man not know about the ruins?

The rain pattered harder against his back, coldly massaging him and easing his tired muscles. Gallant-Stallion hadn't slept at all the night Kalantha stayed with the merchant. He stayed up through the hours talking to Prudent-Flehmen about Paard-Peran and her previous two charges. She'd told him they'd been adults, and that she was glad she hadn't been given a child to shepherd.

The Fallen Favorites are difficult enough at times to under-

stand and to nudge in the right direction. Children? They would be difficult at all times, I would guess, Gallant-Stallion.

Gallant-Stallion hadn't answered her then, though he wished now he would have argued. Kalantha was not terribly difficult to understand. With a snort and a shake of his head to fling the hair out of his eyes, Gallant-Stallion took a last look around the outside of the tower, then he walked through the doorway that indeed did resemble the maw of some beast.

It might have been an impressive entryway at one time, as there were hints of ornate wood trim and pieces of banners ringing the room. It had been a place for men, clearly, and not for horses. A wide staircase wound its way up the wall, the steps as crumbly as the bricks that made up the tower.

Kalantha was sitting a few steps up, beneath a window where only a little light came in when the lightning flashed outside. She looked so small huddled in her wolfskin cloak, like a dirty, scared urchin. She was clutching a piece of precious cheese she'd cut from one of the blocks.

"It's not so wet in here, Rue." She was putting up a brave front, her shoulders no longer shaking.

But the Finest's eyes were keen, and he could see the streaks from tears on her cheeks.

"Wet, but not as wet as outside."

Part of the roof must have been gone, as water ran in thick rivulets down the western inside of the wall, opposite from where Kalantha sat. Water dripped into a puddle in the middle of the chamber, and Gallant-Stallion could make out that the floor had once had a tile mosaic on it. Now only a piece of the floor remained, this showing a knight with a spear in hand. The rest were chips, and it looked as if someone had taken a hammer to the floor to break it all up. There was a ragged gash deep in the stone, and several inches above the knight's head, the gash spread into a spiderweb of cracks that stretched to the west and south. The spiderweb continued up the south wall and disappeared into shadows so thick even his superb vision could not pick through them.

Water drizzled on the sill near Kalantha, but because of the direction of the wind, it didn't rain inside or on the steps. She took a bite of the cheese and chewed quickly, not trying to hide her hunger.

"Bartholomew even put a few pieces of candy in here," she said, gesturing to the canvas bag sitting next to her. "But I'm going to save them. Save the potatoes and the rest of the cheese, too. Maybe I'll have just a little piece of meat, though. I think it might be venison."

Gallant-Stallion was finished inspecting the chamber and turned his full attention to her.

"Maybe I should've gone with Bartholomew. He was a nice man, and he was good to his horses. He said it wouldn't've been a forever thing. Probably just until we got to the next town or so. Maybe I should've. His potato soup was so delicious."

She looked at the punch and finished her piece of cheese, then retrieved a small hunk of dried venison. She made sure all the food was wrapped tight, then she tied the bag and started chewing on the meat. It was tough, and she had to work at it.

"Or maybe I should've listened to Bishop DeNogaret. Maybe Dea Fortress is not so bad a place. He wants what's best for me, right, Rue? Him and Meven? The Bishop said a religious life is a good calling for a girl." She took another bite of the meat, her words muffled as she talked while she ate. "I know I certainly shouldn't've come here. What a horrible place this is. So dark and . . . and . . . empty. I'm scared, Rue. I don't want to be, but I am. I wish Meven were here. Or maybe I wish I was at Dea Fortress. It couldn't be so dark there, could it?"

Done with the venison, she stretched her hands to the sill

and ran them along the stone to wash them. Then she patted them on her leggings to dry them.

"It wouldn't be so empty at Dea Fortress. I'm sure of it. And I wouldn't . . ."

There was a loud thump from above.

"It's the storm," Kalantha said. There was a tremor in her voice. "The wind came in a window and knocked something over is all. Certainly there's nothing to . . ."

There was another thump, then a shuffling sound. Then a faint glow spread down the stairway. Footsteps followed it, slow and heavy, urging Kalantha to her feet. She scooped up her canvas bag and started toward Gallant-Stallion.

"What's the hurry, young one? No use running out into the rain. You'll catch your death." It was a man's voice, high and brittle with age.

Kalantha stood with her back against the Finest, wolfskin cloak pulled all around her and hood over her head.

"My, but you look like a shaggy beast in that thing! Bet it's warm, though."

The man came just far enough down the steps so Kalantha and the Finest could see him. He looked impossibly old, parchment pale skin a mass of wrinkles and age spots, wispy hair floating away from his head like a tangle of cobwebs. He was holding a guttering fat-soaked torch that gave off a rank smell. A black curl of oily smoke drifted upward from it. He was wearing a tattered green robe that hung above his bony knees. His feet were bare, the toes curled and ugly.

He wasn't a ghost, Gallant-Stallion picked up his scent—and realized he hadn't earlier because the man had been entrenched behind all the stone. It was an old-man smell of worn clothes that sweat had leeched into, of camphor and something else medicinal that he'd rubbed on himself, and of urine. He practically clung to the wall with his free hand, as he made his way down. His fingers slipped into the gaps between stones and hung on until his foot was on another step. It took him quite some time to make it to the bottom, emitting a quiet chuffing sound with each step, as if he'd overexerted himself to make the trip to this floor. His shoulders were so stooped forward that a hump had formed on his back, giving him the look of a turtle. He raised his head, like a turtle looking out of his shell and chuffed louder.

"Young man . . ." He held the torch out and squinted, looking at the punch and Kalantha. "Young man . . . what are you doing out on this rainy night?"

"He thinks me a boy, Rue," Kalantha whispered. It was obvious the old man was hard of hearing. "Traveling," she said, lowering her voice and trying to sound like a boy.

"What?"

"Traveling." She nearly shouted this. "Looking for a dry place to pass the night."

He nodded, like a turtle bobbing his head. "I've blankets upstairs, boy. And I'll share them with you. But that horse has to go outside."

Kalantha shook her head. "It's cold and raining and . . ."

"And this monastery is no place for an animal. Dirtying the floor, stinking up everything."

"Sir . . ."

"There used to be a stables around here . . . a big one, it was. But that was before the darkness came. Still, you can find a post or something there to tie him to, where there used to be a stables. Horses don't mind this weather, boy. Animals were meant to be outdoors."

"This is Vershan Monastery?" Kalantha made no move to shoo Rue outside.

The old man bobbed his head again. "Used to be. About seventy years ago."

"So long . . ."

"I was young then, an acolyte. That's why you're here, isn't it, boy? You want to be an acolyte? A priest?"

Kalantha didn't reply and didn't move.

"Well, you'll have to go to the Vershan Monastery to the south. The one they built after the quake brought this one down." The old man wheezed, shaking as a spasm wracked his skeletal frame. "Something very dark came to this place eighty years ago, boy. Something dark and with a dark purpose. It brought down the walls and brought down the homes of the villagers. Sixty years ago, I think it was. The earth cracked open and ate all the sheep and goats and pigs. Folks in the towns around here, old folks, they'll say it was just a quake, that tremors hit every once in a while. But I know different. I was here, boy. It was something dark. Ninety years past, maybe it was."

Kalantha shuddered and leaned harder against the Finest.

"So all the priests and acolytes packed up the books and relics and put them on whatever wagons they could find or could build. And they went south to build a new monastery. Seventy years ago. Said it would be stronger and that no quake would bring it down."

"You didn't go with them."

He shook his head, cobweb hair dancing in the light of his torch, and he wheezed again. There was a fleck of blood on his lower lip. "Someone had to stay behind, boy. This is a holy place. You don't just leave it untended . . . even if there's little to tend. I volunteered to stay, I felt a calling for it. And I've stayed here all these eighty years."

"But what if you . . ."

"Not if, *when,* boy. *When I die.* Someone comes to check on me each spring, someone they send from the Vershan Monastery. Usually a young priest who brings me clothes and fancy things to eat, a new pillow and a blanket. When they find me dead, someone else will have to come here to keep the vigil, I suppose. It is the way with our Order, to leave no holy place abandoned."

Kalantha shifted back and forth on the balls of her feet.

"So you can share my blankets tonight, boy, if you take that horse outside."

"Thank you," Kalantha said. "But I've got to be going. I need to go to the Vershan Monastery—the one that's standing."

"Frightful weather."

"I've traveled in worse."

"Good boy, you'll make a fine acolyte. Maybe you'll be tending these ruins someday."

"Maybe." Kalantha didn't know what else to say.

"Your name, boy, so I when I pray in the morning I can include you."

She paused. "Morgan."

"A good name, for a good boy. Say it again."

"Morgan."

"A good name."

"And you, sir, you are . . ."

He stared at her, eyes squinting, body wracked by another spasm. "Calvert was my father's name, boy. I can remember that, but I can't remember mine or my mother's. So you can remember me as Calvert."

"Calvert," Kalantha pronounced.

"Yes, that's it. A good name, too. Now take that horse out of the grand hallway, Morgan, and be on your way to the monastery. Give them Calvert's regards. The gods watch over you, boy. You'll be a fine acolyte."

He waited until Kalantha led Gallant-Stallion from the tower, then the old man turned and very slowly made his way up the stairs.

11 · A Fowl Gathering

I find the beasts of Paard-Peran amazing in their variety, nonesuch
dwell in the perfect pastures of the Finest Court. The bluebirds~I like
those best, I think, able to fly above their troubles and dance in the soft
rain. Their song, so lovely and soft, everything delicate. Other feathered creatures never held my attention so, their colors and hearts never
as bright. Would that I could take only the bluebirds back to the Court
lands. I could watch them dance forever.

~The Old Mare, from her chronicles

The Old Forest was as dark as the owl's soul. In places the
trees grew so close together a man could not slip between the
trunks. Some hardwoods were as wide around as a cottage, and
many of them were nearly a thousand years old and stretched
three hundred feet or more into the sky. There were few
saplings, as the weave of branches—even in this late fall when
most of the trees had shed their leaves—was so thick little sunlight made its way to the forest floor to nurture seeds. But there
were gaps in the canopy here and there, some of these because
giants had finally succumbed to age or lightning and dropped
their branches and let a little light in. This is where the few
seedlings could be found. And in one of these clearings, near the
center of the Old Forest, Eyeswide gathered his assassin-birds.

He strutted in front of them, slowly, visually measuring
them, and noting in the late afternoon sunlight which ones
trembled at his presence. Some put on a brave front, puffing

out their feathery chests and holding their wings back like knights at attention before their commander. But there was the tremor of apprehension in their eyes, and the owl fixed these birds with his icy stare until they lost the mental battle and looked away. The ones who showed no measure of fear and would not look away were the fools, he thought. Their pomposity could cost them their lives—but not by Eyeswide's talons. His flock was depleted, and he couldn't afford to slay any more as an example. The brave fools could more easily die in battle, likely be the first to fall—overconfident and too certain of themselves, their skills not quite equal to their bluster. He needed desperately to add to his malevolent flock.

The owl stepped back, retreating into the shadow cast by the trunk of a massive black walnut, the fallen shells feeling good against the bottoms of his feet. He hated the daylight, and rarely called his birds and bats during these hours. But there was an urgency to this meeting, and so he struggled to deal with the sun today.

Blackbirds, small kite hawks, black skimmers, herons the color of coal, brown-headed cowbirds, grackles, crows of various sizes, starlings, and more—all of them dark and twisted and fiercely loyal to Eyeswide—were spread out in military formation. Bats hung from the lowest branches; they were also his assassins and hated the light more than he. Eyeswide had enhanced all of them by drawing energy from an enchanted pool that was hidden in the very center of the Old Forest. As the divine Dark Twins—Iniquis and Abandon—increased the owl's cunning and intelligence, so Eyeswide enhanced the members of his depraved army.

He gave many of them the gift of speech, a long lifespan, and a sentience that was nearly the equal of any man. But the owl made sure that none was his own equal, and using his magic and threats, he engendered a fierce devotion in all of them. The owl could not afford to have a subject that would flee when conditions became threatening. He needed birds and bats who would fight to the death for him.

Eyeswide had been a normal creature upon his hatching. The Remorseful Time, as he still looked upon it, days of simple existence when the only thing his small brain considered was survival. But then Iniquis and Abandon touched him.

Iniquis gave Eyeswide speech and wisdom, and Abandon gave him uncanny fast flight and the ability to enhance other winged creatures. Iniquis's tears formed the very pond Eyeswide drew energy from to enhance his own flock. And Abandon gave the owl a mystical ability that let him use the pond as a window so he could look in on anything and anyone he wanted.

Of all the powers, Eyeswide respected only Iniquis and Abandon. The good powers were weak, he believed, not worthy of his prayers. Their greatest accomplishment was the creation of the Finest—and he was certain that Kalantha Montoll's ugly horse was such a creature.

A normal horse could not have slain so many of his assassins.

"Hateful horse," he hissed.

Not one of the birds or bats in the malicious ranks of the avian assassins was as strong as himself. And though they would live twenty or more years—considerably longer than their lesser brethren—they would not enjoy Eyeswide's godtouched lifespan. The owl was nearly three hundred years old, and he hadn't yet noticed any aches from age or loss of vision or speed. He felt as vibrant as a hatchling, and he wondered about Bishop DeNogaret's age. How many years had DeNogaret been walking Paard-Peran? He suspected more than one hundred.

"DeNogaret," the owl said. It was a throaty word, a whisper wrapped around the edges of it. He spoke too low for his flock to hear. "He does not mourn for my lost assassins. He sputters only about the girl. So angry she lives. So angry with me."

Eyeswide tipped his head down. "I will make certain—this time—she dies."

He raised his eyes and returned to the assembled birds and bats. There were less than five hundred; his band had been cut by more than one half, largely due to the big ugly horse. During the last attempt on the palace grounds, the horse alone had killed nearly a hundred.

Eyeswide studied each bird and bat now, noting the fear and false bravery, and the foolish real bravery that Eyeswide detested. Though some of the crows and a few of the hawks had distinguished themselves, there was not one among them Eyeswide would have as a second. None was equal to Fala, the lieutenant he recently lost at the hooves of the punch.

"None of you," Eyeswide said.

A starling cocked her head in question, but the owl did not explain further. He continued to regard them, recalling how he selected some before they were able to leave their nests, and how he slew and dined on their parents before taking the babies to the pool to make them stronger.

"The horse," Eyeswide said at last. "The hateful horse."

Several birds bobbed their heads, knowing the creature he spoke of.

"Cut our numbers," the owl continued.

"Stomped my brother," one crow cursed.

"Stomped my mate," said a hawk.

"Hateful horse," said a starling. "Hateful horse. Hateful, hateful, hateful horse." This last was repeated until it became a chorus.

"Hateful horse," Eyeswide agreed. "Hateful Finest." A shadow passed through his bright eyes, and the birds quieted.

"The horse protects the girl called Kalantha Montoll, sister to the King of Galmier. The girl with the green eyes." The owl noted that most of the birds and bats registered recognition of the girl's name, but a few seemed oblivious. "She is one of the cousins we were ordered to kill."

"We failed!" cried a large blackbird. "We failed Eyeswide."

And thereby I failed Bishop DeNogaret, Eyeswide thought. He didn't share the name of the man with his flock, though some knew the owl served a man. He did his best to protect the Bishop's identity, as he knew the Bishop liked to wrap himself in secrets.

"But we will not fail this time," Eyeswide vowed. "The boy we were to kill . . . we are released of that task. He no longer needs to die." At least not by our claws and beaks, he added to himself. "The threat caused by his presence is no more. But the girl . . ."

"She is a threat." This from a young cowbird.

"Yes, a threat," Eyeswide replied. "She must not be allowed to grow older."

"We will kill her!" cried the cowbird. "For Eyeswide."

"Kill her. Kill her. Killherkillherkillherkillherkillher." The chant was picked up.

When the flock again quieted, the owl fixed the young cowbird with a steely glare. This bird had potential, and might someday make a fine lieutenant, but he was not yet experienced enough, and he was small.

"Our numbers have been cut by the hateful horse. He killed Fala. And so our task is more difficult," Eyeswide told them. "We must be cunning and fast, more alert than ever."

"Fast," a grackle said. "Very, very fast."

"First we must find her," a black skimmer added.

Eyeswide nodded. "I will find her. Then I will order you to strike."

"Eyeswide will find her find her find her," said an old crow.

"We will slay her for Eyeswide," the black skimmer cut in. "And Eyeswide will be pleased."

"We live for Eyeswide. Blessed us, Eyeswide. Please you."

"Yes, please me," Eyeswide said. "I will call you again when I have found Kalantha Montoll."

"The girl with the green eyes," said a crow.

"And we will strike at her together." Eyeswide retreated behind the black walnut, a gesture that dismissed the flock. Then when he was certain they were gone, he edged deeper into the forest, walking slowly rather than flying. It was darker along the ground, and he enjoyed feeling the shells of nuts and tiny bones from long-dead squirrels and rabbits beneath his feet. Too, he was in no hurry at the moment, and walking gave him time to think.

The Old Forest floor was thickly carpeted with the shattered bones of birds Eyeswide had made examples of, husks of dead insects, fallen leaves, and rotted wood. It felt springy and gave a bounce to the owl's steps. He relished the quiet. The loudest sound here was what he made—his talons brushing softly over the leaves, the rhythmic clicking he made with his impressive beak. His breathing, his beating heart; he could hear even those things, so keen his ears were. It was as if the trees worked at Eyeswide's behest to keep any other sounds from entering.

It took him many minutes to reach the center of a circle of stringybark trees. He stood at the edge of a stagnant pond that shimmered darkly in a lone beam of sunlight. A few decades ago he gave it a name—the Vision Pond. There was a dark green film on the water, and as Eyeswide watched it, the green grew as bright as the shade of new grass.

"Talk to me," he instructed the pond. Insubstantial motes of yellow and white appeared in concentric circles, and the rings slowly rippled outward until they touched the mossy banks. Eyeswide reached a talon into the water and gently stirred it. A thread of scum clung to his leg. He hooted long and low, and as the sound trailed off, the pond became still again and the motes of light disappeared. But it was black now, shiny like a mirror, and it perfectly reflected his image.

"Show me the girl named Kalantha Montoll, sister to the King of Galmier," Eyeswide said. He bent until his beak could reach his talon. A quick slice and a thin line of blood appeared. He let a few drops of blood fall into the water. "Show me the girl with green eyes who rides a large brown horse. An ugly, misshapen, hateful horse."

An ephemeral piece of fog hovered on the surface of the pond. The owl tapped a talon at the edge of the water, a gesture that an impatient man might make. As he waited, the fog formed trees, then showed houses on trees.

"The girl," Eyeswide repeated. "Is she in one of those dwellings? I have seen the village before, a place of hunters and summer farmers."

The fog continued to show the stilt village, then that scene faded to be replaced by more trees. Wisps of fog swirled around their trunks, taking on the forms of wolves, then dissipating.

"The girl has been this way, but no more. She was in the village for a time, but left it. Where is she now?"

The fog thinned until it looked like a transparent sheet of parchment stretched over the Vision Pond.

"Is she dead?"

He got the sense that she was not, and he was certain the pond would have revealed her corpse.

"So she is where your magic cannot reach, my Vision Pond . . . at the moment. She is protected by something good, a holy place perhaps."

The owl continued to stir the water with his bloody talon, until the sheet of fog grew as foul-looking as his mood.

"Then I will look at something else," he decided. "Until she moves again and the goodness that wraps around her is gone. Show me birds of prey, my Vision Pond. Young and strong birds, not yet under my control." Eyeswide intended to search for a new lieutenant outside his assassin flock.

The fog divided and divided again and again, becoming dark clouds on the surface of the black pond. The clouds took on the shape of birds—eagles, hawks, falcons, and vultures. Eyeswide studied each one. The eagle was too pale, and larger than himself. He would have no lieutenant that was larger and that someday might pose a threat. The hawks for the most part were too small or reminded him too much of Fala. The few vultures looked ungainly in the air and on the ground, and they ate things even the owl found distasteful. But the falcons, three of those looked promising.

He dismissed the other images with a flick of a talon, and then he concentrated on the three birds. One was brown, its wings and body shot through with black stripes, tail tip almost red. From the look of its feet and its eyes, it seemed to be an old bird. Another was also brown, almost solid save for a white patch on its throat. Its breast was thin, marking it not the best hunter. The third was gray, its belly and the undersides of its wings the color of ashes, the rest of it a few shades darker, unusual coloration for its kind. Eyeswide preferred minions that were black or very dark brown and could cloak their presence more easily at night. But the gray falcon was large and graceful, and he watched as it dipped lower and effortlessly snared a white hare. Obviously an able hunter, it was therefore acceptable—at least until something a few shades darker came along. And it would be singular among his flock. There wasn't a falcon among them.

"This will be my new lieutenant," the owl decided. "Show me where to find her."

The Vision Pond did just that, and—despite the reviled daylight—Eyeswide took flight in pursuit of the falcon, to where the Old Forest met the Gray Woods of Nasim-Guri.

12 · Ninéon

No more perfect creatures exist than we Finest, destined to toil for the sakes of the Fallen Favorites. We struggle through the imperfect yet beautiful woods of Paard-Peran; through the insufferably hot summers and chilling winters; and in the end our sacrifices to put a simple man or woman first will be rewarded. We have long, long lives, keen senses with which to study and appreciate our surroundings, and idyllic pastures to gallop across when our time on Paard-Peran has ended.

Conversely, no more terrible creature exists than that which the dark powers shaped. Such a thing will never enjoy perfection and will be held in contempt. Such a thing should not be. It is an abomination.

~Able Ironhooves, mentor to Steadfast

The falcon circled high above a small polder that was ringed by pin oaks and red maples. She wasn't hunting any longer; her belly was full of rabbit. In fact, she hadn't been able to eat all of it, leaving the rest of the carcass a mile away for carrion birds. She was simply flying for the joy of it. She let the wind bring her the scents of the earth below, pleasantly faded because of her lofty position.

The frosty fall air found its way to her skin. She was cold, despite the thickening of tiny feathers on her body. But it was not intense enough to drive her from the sky. She knew it would get much colder soon, and then she would fly only when she hunted.

So she reveled in the late afternoon sky and watched as the sun crept toward the horizon and touched the trunks and made the bark looked burnished. She circled higher, until she could no longer smell the ground. There was only the scent of the glorious sky . . . and something unfamiliar.

She let out a skreeing sound, pulled her wings in close and dropped toward the treetops. Coming at her from the west, higher in the sky and diving down on her, was an overly large owl.

The falcon was confused. That an owl would be out during the light was puzzling enough, but that it seemed to be hunting her was even more surprising. Where the ancient trees of the Old Forest met these younger and smaller trees of the Gray Woods, the falcon had known no predators. She'd not experienced fear before, and so the tremor that chased through her was unfamiliar and unsettling.

The falcon was fast, but the owl was heavier and so was gaining when he tucked his wings in tight and plummeted like a stone. He started calling to her, in a language she understood but knew *he* shouldn't understand. The falcon had seen owls before, hunting small ground animals at night. None of them spoke the musical skrees and cries of her kind.

Stop, the owl ordered.

She ignored him and dropped past the uppermost branches, angling toward a big familiar oak. Panicking now, she darted in toward the trunk, claiming a thin branch amid a web of leaf-covered branches, thinking the owl would not come in where the branches were so fine and could not support his weight.

But the owl did come closer, skreeing in her tongue and hovering just beyond the weave of wood.

Stop, beautiful falcon, the owl said. *I will not hurt you. I wish only to make you greater than you now are.*

Away! the falcon skreed back. *Away! Away!*

She didn't wholly understand the owl, as it was trying to convey too complex of a message.

Not hurt, the owl repeated, trying something simpler. *No pain.*

Away! Now away you! the falcon replied. Her fear continued to well up, but now it was mixing with anger. The owl was coming closer, risking the web of branches that poked at his shiny golden eyes. He was looming too close, when all she wanted was for him to leave her and her familiar tree alone. He had no reason to be near her or this tree. She was the one to choose when another creature came near. Her decision, not some creature of the evening sky! Her choice!

Away. Away. Away!

No, Eyeswide said. Then the big owl was coming into the weave, snapping the smallest branches with his fluttering wings and his clacking beak. His talons were outstretched, clearly meaning to grab at her. He smelled musty and dusty, and a worse smell clung to him that she couldn't place.

Away you! Away now! She pushed off and shot up through the web of branches. Within a heartbeat she was above the canopy and streaking higher. She would outfly the bothersome owl. He could not prey on something that was faster than his bloated feathery form.

The cold air wrapped comfortably around her again as she flew straight up. The scents of the earth and owl were coming softer now, and for a moment she again relished in the joy of flying.

Free! she skreed.

Never again free! answered the owl.

She looked down and saw him closing the distance.

Not possible! was her cry. The owl should not be so agile and fast. Could not be! No owl she'd seen had ever flown so fast. She beat her wings harder and harder until she felt her body would break from the effort.

Free! Free! Free! . . . No!

Suddenly she was falling, and the owl's talons were digging into her chest. He'd managed to catch up to her, despite her frenzied flying. She tried to flap her wings and break away, but he struck at her beak with his own, holding hers painfully tight as he forced her toward the canopy. Spider-web branches snapped against her back and bit into her wings.

Do not fight so, the owl said. *This will be over soon and you will thank me.*

Away.

Eyeswide clenched his talons tighter and felt the falcon's blood spill over his feet. *Do not fight. I do not want to kill you. I have flown too far. Easy. Calm.*

Calm? No! Stop! Away!

The falcon briefly wondered if this is what the rabbit felt when she pursued it and caught it. Did its heart pound so wildly? Did it gasp for breath? And how would dying feel? Worse than what she was feeling now, she somehow knew, the pain in her chest white hot and the fear driving her heart to beat ever faster. Her anger welled and grew brighter. She struggled harder, giving up her last bit of strength and feeling the air rush from her lungs.

She was growing faint and feeling weaker than she'd ever been. Then she was feeling more twigs and branches strike her, felt the owl's beak slash at her tongue. The taste of her own blood was not so different than the taste of the rabbit's blood, she mused.

For a heartbeat she felt the pain ease and felt her descent slow, then she didn't feel anything.

THE FALCON DIDN'T WHOLLY UNDERSTAND THE CONCEPT OF death or the end of everything. But she expected to be settling deep in the owl's belly, as the rabbit had settled deliciously in hers. She did not expect to wake up. But somehow she managed to open her eyes.

The owl was standing on her chest, keeping her pinned to the ground and keeping the blessed air from completely filling her lungs. She ached all over, her wings especially from striking so many branches.

The forest floor was . . . quite different than she thought it should be . . . unfamiliar. It was covered with rotting bits of wood and the husks of insects. There was a thick layer of moldy leaves, and the scent of everything was heavy and unpleasant. This was not her forest, and she was not near the familiar oak. The owl had somehow taken her . . . where? This place smelled unknown, and what little she could see of it from her forest-floor vantage point was peculiar. There was a stringybark trunk, and another beside it, both so thick and looking terribly, terribly old.

Mine. You are mine, gray falcon, the owl told her, trying to keep his ideas simple so she would understand him. It would not be much longer and he could address her as he could any in his flock. *Mine to command. Mine.* He lowered his face until all she could see were his golden eyes. So large and round, they looked like twin moons. So bright! Something dark passed through them, the way a cloud moves quickly through a windy sky. Then there was only the gold again, and inexplicably she began to feel better.

The ache in her wings receded, and the weight of the owl on her body didn't seem so hurtful. Despite that weight, she was breathing easier.

She began to feel stronger, and her senses were becoming more acute. She could see more detail in the owl's feathers— beautiful browns and creams and stripes of black. The golden color of his eyes grew even more bright, hypnotic now. She could smell so many, many things. The moldy, musty leaves, of course, and the damp earth inches beneath them. But she could also smell the insect husks, and she'd never noticed such things before. The owl's scent was stronger, too, and he was no longer frightening—though he still loomed above her.

His eyes.

Mine, gray falcon. Mine to command.

His eyes became everything again. Wonderful and mysterious. She could see her reflection in them.

Mine.

The owl left her for a moment, and she didn't stir. But she could see him. He walked to the edge of a scum-covered pond and stirred a talon in it. She thought she saw him slash his foot with his beak and dribble his blood in the water. But then she thought she was mistaken, for that would be a foolish thing to do.

She saw the pond grow lighter, though the sky was darker overhead. The sun had set and twilight had taken over the sky. What had happened to the time between daylight and now? The time between when the owl captured her and now? Just how far from her familiar tree had he flown her?

There were motes of light dancing above the pond, like insects though they had none of the insect sounds. Indeed, the only thing the falcon heard was her own breathing and the faintest shush of oak leaves brushing against each other. No flapping of wings from other birds, no skrees, no scampering of animals along the forest floor. In fact, she could smell no other creatures besides herself and the owl. So animals did not like this place.

She thought, perhaps, that she shouldn't like it either and that she should turn over and get to her feet, push off from this unfamiliar ground, and fly away. But something held her in place, and so she waited for the owl to return.

In his beak he held one of the motes of light that had hovered over the pond. He brought it to her own beak, then jerked her head. It was as if she were a hatchling and he a parent regurgitating food into her mouth to feed her.

The mote of light slid down her throat, warming her. She closed her eyes and still saw the owl's large golden eyes.

Mine, he repeated.

She was on her feet now, though she couldn't remember getting up. There were a lot of things she couldn't remember, and the rabbit she'd eaten earlier today was fading from her mind, too. But in the empty places in her mind were other things, and these she found . . . amazing.

Yours, she told Eyeswide. *Yours to command.*

Her mind was reeling, flooded with images, odors, and sounds more intense than she'd ever experienced. It felt as if she were flying, then diving and spinning, the earth rushing up to meet her. She tried to sort through it all but couldn't make sense of everything.

He fed her another mote of light from the pond, then coaxed her to the water's edge. She felt the water touch her feet, then she edged in deeper until it touched her belly and swirled around the wound the owl's talons had inflicted. The water should have been cold this late in the fall. But it was as warm as a summer day, and it soothed the last bit of pain away. The motes of light moved toward her, rose, and melted against her breast. The warmth increased, and suddenly she could manage all the sounds and sights and smells of this very Old Forest.

Eyeswide stood behind her, pleased that the pond had enhanced her. He never took any other member of his assassin band directly to the pond—save Fala years upon years ago. The birds were fed only motes of the pond light that he'd brought to them. Eyeswide wanted them smart and strong, but not too smart and not too strong. He could have none challenge him.

The falcon stared unblinking at the pond's surface, seeing her reflection and not recognizing it. She wasn't the same creature who flew where the trees of the Old Forest met the smaller trees of the Gray Woods. That creature was not so keenly intelligent, and had no purpose beyond eating and flying. She was better than the image she saw. More powerful.

She would have a purpose now.

"There is something I would have you do—Ninéon," Eyeswide said. The owl was speaking in the tongue men used, and the falcon understood each word save the very last.

"Ninéon?"

"It is your name," the owl explained. "I name each member of my flock, and I have chosen Ninéon for you."

"It means . . ."

The owl swiveled his head nearly completely around, then turned it back to face her. "It belonged to a woman I saw in a secret temple to the dark powers many years ago. The priest there called her Ninéon. She was special to him, and I found the word to have a pleasing sound. I have been saving it, and now I give it to you."

"This woman? What was she like? What did you know of her?"

The owl's eyes narrowed. "Nothing, really. She was cleaning the colorful glass windows, and then I watched her polish the image of a large crow, one of the dark power's symbols. But I liked her name."

"Ninéon," the falcon pronounced. "Ninéon. Ninéon." She ruffled her feathers and stretched her wings. Then she stepped back from the pond. She'd heard wings flapping, lots of them, and the soft crunch of talons landing on insect husks and fallen leaves. More than a hundred birds had gathered in a clearing beyond the stringybarks.

"I have something for you to do, Ninéon," Eyeswide said.

"You will lead three dozen of my assassins to the north, where the countries of Nasim-Guri and Galmier touch. It is a long border, marked on maps and unseen on the land, but you will know the spot because there is a dead oak, as thick as any of the trees around my Vision Pond. Its bark has turned white and brushes off like snow, and it has no limbs. Men cut them off some time ago, but they left the trunk behind to serve as a landmark."

"I will find that tree, with three dozen of your birds behind me."

"Yes, Ninéon."

The falcon let out a deep breath. "And do what, Eyeswide?" Somehow she knew his name, though he hadn't spoken it.

"Lead the birds and slay the small patrol of men stationed there. You hunt other quarry now, Ninéon. Hares and ground squirrels are beneath you. I will show you more challenging prey. More delicious and rewarding. Do not risk yourself this evening. Just command the birds to do the killing for you."

SHE CHOSE MOSTLY CROWS, AS THAT WAS ONE OF the symbols of a dark power, a power Eyeswide told her a little about and promised to tell her of more. The woman she'd been named for, Ninéon, had been polishing the crow symbol, and so the falcon decided crows would be important to her.

She'd spent so many hours with Eyeswide, listening to him discuss the dark powers and how they gave him the ability to bless the birds of the forest—and bless her. Eyeswide paraded her before the birds and bats, explaining to her that there were more in his force, but he hadn't summoned them all today. She studied each one, finding it took little time to note their features and to find something about them to tell them apart, one crow from another, one cowbird from the next. There was a paler patch of feathers on one, a crooked beak, and a wing slightly longer than another.

"I see so clearly," Ninéon had said. She was certain Eyeswide thought that she meant her vision was so keenly acute. It was, but instead she meant that she understood so much, and so easily now. She understood everything.

Because she'd spent so much time in the clearing, and because it was so many miles to the branchless oak, it was well past midnight when she reached it and spotted the patrol. There were four men.

"Only four," she whispered. She had expected more, had hoped for a formidable test. But it was late, and a patrol, not an army, was stationed here.

Two of the men were awake and yards apart, one of them facing Galmier, and the other Nasim-Guri. Another was soundly sleeping at the base of the branchless oak. The fourth was near the sleeping man, curled under a blanket, eyes open.

"We strike the man facing north," Ninéon said. "Him first, then the man looking to the south. The ones on the ground after." She realized the birds understood the gist of what she said. And she realized she was far superior to them.

There weren't enough of them to fly in a formation resembling something else, such as a man or a horse. Eyeswide had told her when the flock numbered more than a thousand they would fly in the formation of men on horseback. They'd struck at Prince Edan and the wedding party that way, and at two people named Kalantha and Meven. But she had only three dozen birds with her at the moment, so she couldn't attempt such an illusion.

"Slay the man facing Galmier first."

"We slay the man for Ninéon," the largest crow said.

"That man first, then the other," another cawed.

The cloud of black descended, beaks open and claws

stretched forward. The sentry heard their caws, whirling and looking up and throwing his arms up to cover his face—too late! The birds were scratching at him furiously, first at his eyes and then his throat. He was on his knees and flailing with his hands at the birds while the other sentry, who had been facing south, drew his sword.

"Up!" the southern sentry hollered to the men lying by the branchless oak. "We're attacked!" Then he was rushing toward the birds, who had his fellow on the ground.

"Slay him!" Ninéon flew toward the man with the sword, swooping around him and avoiding the slashing blade, coming at him from his back and raking her talons through the heavy tabard. "So sharp!" she cried, amazed that her talons could slash through material that appeared so thick. Then she tested her claws again and again and again, while half of the birds joined her.

The screams of the sentries joined the shrieks of the crows, filling the air with a horrid cacophony that was beautiful music to the falcon.

Two sentries having fallen, the birds flew toward the other two men, who were now standing and fumbling for their weapons. The one who'd not been sleeping was having the harder time, caught in his blanket and stumbling, and flinging his hands around trying to find his sword. The man near him was more agile and had a sword in one hand and a dagger in another.

"That one," Ninéon ordered. "The one who is the threat. Kill him quickly." Ninéon thought the noise might travel to other sentries farther down the border. With only three dozen birds at her command, the sensible part of her didn't want to risk taking on another group of sentries. However, she was enjoying this assault, she realized, and she would like it to go on longer.

But she also wanted to return victorious to Eyeswide—and without a loss to her meager force.

The man was good with his weapons, but the birds were practiced and too many for him to manage. They brought him down, and his screams were short and disturbing to Ninéon's keen ears.

Then the flock was streaking toward the last man. He was bearded and the largest of the four, and still ungainly, dropped his sword as he tried to swing it. He was dressed differently than the others, not in the crude uniform of dyed leather tabards. He was wearing a deerskin jacket, and Ninéon realized she'd seen him before—when she was a simple falcon hunting for ground squirrels. He hunted, too, where the Old Forest met the younger trees of the Gray Woods.

He was a woodsman who'd likely thrown his lot in with the sentries when the weather turned cold and hunting turned poor.

"Leave him alone," Ninéon ordered.

"Not kill?" this from the largest crow.

"Not this one," Ninéon answered. "Not this night."

13 · Vershan Dreams

On the ground of any forest floor there are layers and layers of oak and maple leaves, a veritable fall cushion filled with interesting smells and shades. It is that way with most of the Fallen Favorites~there are layers to them. They show one layer when they are with their family, another layer when they are with men they do not like. There is a different layer when they are at large gatherings. A layer when they are happy. And yet one more layer when they are sad. It is only when they are alone, with none of their kind to see them, that they are leafless and reveal their true selves.

> ~Mara, guardian of Bitternut, in a report to the Finest Court

Kalantha was not in a hurry, so Gallant-Stallion took his time following the old priest's directions to reach the rebuilt Vershan Monastery. The Finest was pleased to not be in a hurry for a change, and to not be fleeing from something.

From the looks of the sky directly above and to the south, it appeared the threat of rain was well behind them for the moment. Even the ground beneath his hooves felt solid and had only a trace of dampness. Gallant-Stallion decided he'd had enough storms to last him well into his next assignment as shepherd—though he admitted he found all the lightning and thunder interesting.

It was warmer where they traveled now, though not terribly so. But not being soaked all the time made it *feel* much warmer, and the Finest relished the sensation of the wind playing against his dry hide. He'd decided two nights past, in the midst of a downpour, that he liked summer the best on Paard-Peran. The rain didn't bother him so greatly then, and there didn't seem to be as much of it.

Kalantha seemed to appreciate the drier weather too, as she'd been riding all of yesterday and today without her hood pulled up over her head. She hadn't talked much, and neither had Gallant-Stallion. He was certain she was thinking about her brother. He was thinking about the Finest Court and Prudent-Flehmen and if they might cross paths again. He missed the company of another Finest.

Steadfast, I do not know what the future holds for Kalantha and me, and I never thought to ask you if . . . Gallant-Stallion's nostrils flared, and he looked behind him.

The wind had shifted, not the way it did when Steadfast's spirit came to visit. It brought new scents to him, of the rain that still fell somewhere to the north, and of a horse and a man—neither of them familiar.

The Finest changed his course, angling away from a branch of the Sprawling River and paralleling a merchant's trail that wended its way toward a forest in the distance. After another hour, the scents persisted, and he decided to let that bother him.

Steadfast, is someone following us? Does someone have the skills to track me?

The spirit of Steadfast did not answer, nor did Gallant-Stallion truly expect it to. He hadn't felt his mentor's presence for a few days.

Gallant-Stallion broke into a trot as a precaution, and changed his course yet again. Fleeing once more? he wondered. Running from nothing?

He was careful not to alert Kalantha, who seemed lost in her own thoughts, and who seemed ever on the lookout for dark birds. This time he returned to the river and walked through its shallows to cover his trail. Then after a few miles he returned to parallel the merchant's road. Miles later the wind shifted again, and he lost the scents that had been bothering him.

The Finest hoped he'd lost their pursuer—if indeed they had been being pursued.

I could be paranoid, Steadfast. So many things have befallen this girl, that I could be overly nervous and . . .

"Rue, look!"

He'd been so distracted with what was behind them that he hadn't paid enough attention to what stretched ahead. Kalantha tugged on his mane and leaned forward, pointing so he could see what she'd spotted.

Off to the side of the merchant's road was a large weathered sign. It sat squarely on two posts driven into the ground, and the words on it had been cut into the wood and then painted green and black. The paint was faded, but legible, despite the dead vines that twisted around the sign's edges and draped it like a veil on its right half. It read:

Around the Next Bend Please Find You
THE VERSHAN MONASTERY
Holy Sanctuary and Library
We Welcome the Faithful

"Finally," Kalantha breathed. "It's the library we want, Rue. There will be a book about the evil birds, and I will read it. Then maybe we'll learn why the birds killed my cousin and tried to kill my brother and me." She dug her knees in and slapped her feet against his sides, urging him to hurry.

"Maybe we'll be there in time for breakfast. It's early still." She'd eaten the last of what Bartholomew had given her yesterday morning, handing the pieces of dried apple she'd found in the bag to the Finest. "I could use something warm to eat. And I can even pay the priests for it with one of those pretty trinkets."

Gallant-Stallion waited until her hands were clenched in his mane, then he broke into a gallop. The dry road, despite the ruts from wagons, was easy terrain to navigate. The wind and his speed sent his mane flailing into Kalantha's face, and she closed her eyes and nudged him faster still.

The road split, and Gallant-Stallion took the narrower branch that led to the west, as the sign had said "around the bend." Birch trees were spaced evenly along both sides of the road, as if someone had planted them. There were only faint traces of wagon ruts here, meaning few merchants came this way. There was another sign and an arrow, directing, ALL FAITHFUL FOLLOW THIS PATH TO ENLIGHTENMENT. This sign, too, was weathered, and Gallant-Stallion gave its lack of upkeep no concern until he continued around the twist in the road and came upon the Vershan Monastery.

It looked abandoned and more weathered than the signs that had led them here.

"No!" Kalantha moaned. She slipped from the Finest's back, canvas bag of trinkets falling. She raced forward and disappeared into the entryway of the monastery.

IN THE HEART OF THE OLD FOREST, EYESWIDE STOOD AT THE edge of the Vision Pond. He detested the morning nearly as much as he detested the afternoon sun. But the sun hadn't yet climbed straight overhead, and so he was mollified somewhat with the diffused light. He'd been consulting the pond on and off through the night, watching Ninéon find the small patrol and lead the attack against the men. He didn't watch the entire battle, as the patrol was insignificant, and therefore the fight would be brief and unexciting. He didn't know that the falcon had left one alive.

Instead he consulted the pond on another matter. He tried to find Kalantha Montoll, this time painstakingly describing her face and hair and the scattering of pale freckles across her cheeks. He described the ropy scar on her neck that his former lieutenant Fala had given her, and then he detailed the big punch, which he was certain was a Finest.

"The most unprepossessing Finest I have seen," he said. "An ugly, ill-shaped horse. Its legs are too short for that big body."

Fortunate that the dark powers shaped him into a beautiful, large owl, more impressive than any other bird in any forest in Paard-Peran, Eyeswide thought. "I am blessed. The Finest is cursed with his ungainly form."

He hadn't found a trace of the horse or girl through the evening, but he wasn't dissuaded. The pond sometimes had to be consulted multiple times to find just what he was looking for.

Eyeswide slashed at a foot with his beak, drawing blood and letting it drip on the surface of the murky green water. "I shall try once more," he announced. Then he again described Kalantha and the Finest.

And this time, after several long minutes, he was successful.

The green surface became shades of olive and brown, forming a picture filled with late fall trees and a carpet of leaves and twigs. There was a trail, and the homely Finest was paralleling it and was furtively looking behind him.

"Nervous. About something. About what?" After a moment, Eyeswide decided the source of the Finest's discomfort was inconsequential. "Where are you going, punch?"

Eyeswide was exhausted, as he hadn't slept in days, so preoccupied with finding Kalantha and sculpting a new lieutenant. His round, golden eyes blinked, and he felt a wash of dizziness that told him he needed rest. But not yet, the owl railed.

"Where are you? And where do you go, punch of a Finest?"

The owl watched the horse change its course again and follow a branch of the Sprawling River, then return to the trail before going back to the river once more. He watched the horse try to lose its hoofprints in the shallows of the river, then watched it stop before an old sign.

"So you fear you are being followed? Is it me that worries you, ugly punch? And that sign, what does it say?"

The owl couldn't make out the words, and no amount of his coaxing the magic helped. Then the horse was galloping, and Kalantha was holding on tight. They followed the trail as it twisted through a line of paper white birch trunks, and past another sign the pond could not clearly display.

The owl's tired eyes never left the surface of the pond, as Gallant-Stallion and Kalantha came to a massive stone building that seemed very out of place amid the trees and that looked a little hazy in the image. There wasn't a village for miles that Eyeswide could tell. There was a wooden fence that circled the place, though much of the wood had rotted and there was evidence part of it had burned. The remains of two wooden outbuildings were indistinct.

"What is this place?" Eyeswide wondered, realizing the pond could not answer the question. He tried to concentrate harder on it, finding instead that the bricks grew even fuzzier and everything was becoming blurry—like a chalk painting ruined by the rain.

"What is . . ." Eyeswide sucked in a breath and his heart smoldered with ire. "A holy place! The girl is in a holy place." And the pond couldn't often probe such a place that was fashioned and blessed by good men in the name of the good powers of Paard-Peran. "No! No! No!"

Eyeswide instead concentrated on the Finest. Though the punch was a creation of the good powers, he knew the pond would not be blocked from watching the horse. In response to the owl's efforts, the horse came to the fore of the image, and the details grew sharper. The punch's mane was tangled and bits of twigs were caught in it. Mud was spattered on his legs and belly. The girl hadn't been grooming him, not that she likely had anything to groom him with. But his motley appearance only added to his homeliness as far as Eyeswide was concerned. He suspected the horse stank, too.

"Where are you, Finest?" Eyeswide stirred the pond and tried to draw back from the horse, so he could find some landmarks and thereby give his birds something to look for. "Where is this ruined holy place? And where are you ultimately going?"

The horse was moving now, slowly, picking his way over a section of burned fence and then trotting down a pebble-covered path that led up to the misty image of the big stone building.

"No! Do not enter that place!" the owl hooted angrily. But his words could not reach Gallant-Stallion.

The horse stepped through the entryway Kalantha had taken moments ago.

The pond turned mirror-black, reflecting the owl's angry visage. Then the water returned to its normal murky green appearance.

THE BUILDING HAD NOT BEEN EMPTY MORE THAN A HANDFUL of years, he decided, as the smell of men still clung to the stones. There were banners high on the wall following the staircase, and they were musty from the wind that roamed the halls and the constant damp that hugged every inch of everything. The cloth was singed, but it was not age-tattered. One banner displayed an armored man holding a sword in one hand and a white rose in the other. A second showed a man in a white robe polishing a sword, with a dozen more swords at his feet. The third and fourth depicted other men in white robes with purple sashes around their waists, likely priests praying.

He could see where furniture had filled the hall. A splintered bench was to his right, and a broken chair was straight ahead and to the left. There was a square on the tile floor that was darker than the rest, and he guessed a rug might have lay there, keeping the sun from lightening the stone chips. The hall smelled fusty, but not overwhelmingly so, and the scent of something burnt came from a door at the back of the hall. Gallant-Stallion plodded toward it, his hooves clopping against the tile.

Kalantha, he called as he went. *Where are you?*

He didn't get an answer, and so he began to worry. He wanted her with him in this abandoned place. The door frame was barely wide enough to accommodate him, and he scraped his sides as he went through. This had been the kitchen.

Gallant-Stallion had never been in a kitchen, but Kalantha had described one once, and he could see where a pot would have simmered in the fireplace. A long table was blackened by fire, as were the benches pushed under it. A tapestry against the far wall was burnt, save for the very upper section stretched along a pole and fastened into the wall. A wooden cupboard was likewise burned, and there were scorch marks on the floor. The Finest recalled seeing that a piece of the fence outside had burned. Could a fire that had started in the kitchen spread that far outside?

Kalantha had not come this way, as her bootprints were not in the scorch marks—and his hoofprints were. The room itself was intact, the fire not able to harm the stone. He clomped forward and shoved his head against a cabinet door. It crumbled and Gallant-Stallion saw that foodstuffs and clay cups had been ruined in the blaze. It was interesting, and something he might puzzle out on another day. But he had to find his charge, and so he awkwardly turned around and retraced his path, again scraping his sides as he went to another door.

This time Gallant-Stallion discovered a room twice the size of the entry hall. It was easy to walk here, as the only pieces of furniture were chairs, and these were either burned or in pieces along the walls. There had been tapestries and banners on painted walls, but all of them had been burned, and the paint had curled and flaked, looking like dried fish scales.

Kalantha! Gallant-Stallion called. There were other doors off this room, more doors off the entry hall that he hadn't stepped through. Too many doors, and too many choices!

Kalantha, this isn't a place for me. I do not like it here. The Finest felt uncomfortable. He relished the feel of the earth beneath his hooves, no matter how soggy and cold the weather made it. And while he hadn't minded stables, he did not like traipsing through a place that men had built for themselves. The doors were too, too narrow, and though this room was immense, it felt confining.

Kalantha!

He heard footsteps overhead, faint because of the distance and the stone that separated him from her.

I do not like this place, Kalantha.

Gallant-Stallion went back to the entry hall and stared at the wide stone steps that curved up.

And I do not want to climb these stairs. I was not made for such as this. And we should not be here, he continued, even though he doubted she could hear him so far away. *This place caught fire years ago, and no one remains.* For a moment he remembered thinking the same thing at the previous Vershan

Monastery. There was a very old priest there. Perhaps Kalantha would indeed find another. And perhaps this one would send them to another abandoned place.

Cautiously he put his front right hoof on the lowest step, then followed it with his left. It couldn't be much more difficult than taking a trail through the mountains, could it? he wondered. There had been a very steep pass in the Galmier Mountains that he'd navigated with Meven and Kalantha well more than a year ago. This should be easy compared to that. But this was inside a place he didn't want to be.

Gallant-Stallion waited another moment more, then he slowly—and awkwardly—began to climb the stairs. He was halfway up when Kalantha appeared at the top. Her face was streaked with tears. But suddenly she was laughing, and her smile managed to reach her bright green eyes.

"Rue! Whatever are you doing? Horses aren't supposed to climb stairs! You probably shouldn't even be in here!"

She continued to laugh, and though Gallant-Stallion found it pleasing to listen to, he was very much not pleased with being on the curving staircase. He watched her as she came down and slid around him, then helped to guide him back down, one laborious, graceless step at a time.

"Poor Rue, you were worried about me, weren't you?"

Yes, he answered. *We should not be here.*

"Why not? No one else is using this place. Lied to, we've been. The Vershan Monastery is empty." She paused. "And it can be all ours. There's a bedroom upstairs that's not been burned too badly. I can sleep there. And there's lots of land, we can find seeds somewhere and plant a garden. We could live here."

She couldn't stay here, the Finest thought. A child in a place like this? So big and empty and in the middle of nowhere. She would be too vulnerable here. It didn't feel right to him, and he doubted the Finest Court would approve of him going along with it. Still, he could not force her to do anything. He was a guide and a guardian—not a parent. And she wasn't thinking straight. There was no food here. How would she eat?

She seemed to pick up his thoughts. "I could hunt rabbit, like I did in the mountains. And there must be a stream nearby where I can fish. We'll have to find something for you to eat. And you can stay here, in this big hall, just like it's a stable. It'll keep out the winter pretty good."

She needed to be with people, Gallant-Stallion thought. A child should not want to be alone.

"Yes, I think I'll stay here."

You should be with people, the Finest finally told her. *Don't you want to be with people?* There, he wasn't forcing, just suggesting, guiding her as he was supposed to do.

She shook her head and folded her arms tight against her chest. Again, she looked very much like a child to him.

"I don't want to be with people. What good have they ever done me? Except for Morgan. Bishop DeNogaret made me work on embroidery stitches, then decided I should go to Dea Fortress and be an acolyte. My brother wouldn't let me stay at the palace with him. He wanted to send me to Dea Fortress, too. Oh, the people in that stilt village were nice enough, and they would have let me stay there. But I probably wouldn't have liked that either."

Gallant-Stallion nudged her with his nose, and she reached up and stroked his muzzle.

"Besides, I can talk to you, so I don't need people to talk to. You're not going to tell me what to do with my life. Are you?"

No, he agreed.

"So you're all the company I need."

You need to be with people. You're a child.

She made a huffing sound and dropped her hands from his muzzle, folding her arms across her chest again.

"I'd like to be with Morgan," she admitted. "I'd work in the garden with him. I could be a gardener just like him." She paused. "But there are priests at High Keep. I don't think I like priests much, Rue. The Bishop was going to send me away. That priest in the stilt village—Ergoth—he told me where to find the Vershan Monastery. Well, the first one was pretty much ruined, wasn't it? And the only soul there was a very, very, very old man who lied to me just like Ergoth. He told me where this monastery was, and he said there'd be a great library and lots of priests and acolytes. Well, there's no library and no priests. There's not even a very, very, very old priest to watch over these ruins. I've no use for priests, Rue, I say. They talk and lie and . . ."

"I wasn't lying, Kalantha."

Kalantha and Gallant-Stallion turned to see a young man standing in the entranceway, backlit by the morning sun.

"Ergoth," Kalantha said.

Behind him was a swaybacked horse, one the Finest had spotted in the pen outside of Stilton. So that was what he'd smelled earlier when he thought they were being followed—the priest on a mud-covered horse.

The priest was nearly out of breath and leaned against the frame, taking the weight off his bad left leg. "I've been following you for days, fast as Boots would take me." He gestured to the horse. "I thought you were going to let me escort you to the Vershan Monastery. Isn't that what we agreed on?"

"To a ruins?" Her eyes smoldered. "That's what I found, a place in ruins and a very, very, very old man guarding a crumbling tower."

"If you had let me finish my tale several nights back, I would have told you that an earthquake claimed the first monastery, a fire the second, and that the third stands many miles south of here, just inside the Gray Woods."

Kalantha stood silent, and Rue carefully measured the priest.

"There really is a library there?"

He nodded, still catching his breath. The horse behind him was winded also.

"I promise. There is a library there. And plenty of people. My brother is among them."

She remained skeptical. "And I can use this library?"

Another nod. "Yes, I promise. As my guest, you can use the library."

"Then you'll take me there now, please."

He shook his head and gestured to the horse. "Neither Boots nor I are up to any more traveling today. We've pushed ourselves very hard to catch up to you, Kalantha. How about we leave tomorrow morning?"

She tapped her foot and looked at Rue, then after a moment glanced back to Ergoth. "All right," she said finally. "In the morning. Did you bring anything to eat?"

14 · Meven's Peace

I have learned that the people of Paard-Peran are like apples; one is crisp and sweet, and another is tart and interesting. Many are simply beautiful and shiny. But some are terribly sour, though outwardly they are pretty. It would be simpler if apples and people were all the same flavor.

~Zephyr the Heedful, shepherd to Bellcow Keth Polstar of Saphren Harbor

Bishop DeNogaret, I've decided I will not go to war." Meven was bending over the table, the top of which displayed a detailed map of Galmier and the kingdoms to the north and south. "I shouldn't have to start a war if I don't want to. And, indeed, I don't want to."

He carefully moved one of the miniature figures, then picked up the one next to it and held it up to his eyes. It was one of the newest figures the Bishop had given him. It was a Knight Commander in silver plate mail. The figure was wearing a tiny piece of blue cloth representing a tabard. It was the Bishop's colors. In its right hand was a sword, and its left gauntleted fist was clenched. Meven marveled at the detail in the small piece. He considered it the best of his collection.

"I suppose you don't have to go to war, Meven. Not if you don't want to have a stronger, better kingdom. Not if you don't want to make your people richer and happier." The Bishop stood behind him, surveying the map and the pieces arrayed at the borders, near the bridges, and along the most-traveled roads. "So, you don't need to go to war. But don't you think you should? For the betterment of Galmier?"

Meven shrugged his shoulders and placed the Knight Commander just to the south of Nadir. There were five other miniature soldiers there, painted to look like they were in chain mail. Shields that appeared to be tiny metal buttons were affixed to their backs. Some wielded axes, which were slivers of wood with iron filings atop them. Others had swords that somehow had been carved out of wood, then painted to look like steel. Meven could pick out the figures that had been more recently given to him; all of those were more detailed, evidence the artisan was improving. Still, he appreciated all of them, and wished that Kalantha could see them. She would move the soldiers around the map and wage mock battles.

"The Knight Commander figure is the most impressive, Bishop DeNogaret. The detail is incredible. I think I would enjoy creating miniatures such as these. Perhaps I could learn to sculpt."

"Perhaps you could." The Bishop stepped to the other side of the table and adjusted some figures along a road paralleling the Sprawling River southwest of Nadir.

"Don't you think I'm too old for this, Bishop DeNogaret? Moving miniatures around on a map? In a way, it seems a childish thing."

The Bishop shook his head and made a soft tsk-tsking sound. The lines on his face seemed a little deeper this afternoon, and his pale skin even more white. "The King of Galmier is never too old for anything, Meven. The King can do as he pleases."

Meven smiled and turned his head toward the window. A glass pane was closed over it to keep the cold air out—something he'd ordered commissioned a week ago. And the sun streamed through it and felt a little warm against his face and on his ears. He'd had his hair cut this morning, shorter than it had ever been before. His scalp felt itchy, but he didn't want to scratch it and risk loose hairs falling on the map and the miniatures.

"I don't think a war will better Galmier. And so I will not wage war," Meven said with a surprising measure of authority in his voice. He stood back away from the board and crossed his arms in front of his chest. It was a gesture he'd seen Kalantha make innumerable times when she was trying to get her way on something. "The King of Galmier has decided we will not fight Nasim-Guri or any of our neighbors. As you said, it would take a year to build up troops, train them all. The time and wealth . . . it would cost a lot for weapons and armor and food . . . could be better spent on other matters. And so we will be at peace."

The Bishop's hands gripped the edge of the map, his nails digging in and crushing a ridge of mountains on the west. "Meven . . . look at me."

Meven reluctantly turned away from the window and met the Bishop's stare. The elderly priest's eyes seemed brighter and larger, and Meven found that though he wanted to, he couldn't look away.

"Meven . . ."

"Yes, Bishop DeNogaret."

"You do indeed want a war with Nasim-Guri. Very much want it. We've been plotting the war for some weeks."

Meven's mouth was dry and his tongue felt swollen. He tried to work up some saliva. "But Bishop DeNogaret, soldiers will die. I've been thinking about that. I remember all the soldiers who died when those horrid birds attacked Edan's wedding party. It was awful."

"Think about gaining more land, Meven."

"That would be nice, Bishop. But what about the soldiers dying? And what about all the coin it would take to support an army?"

The Bishop's eyes narrowed and another mountain ridge crumbled beneath his squeezing fingers. "Coin? You have more than you could spend in your lifetime. You'd need only a fraction of your wealth to turn commoners into strong, skilled soldiers. And they will have surprise, remember? Nasim-Guri thinks we are at peace. Now is the time to strike."

Meven swallowed and worked up more saliva. He tried to look away, but the Bishop's eyes held his. He managed to find the will to protest again. "I know we've been planning this war, Bishop DeNogaret. And it seemed like a good idea for a while. But I've been thinking about it lately, a lot. And I truly don't think it's a good idea anymore."

The Bishop snarled. He'd been lax about the boy, forgetting to re-exert control over him.

"The history books I read. You gave them to me, Bishop DeNogaret. They prove war is wrong."

"Not this war, Meven. This war would be the right thing to do. Think about being King of a larger Galmier, and of having many, many more subjects."

"I would like that, Bishop DeNogaret. But . . ."

"A war would please me, Meven."

All Meven could see was the Bishop's eyes. For a moment, he saw himself reflected in them, then he felt like he was swimming in them. A wave of dizziness washed over him, and he grabbed the table to steady himself.

"It would please me very much if you publicly supported this war, if you signed the papers declaring a war against Nasim-Guri, if you spoke to the nobles and announced the war, first to them. It would please me."

"This war?"

"Yes, it would make me happy, Meven."

"I want you to be happy, Bishop DeNogaret."

"Then you want this war, don't you Meven? As King, you need a larger country and more subjects. Nasim-Guri to the south would not suspect an attack and would be vulnerable. The time to strike is now, Meven." The Bishop smiled and nodded, and his eyes lost a little of their brightness, releasing Meven.

The boy blinked and wiped at his face. He still felt like he was swimming.

"Bishop?"

"Yes, my child?"

"You want me to sign some papers? A declaration of war?"

"Yes, Meven."

"And you want me to tell the nobles, so they will have men to add to our army?"

"Of course, Meven. I can see to it that the nobles are assembled."

Meven smiled, his eyes glimmering arrogantly. "I would like to do things to make you happy, Bishop DeNogaret. Signing the paper, declaring war."

"Good, Meven."

"But I can't. Not now in any event. I don't think this war is a good idea."

Bishop DeNogaret made a sound like an animal growling. He took a step toward Meven, then stopped when an attendant softly rapped on the door.

"Bishop?"

The elderly priest turned to acknowledge the attendant in the doorway.

"There is someone in your study. I'm not sure how he got past the palace watch, and he refuses to leave sir."

"His name?"

"Herbert," he says. "He's a bear of a man, sir, with a large bird on his shoulder. The man's quite large and imposing and . . ."

"He sounds interesting, Gerald. I'll see to him."

The Bishop glided from the room.

"Perhaps we can go to war some other time, Bishop DeNogaret. When I am a few years older," Meven said. There was no emotion in the young King's voice, but his dark eyes continued to glimmer.

15 · Brothers

When I study some of the families of Paard-Peran, I see people forced
together because of their blood ties. Their friends are closer to them
than their brothers. Perhaps the Fallen Favorites should be able to select their relatives. The families might be tighter. What matters blood
anyway?

~Prudent-Flehmen, shepherd to Bartholomew the merchant

Kal, if you would have stayed in Stilton a little longer, and
listened to me . . . Or if you were older and educated, you
would have known what happened to the first two Vershan
Monasteries. It's as if some dark force was after the priests
then. They were bad times."

"An earthquake? A dark force?" Kalantha sounded disbe-
lieving.

"Kal Morgan, when you consider that the second monastery,
this one we stand in, suffered a horrible fire. Many of the
priests were killed trying to save all the books and the holy
relics. Two disasters, both against my Order? When nearby villages and farmers suffered no losses? I consider that unnatural,
Kal Morgan. A coincidence? I hardly think so. Fortunately, the
monastery we head to has been standing for well more than a
few years. I'd hate to see something happen to the third one."

"I like it when you just call me Kal. It's what my brother used to call me. I like it best."

"Kal. All right. So you've a brother?"

She shook her head. "Not anymore."

"Oh, I'm so sorry to hear that." Ergoth seemed genuinely sad, and he reached out a hand and put it on her shoulder. He was missing the last two fingers on his right hand. She'd not noticed that before. "What happened to your brother, Kal? Was it an illness?"

She shook her head more sternly. "I don't want to talk about it."

"Well, I'll be happy to see my own brother, Kal. And you're just the excuse I need for the trip. I think you two will get along well. He'll be amazed that a girl of your age can read and is so interested in books!"

She drew her face together until it looked pinched. "Why shouldn't I be able to read?"

"Oh, it's not that you shouldn't. I think everyone should." He paused, searching for the words. "It's just that . . ."

Ergoth looked much better this morning. Kalantha had volunteered the bed she'd found, since he looked so haggard and even more tired than she did. He didn't argue much, and he quickly fell asleep. She considered leaving him during the night and striking out with the punch for this third Vershan Monastery on her own—or maybe just striking out and going . . . somewhere. But for some reason she trusted Ergoth, or wanted to. She needed to trust someone, she decided. So she slept on a mostly intact rug in another room, her wolfskin cloak pulled up all around her.

"So . . ." she pressed. "You were saying . . ."

"Not many women . . . girls . . . can read. Not all men can for that matter. In fact, in Stilton, there's not more than a handful of men who can read. It's just not called for, and there really aren't many books in any given village."

"Not called for? For girls especially, huh? Girls . . . women . . . aren't taken seriously, Ergoth. They're taken for granted and considered less than men, aren't they? Oh, I'll bet there're women acolytes at your Vershan Monastery—if it still stands and hasn't crumbled to some *dark force*. But I bet there are no women priests. They aren't allowed, are they?"

He didn't answer that. "I just think it's fortunate that you know how to read. That's all I'm saying."

"So why'd you leave Stilton, Ergoth? You could stay there and protect and educate them at the same time. Get them some books and teach them all."

He grinned. "My, my, Kal, quite the tongue you have for someone so young. Speak your mind, don't you?" He ran his fingers through his hair and let out a deep breath. "I intend to go back and work on just that. But, as I said, you're an excuse to visit my brother. I haven't seen him in two years, and I think it's important to stay in touch with family."

She scowled at this.

"Besides, I couldn't let you wander in the woods alone. It's not safe for someone your age."

She opened her mouth to say, *I'm not alone. I have Rue.* But she stayed silent.

"Especially when you didn't listen to my whole story about the Vershan Monastery and didn't know exactly where you were going. I think you need me around to find the place."

"I still don't think there were any evil forces at work here." She pointed to a burned tapestry. "Just a fire, Ergoth. Just an earthquake at the other old monastery. Bad things happen." A little louder: "Bad things happen all the time."

He brushed at his robe and made a move toward his horse,

awkwardly dragging his left leg. The two made an apt pair, she thought, Ergoth lame and the plow horse swaybacked.

"And what about the birds, Kal? I suppose there was no evil force at work there, either." He looked over his shoulder and saw she was staring at a spot on the ground. "C'mon, Kal. We've a long way to go . . . all the way to the Gray Woods to find the standing Vershan Monastery."

Kal wasted no time finding the canvas bag of trinkets she'd dropped yesterday and climbing onto the Finest. She stared at Ergoth's horse and saw a ring around its neck where the harness for a plow had rubbed. The horse's ears were overly long and she was wearing a saddle that appeared to be made especially for her sloping back. Her mane was short, and her feet on the small side, like a donkey's.

She was sandy brown, with a white stomach and a white patch on her neck.

"She's no marking on her legs," Kalantha observed, as they headed away from the abandoned monastery.

"No."

"Then why do you call her Boots?"

Ergoth chuckled. "She's not my horse. I borrowed her from Hedge. Remember him from Stilton?"

"The big man."

"He uses her in the field. Well, he doesn't consider Boots too cooperative, and she hates pulling a plow. He told me one day that he named her Boots because that's what he was going to turn her into if she got any more cantankerous. That's why he let me borrow her. Said he wanted her out of his sight for a while. He's not going to need her until the spring planting."

Kalantha stretched over and patted Boots's neck. "She's pretty for a plow horse."

The Finest studied Boots for a few minutes.

I am Gallant-Stallion, he said in her tongue.

She made a sound that was a cross between a bray and a whinny. *Cold,* she said. *No one to stand against to stop the cold. Nothing to stop the wind. Cold. Cold. Cold.*

We travel south, Boots, so it should get warmer.

I do not want to go.

It will be warmer and . . .

And I do not want to go. And I do not want this man on my back. And I do not want this saddle, and this thing in my mouth. And I do not want to walk next to the girl in the smelly wolf cloak. And I do not want to talk to you . . . ugly horse.

Gallant-Stallion snorted and looked to the road ahead.

BOOTS ADOPTED A SLOW, STEADY PACE, REFUSING ERGOTH's urgings to go faster and complaining in her braying-whinnying tongue.

"Maybe we can get you a saddle for your horse at the monastery, Kal. You could do some chores to pay it off. That's how things are done there."

"I don't need a saddle, Ergoth. I don't think Rue would like it. Boots probably doesn't like her saddle either."

Cold, she complained. *Don't like the saddle. Don't like the man on my back. Don't want to walk anymore. Want to go home.*

"It shouldn't be too much farther to the monastery," Ergoth told Kalantha the next day. And the day after that.

"It should have taken only two days, I think," he told her on the third day. "Boots went much faster when I was trying to find you. Maybe we're just not making good enough time. Or maybe I'm slightly off on my directions."

Kalantha didn't reply, and had stayed silent for nearly the entire journey, as Ergoth tried to draw her out and ask about her family. She didn't want to talk about that. She only wanted to talk to Rue, but she didn't do that either. She wasn't sure why, but she didn't want to have Ergoth get suspicious and learn about her magic horse.

But on the evening of the fourth day she let out a surprised gasp and showed more energy than she'd displayed since they started traveling together. They hadn't yet come across the standing Vershan Monastery, but something caught her eye.

"Look, Ergoth. It's . . . beautiful! Hurry." She kneed Gallant-Stallion, and he took off at a gallop.

The ground in front of them was covered with stars.

16 · The Hollow Man

Plots and plans, I never could understand it all . . . and in that respect I considered the Fallen Favorites superior to we Finest. They have so many plots and plans and schemes, my head spun each time I tried to unravel it all. Complexities were not in my nature, and so I had only one man to shepherd, this a merchant's guild head from Dolour. After I guided and guarded him, I shook off the scent of men, cleared my mind of their manipulations, and thankfully returned to the Court lands. Forever.

~One-Ear Sleekcoat, messenger for the Finest Court

Bishop DeNogaret stared at his visitor. The man resembled a bear with his barrel-like chest and thick arms, and his black beard came to midway down his chest and was well-groomed, though unevenly streaked with gray. Short hair flared away from a flat face, and his puglike nose looked like it had been broken more than once. His eyes were a watery blue, and his skin looked like the shell of a walnut, tanned and deeply weathered. The Bishop might be looking at a sailor, from the condition of the man's skin, but after studying him a bit longer, the Bishop doubted the man had ever been to sea.

Standing proud, he had the look of a woodsman with his deerskin jacket and trousers, with an axe hung from his right hip and a shortsword from his left. His right arm was extended straight away from his body (like a scarecrow posed in a field), a falcon perched on it.

The Bishop sniffed. He expected the man to carry the stink of the forest, but instead, the man smelled clean, of a pleasant musk-scented soap, and his clothes carried not even a trace of dirt. Bishop DeNogaret had been intrigued when Gerald announced this fellow. Now he was doubly curious.

Few of his own men were this fastidious.

"Herbert . . ."

The man turned slightly so he squarely faced the Bishop.

. . . But he didn't answer.

"What does a falconer want with the High Bishop of Nadir? You must have been persuasive to get an audience today. I'm a very busy man and . . ."

Herbert shook his head. "I had to come here to see you." His voice was hollow sounding, almost haunting. His eyes looked vacant.

"Obviously you wanted to see me." The Bishop was becoming irritated now. First there was Meven's impudence, and now this man. The falconer was being slow to provide the answer the bishop wanted. "I said . . . what do you want?"

"To see you?" The man shrugged, and the falcon on his arm opened her wings to keep her balance. "I wanted to see you, I said. It was important I come here." He scratched at his beard. "But I don't remember why it was important. Who are you again?"

"Bishop DeNogaret. I'm a very important man, and my time is precious. Why did you come here?"

"Because I said he had to bring me," the falcon answered. "I required an escort to this palace."

Bishop DeNogaret stepped back, startled, but he quickly regained his composure.

"I sent for Eyeswide."

The falcon flew from Herbert's arm and landed on the back of the chair that Eyeswide often used for a perch.

"Eyeswide is otherwise occupied, Bishop DeNogaret. He is personally searching for a girl named . . ."

"Kalantha Montoll." The Bishop lowered his voice. He didn't think anyone was out in the hall, but he was careful nonetheless. There were always servants about somewhere.

"Kalantha Montoll." The falcon's voice was also soft now, sounding as if a breeze was whispering through leafy trees. "He seeks her personally—he and three elderly crows—and he sends me in his stead. Kalantha Montoll is an important matter to him."

The Bishop waved a hand in front of his nose as if this meeting was offensive to him. "And what of him? Herbert?"

The falcon made a gesture reminiscent of a man rolling his shoulders. "I thought it inappropriate to knock on the palace door and seek an audience with you on my own. I thought that might rattle some of the servants . . . unless they are used to talking birds."

Was there a hint of snideness in the falcon's feathery voice?

"Good of you to bring Herbert then," the Bishop said. "You and Eyeswide must live a life in shadows, you know." He walked toward the chair and stooped a little so he could look closer at the falcon. "And what do I call you?"

"Ninéon."

Bishop DeNogaret's forehead wrinkled. "A familiar name. Long ago I knew a devout woman called Ninéon. She especially revered Iniquis and Abandon. I had a particular fondness for her."

"It is a good name I have then. And it is good of you to know the name," Ninéon said. "I wish to be familiar to you. Easy to remember."

The Bishop turned to look at Herbert. His arms were at his sides now, and there was a serene look on his face.

"I am pleased Eyeswide is attending to the matter of finding

Kalantha, Ninéon. But there is more work to be done than looking for one girl. Many things are falling into place, and time is crucial."

"So, Bishop DeNogaret, Eyeswide should cease this . . ."

"No!" the Bishop cringed that he'd spoken so loudly. He instantly lowered his voice again. "No. I want the girl found. And killed. Now would be far easier and less complicated than if she were to grow any older. And, as I said, I am pleased that Eyeswide is seeing to this personally. But I need something else addressed, too. I want the flock to scout throughout Nasim-Guri and study the King's soldiers and defenses. I want a precise and detailed report of the soldiers' locations and patrol patterns. Do you understand, Ninéon?"

"For your upcoming war," the falcon replied. "I will get you this information, Bishop DeNogaret. It will be useful in your plans for Galmier's soldiers, yes?" Ninéon looked to Herbert. "You will take me out of the palace now, woodsman. I have work to do."

Herbert extended his arm, and the falcon took her perch.

"I will return when I have your answers, Bishop DeNogaret."

The elderly priest watched the pair. He was a little concerned that the bird had enough presence to subjugate a man. But perhaps it was a sign that Eyeswide was giving more authority and putting more trust in what was obviously his new lieutenant.

"Ninéon . . ."

The falcon stopped Herbert from opening the door.

"Yes, Bishop?"

"Where are you from, Ninéon? Your feathers are too light to mark you from Eyeswide's normal flock."

The falcon and the Bishop were so engrossed in studying each other for a moment that they didn't notice the rear door to the study open and King Meven enter.

"I am from the land men named the Gray Woods. Years past,

I understand, a type of tree grew there that gave off a pale gray mist that looked like fog. The trees are gone, but the name of the place remains."

"The Gray Woods. In Nasim-Guri."

"Yes, where Nasim-Guri touches the country Vered. I hunted where the Gray Woods joined with the Old Forest."

"And Eyeswide found you there?"

The falcon nodded. "The great owl rescued me, Bishop DeNogaret."

The Bishop raised an eyebrow.

"I was a simple creature before the owl caught me and awoke me from my humble existence. Now I am much, much more than that, priest. I am . . ."

"B—B—Bishop?" Meven was staring slack-jawed at the bird. The youth was trembling and brought his hand to his throat. "Bishop DeNogaret!"

The Bishop brushed by Herbert and Ninéon, moving more quickly than Meven thought someone of his advanced age could.

"The bird," Meven continued. "The bird talks. Like the birds that attacked me and Kalantha and Edan. Killed Edan and the soldiers. Almost killed Kal." He took a step back toward the door, and his shaking hand fumbled for the knob. "The guards . . . I must get them. They'll save us."

Like a blur, the Bishop slipped between Meven and the door and grabbed the youth's shoulders. His nails dug in painfully and caused Meven to squeal.

"You do not see a bird in my study, King Meven. Do you understand? There is no bird." Bishop DeNogaret gripped Meven even harder, and the youth cringed. Tears formed in the corners of his eyes.

"Bird," Meven said. His eyes were staring into the Bishop's. They were the only things he could see, and again he found himself swimming in them. Except this time it felt like he was drowning. He gasped for air. "Bird? There is no bird here, Bishop DeNogaret." Meven's voice lacked inflection and was steady, like an acolyte chanting.

"You see no other man here either, Meven."

The King shook his head. "No one but you, Bishop DeNogaret."

The Bishop stared deeper into Meven's eyes just to be certain. "Meven, I have an important task for you this morning."

Meven's eyes brightened a little, but his face still held the pain. The Bishop hadn't eased up on his grip. "Important. Something for me to do."

"There is a vital dinner engagement this evening with the lords of the northern territories."

"I remember. It's important."

"Very. And you must tend to your wardrobe. You must look your absolute best."

"I like dark colors," Meven said flatly.

"Then you must find something dark to wear."

17 · Astrologers

I shepherded an astrologer once, decades past, in the time before they were hated. He looked to the stars and claimed to see the future. I thought him wiser and more interesting than other Fallen Favorites I knew. But the stars did not tell him that people would come to distrust his kind. And they did not tell him that he would die soon to a sweating sickness. I looked to the stars and saw only cold, bright shining beauty. And the stars made me think fondly of him.

~Steadfast, veteran Finest

All of these stars! Amazing." Kalantha slid off Gallant-Stallion's back and stood at the edge of the field of stars. Her breath caught, and she steadied herself against the punch's side. "I've never seen anything so incredibly beautiful. I feel dizzy looking at them."

All thoughts of the Vershan Monastery disappeared.

She saw only stars.

It was as if a piece of the night sky had been torn free and spread out on the ground in front of her.

The world was dark and sparkling, and she stretched out her fingers, thinking she could actually touch one of the stars. They looked so close and delicately brittle.

Gallant-Stallion stood beside her, equally amazed. Though he'd considered many places in Paard-Peran beautiful, he'd not considered any of them equal to the lands of the Finest Court. Until now. He sucked in a deep breath and stared. Nothing in the Court lands came close to this. It was as if he was floating in the night sky.

The Finest was so stunned by the tableau that he didn't hear Ergoth and Boots approach. After a moment he vaguely registered that the priest was talking, but he thrust the words aside and concentrated only on the stars.

There were constellations—of Paard-Zhumd, Peran-Morab, the Old Mare, Grand Andalusian, Mother Cob, Dartmorland, and more. Not a single cloud intruded.

"How is this possible?" Kalantha asked in a hush. "Rue, how could such a place be?"

The Finest's throat was dry, he was so overwhelmed. So he said nothing and watched as a shooting star, brighter than anything else, arced in the distance and was mirrored on the ground.

"The Lake of Stars," Ergoth managed. He was on his knees, and had been praying. "I was indeed off on my directions a bit." He chuckled lightly. "But not a bad thing, eh? Traveled a little too far east, Kal. But now I know for certain where we are. The Lake of Stars."

Kalantha was inching forward. The tips of her boots touched the starfield on the ground, and it rippled. "It is a lake, isn't it? But I've never seen water reflect the sky so. Ever. Especially at night."

Ergoth got to his feet. "This is a special place, Kal. Maybe the gods directed I get lost just to show it to you. I have trouble finding my way sometimes. I . . . tend to get lost."

She nodded and bent over, twirling her fingers in the water and thereby stirring the stars. "And you thought *I* shouldn't be traveling alone?"

Tired, Boots complained. *Hooves are sore. Back aches. Tired. Tired. Hungry. Thirsty.*

Then drink from the lake, Boots, Gallant-Stallion said. *The water smells cool and clean. It will not hurt you.*

The plow horse made a noise that sounded almost like a dog growling, but she edged forward and dipped her muzzle. *Water is too cold,* she groused. *Tired. Hooves are sore. Man was on my back too long. Hungry. Hungry. Muzzy looking at the starry water.*

Gallant-Stallion snorted his disgust at the plow horse and came forward until the water lapped around all his hooves. He didn't mind the cold. He fancied himself standing in the middle of the constellation of Mother Cob. He took a long drink and imagined he was swallowing stars. He was a little dizzy, too, trying to take it all in. But he was enjoying the sensation.

Too many bright spots. Boots was still complaining about the stars and their reflections. *Dizzy. Dizzy. Dizzy. Too many, many bright light spots. Home. I want to be home, punch. Make the man take me home. Make him take me home now.*

"There is a village on the east shore, Kal." Ergoth was unaware his horse was upset by the lake. "I visited it a few years ago . . . when I again got lost trying to visit my brother at the Vershan Monastery. Some of the people there are a little peculiar. And sometimes they chase people away from the lake." He paused, and his breath caught as something grew brighter in the sky, then vanished. Ergoth was still staring at the stars. "But they're nice enough, the people. And maybe we can pass the night with someone there. I'd rather do that than sleep out in the cold again. I've no desire to catch a sickness."

He didn't see Kalantha nod in agreement. She reluctantly stepped back from the lake's edge and reached for Gallant-Stallion's mane. "I wish Meven could see this," she whispered. "And I wish Morgan could, too. My friend Morgan would want to live here forever."

I wonder if Steadfast ever saw this, Gallant-Stallion thought. I hope he did. I hope Mara and Prudent-Flehmen did too.

Then they were working their way to the east, following the shore and still watching the stars.

I want to be home. Too many bright spots. Cold. Hungry. Hungry.

"On my last visit here . . ."

"Where, Ergoth?"

"Here, at Salshad. That's the name of the village we're going to." Ergoth paused and watched another shooting star, this one fainter. "Salshad is short for Salern's Shadow. The village, nothing more than a collection of cottages actually, was named after . . . hmm, let's see if I can remember the name . . . hmmm . . . Salern Weldon, an astrologer who fled across the Esi Sea from Minau-Pia. Yes, that's it! Salern Weldon. He settled here at the edge of the Gray Woods with a handful of apprentices. They favor the place to this day because of the Lake of Stars, which supposedly aids their arcane studies. The village grew with the falling of the first and second Vershan Monasteries, the stablehands and some of the acolytes moving here. An acolyte told me about the lake. Said the bottom is white sand. It makes the water an intense blue during the day. Hopefully you'll see that, Kal. If they put us up for the night. It reflects the clouds and sky during the day, like any lake would. But at night this lake reflects the sky just like a mirror. Anyway, on my last visit here, I was received warmly enough. I slept near the lake."

"The Lake of Stars."

"Yes, of course, Kal. The Lake of Stars."

Several minutes later Ergoth pointed to a scattering of thatched and wood-plank homes. There wasn't a stone building anywhere, but the homes looked like they had quite a bit of age to them. A few were shaped like a turtle's shell, made out of mud and grasses, the doorways where turtles' heads would come out.

A few dozen people were outside, which seemed odd given the time of year and this being so late at night. They sat apart from each other, blankets and cloaks wrapped around them, all of them staring up at the stars, or looking to the west where the stars reflected so keenly in the lake.

"Wh—what are they doing?" Kalantha whispered to Ergoth.

"I don't exactly know, and I've never tried to understand it. Suffice it to say they're astrologers," he answered in an equally hushed voice. "And astrologers look to the stars."

Kalantha shivered, and not from the cold night air. She'd heard Bishop DeNogaret tell stories of how astrologers encouraged wars or trade, all manner of things, based on the position of the stars. She remembered him saying they were right sometimes, the astrologers. But they'd also been wrong and catastrophes resulted. In ages past it was said an astrologer encouraged a war between Uland and Galmier, and that both sides lost more than half their forces before a truce was declared. Kings on both sides died in the battle, and riots and power struggles ensued. It was the beginning of the end for consulting astrologers about anything of political importance. They became distrusted·and shunned, and Bishop DeNogaret said more than a few of them were hanged in Galmier, "and their bodies left for the crows to feast on."

"This might not be a good idea," Kalantha said. "The lake is beautiful and all, but I'm not sure we should . . ." She stopped when four of the astrologers rose in unison and like soldiers marching started coming toward her. "Not a good idea at all, Ergoth." Much softer: "Rue, I knew I shouldn't have trusted this priest. Any priest."

The four men took long quick strides to reach Kalantha and

Ergoth. The tallest among them nodded to the priest. All of them seemed intent on Ergoth, paying no regard to Kalantha.

"We travel to the Vershan Monastery," Ergoth began. He smiled and tipped his head to the tallest astrologer.

Too many people, Boots continued to grumble. *But maybe they will feed me. Hungry. Cold. Hungry. Tired. Tired. Please to feed me something sweet.*

Kalantha noticed that other people were poking their heads out of doors and windows, and a few were coming outside. She and Ergoth hadn't made much noise, certainly not enough to wake all of these people. But maybe astrologers did not sleep at night, she thought.

"Vershan is to the southwest," the tall man said. His words were clipped, and there wasn't a hint of warmth in his voice. "If indeed you were looking for that . . . castle . . . you have ventured many, many miles out of your way."

Ergoth ground the ball of his foot against the earth. "Well, I'm not the best . . . navigator, if you will. I got us a little off track. I've made a habit of getting myself lost. We're from Galmier. I'm from Stilton."

"A long way from here," the tall man grudgingly returned. "Had you looked to the stars, they would have led you correctly."

Ergoth kept grinding his foot. "Well, yes. If I knew how to read them."

"You are welcome to spend the night here. . . ."

"Ergoth Thistlebrook, as I said—lately of Stilton. And this is Kal Morgan."

"Not your daughter."

Ergoth shook his head. "No, no relation to me. And I'm not quite old enough for a daughter of her age. But she's a friend. And we're traveling together."

Then the tall man studied the two horses and finally dropped his gaze to Kalantha. "I suspect you could use something warm to eat."

It was Kalantha's turn to nod. She still shivered nervously, and she moved close to Rue when the tall man brushed her hood back to get a look at her face.

"I am Innis Soto, Kal Morgan . . . Ergoth Thistlebrook. Welcome to Salshad." He wrinkled his nose at Kal. "You could use a bath, child."

Kal and Ergoth were permitted a bath, a luxury for a village this small. Then they were given venison stew and goat milk.

Gallant-Stallion and Boots were kept under a lean-to attached to Innis's home and provided buckets of oats. The plow horse didn't complain when she ate, and the Finest was thankful for that and wished that the oat bucket was bottomless so she'd eat all night and not say a word.

Kalantha thanked Innis and remarked how good the food was. But in truth she found the venison tough and the broth greasy and not nearly warm enough. She didn't care for the goat milk; still, she was thirsty and knew it was good for her. It was not as good of fare as she had enjoyed in the company of Bartholomew, or even in Stilton. But she ate as much as she could manage, as she wasn't certain when her next meal would be.

She and Ergoth were given blankets and invited to sleep on Innis Soto's kitchen floor. And though she was comfortable and terribly tired, she slept only fitfully.

It was early in the morning, the sky still dark and the riot of stars still reflecting in the lake, when Kalantha slipped out to stare at the water again. Sitting at the eastern edge of the lake, inches from the water, she was so caught up in the lights that she didn't hear someone approaching until the woman sat down next to her.

Kalantha was so startled she almost bolted forward into the

lake. But the woman put a hand on her knee to reassure her. Kalantha had met her earlier—Belda-Derora Soto, the mother of Innis. Belda did not appear much older than her son, except for around her eyes where tiny wrinkles spread away like spiderwebs. Her hair was dark, though in the starlight strands of white shimmered at her temples.

"Child, you are uncomfortable here."

Kalantha looked at Belda's hand. The skin was smooth, but there were a few brown spots on the back and near her wrist, a hint to her age. "A little," she admitted.

"Because astrologers live here? Not everyone in this village is an astrologer." Belda's eyes looked kind, but there was also something mysterious there.

"No . . . But I'm not comfortable a lot of places. Not anymore."

"Astrologers shouldn't make you quake."

"I've never met astrologers before. And they don't make me nervous. I saw a big bird a few minutes ago is all. It spooked me." She wasn't lying about seeing the bird.

"And birds make you nervous . . . and astrologers do not?"

"I've heard stories about astrologers," Kalantha said, not wanting Belda to press her about the birds. "Bishop DeNogaret said a long time ago one started a war between Galmier and Uland."

Belda's eyes showed sadness now. "That story, and probably many more that you've heard, are true. A hundred or more years ago astrologers had quite a bit of power in this world. But that power wasn't enough for some of them." She laughed. "For most of them, actually. Hungry and manipulative, they championed wars and encouraged rebellions. They brought suspicion and hate down upon themselves as a result. Down upon all the astrologers."

Kalantha nodded a little too quickly.

"But not all astrologers were like that. I'm not like that."

Kalantha's eyes grew wide and she scooted away so Belda no longer touched her. "You're an astrologer?"

Belda laughed again, longer and high-pitched. It sounded like crystal wind chimes blown by a slight breeze. "You find it odd that a woman does something other than care for her family?"

"No. No, that's not it. Well, yes, that's partly it. You just don't seem like . . . like I would picture an astrologer."

"Perhaps, Kal Morgan, I should take that as a compliment."

They fell silent for several minutes, watching the stars and seeing a gust of wind catch the surface of the lake and make the reflected lights dance like agitated fireflies.

"I dream of stars, Kal Morgan. But my dreams cannot equal this." The woman cupped her hands in front of her face, then made a scooping motion as she inhaled. "Stars and dreams are sweet, child. Stars atop stars and dreams within dreams." She let another stretch of silence settle between them. "I was dreaming of you yesterday, child. I knew you would come to our village."

"Can you tell the future, Belda?"

"Call me Bel, child."

"Bel."

"Maybe I dreamed you here—with the help of the stars." There was a distant look on the woman's face. "The astrologers who live here, there are thirty-seven of us, perhaps all who are left with the art on this island continent. We're not hungry for power, like so many of us who went before. Myself? I am too old and tired to do anything other than live by this lake and study the constellations and dream that a girl will pass through, touching me." She drew in a deep breath and slowly released it, a misty cloud that dissipated before it reached the reflected stars. "None of us are interested in politics and governments. And religion? Some of us worship the gods, some the stars. Ah, but others . . . religion is a private thing, isn't it, Kal Morgan?" She moved closer to Kalantha again, and took the girl's hand.

"Bel, can you . . ."

"Yes, child, I can tell your future." Bel cast her head back until she was looking directly overhead. "A waking dream it is. A little look at tomorrow and tomorrow." She stared unblinking for a few moments, and then she closed her eyes and her fingers tightened.

Kalantha thought the wind that had been stirring the reflecting lights faded at that moment. From somewhere in the village a dog barked anxiously. Another howled softly. She considered pulling away, finding Ergoth, and urging him to leave with her at this very moment. But Bel thrummed her thumb against the back of Kalantha's hand, hummed softly, then spoke.

"So much moves around you. Constantly shifting it is, and so very difficult to pinpoint. But I can see that a dark power works to start a war on this island continent, girl. Royal blood will cause the shedding of common blood everywhere. Too much blood for the ground to soak up." Bel shuddered. "Blood enough for the people to drown in."

"That has nothing to do with me. War and death, that's not about me at all." Kalantha was curious, though, and scared. The thought of a war terrified her; a battle between soldiers would be worse than a flock of assassin-birds. She looked at Bel and saw the stars reflected on the front of the woman's dark cloak. "I don't like fighting. That's not my future at all. I'm not a part of that. It has nothing to do with me, I say."

"It does, child. Somehow. The stars have never lied to me. The same dark power that wants this world . . . it wants also to rid this world of you. It seems your royal blood poses a threat, and your enemy will not stop until you stop breathing. You are a threat to that dark power, child. You only will be safe if you leave this island continent." Bel relaxed her grip on Kalantha's hand, but she didn't let go. She opened her eyes and stared at the lake. "Run, child. Find your way to a small island. Farmeadow or Minau-Pia. The stars tell me that your foe will not or cannot reach you there. You can find ports far to the south, and you can find passage there to one of the small islands."

Bel finally released Kalantha's hand, and the astrologer reached to the back of her neck and tugged free a long silvery chain. A small, clear stone that glimmered as brightly as a star hung from it.

"This has considerable value, child. From my mother's mother. Barter it with a jeweler or silversmith in one of those port towns to the south. You'll get the best coin for it that way."

Kalantha shook her head. "It's a diamond, Bel. It is too valuable. You can't give it to me. I'm a stranger to you."

The woman shook her head vehemently. "I dreamed you, child. I knew you were coming, and I have looked to your future. We are not strangers."

"I can't accept it anyway. You could feed this village for . . ."

"We've plenty to eat. And none of us have royal blood that makes us a target." Bel pushed off the ground, steadying herself on Kalantha's shoulder. "And I am an old woman who doesn't need such things anymore. I have no daughter or granddaughter to give this to. Better I look at the stars in the lake than to the one around my neck. Better you use the diamond to stay safe. Although, know you this, child—being safe isn't always the safest answer to a dilemma."

She shuffled back toward her cottage, Kalantha following and trying to puzzle out the astrologer's final message.

Neither saw three large crows fly across the Lake of Stars, searching.

18 · A Change of Heart

I guided and guarded King Galvin of Minau-Pia. He was my first to
shepherd, a remarkable man who spent his days creating laws he
thought would improve the lives of his people, and his nights praying
for their souls. My final assignment was shepherding the elder of a
small coastal village. He spent his days fishing, and he spread his catch
among his people. At night, he taught the youngsters how to make
hooks and nets, so they could fish too. Sometimes simple acts garner
the greatest results, and the simplest of men are the wisest.

~Walker Blacktail, second son of the Old Mare

Meven fought a yawn and tipped his head back to look at the
stars, but only a scattering shone through a gap in the
clouds. He wasn't certain of the constellation—Acacia or
Greater Acacia, he thought—as he made out twin lines of stars
that likely defined a tree trunk . . . but the lines could also de-
fine the belt of Peran-Morab.

It was cold, even though it was spring, and the wind was
strong and whistling. It stung his face, and brought with it a
clean scent that settled pleasantly in his mouth. When he
peered over the balcony railing he saw patches of snow as far as
the grounds stretched. In the distance, he could see snow on the
roof of the stable where his prized norikers slept. Meven remembered there being snow on the ground this late in the
spring . . . but he'd been a child then. The cold weather hadn't
hung on so fiercely in more than a few years.

The balcony he stood on wrapped around the northeast corner of the palace. It was larger than his principal study, and he slowly followed it along the railing, thrumming his fingers against the stone as he went.

He hadn't thought of Kalantha for a few weeks, but he did so now, as today—if she still lived—marked her thirteenth birthday. He wondered if she and the ugly punch had made it through the winter, and if so, where they were. Someplace warmer, he hoped, but someplace not too far away. He knew she'd like this balcony and would no doubt spend a lot of time on it if she were here. If she came back to visit, he promised himself he would not chase her away again.

"Should I get a coat for you, King Meven?"

Meven glanced to his right, where his attendant Gerald stood so straight it looked like he was a soldier at attention. The older man shivered and his breath puffed away from his face. He'd been following Meven since dinner, his night to wait on the King.

"No, Gerald, but thank you. The cold feels good to me right now. I spent too much time in front of the fireplace. You would've sworn I'd had a fever, my face was so hot and red. And the heat made me sleepy. The cold's a good change."

"You could catch . . ."

"I don't plan to stay out much longer anyway. So don't worry. I'll not catch some ailment."

"Of course, King Meven."

"Gerald . . ." Meven wrapped his fingers around the railing and leaned hard against it and looked straight down. He didn't see the attendant pale and reach a hand out, as if to grab him, but he heard Gerald suck in a nervous breath. "Gerald, you don't have to hover all the time. You're like my shadow. I can do for myself, you realize. It's not that I don't appreciate you. I just . . ."

"I am your assistant, King Meven. It is my job to hover."
Gerald relaxed when Meven leaned away from the railing.

"But you don't have to stay out here with me, Gerald."

"Of course, King Meven. I understand. However, I, too, like to look at the stars."

Meven shook his head and smiled thinly. "Of course you do, Gerald." He followed the balcony back around the corner and returned his attention to the constellation. It was a little more visible now because the wind had blown a larger gap in the clouds. "I was right. That's the Greater Acacia. Legend says the first King of Uland named it for an ancient tree that grew outside his bedroom window. That was hundreds of years ago, a thousand years ago. And they say the tree still thrives. It was when Uland was larger and Galmier was only a city on the coast. Before Galmier declared its independence, and a soldier took charge of the army and starting taking some of Uland's provinces. That soldier was the first King of Galmier, Gerald. And I'm the youngest king Galmier's ever had."

Gerald didn't reply, but he nodded as if he was interested in what the King was saying.

"I should like to visit Uland in a few months, when things warm up, and see the tree for myself. I could visit the King too, and we could talk about the stars. I think I shall name a constellation, too. It will give the people something else to remember me by. Maybe I will name it after my favorite noriker."

Meven continued to stare at the constellation, and Gerald continued to watch Meven. Neither of them saw four dark figures glide around the corner of the balcony, hugging the palace wall, difficult to distinguish from the night's thick shadows. The whistling wind covered the flapping of their cloaks and their whispers.

"I understand Uland's King is a little more than twice my

age, inheriting the crown from his father nearly three years ago. He has five daughters, and his wife is pregnant again. I'm certain he prays for a boy, someone to pass the crown to. But I'd wager they have another girl. The crown might end up on the head of a nephew . . . like this crown ended up with me." There was a hint of arrogance in Meven's voice. "And that would not be a bad thing."

"Fortunately, King Meven, you are young enough not to worry about heirs."

"For some time, I'd like to think!" Meven chuckled. "And I pray I will have a long, long reign, Gerald."

"Of course you will, King Meven. And a distinguished one, I am certain of it."

"Do you think I am a wise King?"

"Most wise, Sire."

"I'm wise enough not to start a war." Meven cupped his hand across his brow when the wind shifted and blew his hair into his eyes.

The four figures separated and slowly moved behind the King and his attendant. They were tall and clad entirely in black, as inky as the shadows that spread out from the palace walls and wrapped around their feet.

The wind gusted stronger, the clouds separated further, and the stars spilled more light onto the snow and the balcony. The quartet remained indistinct.

"I know a war could make Galmier bigger," Meven said. "More land means more people, which means more taxes. The coin could build schools in some of the smaller cities. That would be a good thing. And it would add to my coffers so I could enlarge the palace."

"Yes, it would."

"But a war . . . lots of people would die, Gerald. And a war would cost a considerable amount of coins."

"I think you're right, King Meven, to not start a war. There's no cause for such bloodshed."

Meven smiled broadly, the smile reaching his eyes. He hadn't been so pleased with himself for some time. "I needed someone to tell me that, Gerald, that a war is a bad thing."

"Why, Sire? Had you been contemplating one?"

Meven firmly shook his head. His talks with Bishop DeNogaret had been private. "No, not really."

The shadowy men edged closer, cloaks fanning out in the wind. Two figures slipped directly behind Gerald, the other two behind Meven.

"In fact," Meven continued, "I can't even say what made me think about war just now."

"Maybe because all countries have a history of it, Sire. And you are well versed in history."

"Maybe, but Galmier won't be adding to that sort of history. Not if I have . . ." Meven's words trailed off into a scream, as the two figures scooped him up and leaped off the balcony.

"Guards!" Gerald hollered. "Guards!" Then he was swept up too, and carried over the side of the railing.

The figures holding Meven floated impossibly skyward, while the ones carrying Gerald somehow hovered, then dropped the struggling man. He fell awkwardly, and a moment after he hit, the hovering dark figures appeared to shatter, and the pieces dove on him.

Wings tucked into their bodies to give them speed, beaks pointed like daggers, the avian assassins slammed into the King's attendant. Gerald's shrill cries turned into helpless whimpers, as the birds clawed and pecked him.

"Birds!" Meven cried. His attackers were not men at all! The birds held him in a perfect position to see the carnage below. He struggled against them while he watched in horror. "No! Stop! Gerald!"

Meven felt needle talons digging deeper into his arms and legs and slicing through his fine velvet shirt to skewer the flesh on his back for a better hold. He'd not felt such pain before, and he gritted his teeth and fought to stay conscious. At the same time, he kicked wildly, hoping to dislodge some of the birds so he could get free of them. Free and . . . what? Fall. The thought raced through his mind. Fall like Gerald and be pecked to bits!

They took him higher still, and he began shouting for the guards, wondering if he could possibly be heard over the flapping of their wings and the whistling wind.

All the while he stared down where he knew Gerald was. He couldn't see the man anymore, could only see a cloud of black swarming against the patches of snow. Tears spilled from his eyes, freezing against his skin.

"Gerald."

"Kill him," one of the blackbirds holding Meven said. The bird was at Meven's shoulder and pecked at his ear. "Kill him. Kill him."

"Drop him," another said. "Drop him. Drop him. Drop him. Drop him like the other man."

"Kill the King." This was higher-pitched and softer, coming from somewhere above. "Slowly, we will kill Meven Montoll."

Meven's eyes grew wide with greater terror, as the birds spun him around so he was looking up at the clouds and the stars. A small brown and black bird hung practically motionless above his face.

"Slowly, we will pick the flesh from the King's royal bones," the small bird said. "A royal feast for us."

"Nooooooo!" Meven screamed. The word came out a strangled croak, as his throat had gone dry and his tongue was suddenly thick and unwieldy. "Please no!" The words a whisper now.

"Drop the King," the small bird ordered.

Meven felt the dozens of talons release him, and he was falling. The cold air whipped around him, stinging his skin, and whistling so shrilly he could hear nothing else. He squeezed his eyes shut and waited to hit the ground. But then the talons dug in again, grabbing at his legs and arms, cutting through the velvet and burrowing into his chest and abdomen. He was wrenched to a stop, then was lifted higher again.

"Kill the King," a crow cooed.

"But play with him first," another said. "Play with the King."

Meven tried to call for the guards, but nothing came out this time. He gulped in the frosty air and clenched his hands, his nails digging into his palms in a last effort to stay conscious.

Through a haze of fright and pain he thought he heard something beyond the wings and the wind. Faint, someone calling to him, calling to him from wherever it was spirits drifted after their bodies died. The voice was familiar and comforting. Would it be so bad to die? he wondered. Would he see his parents again? His cousin Prince Edan? Kalantha, if she'd died during the harsh winter?

Again, Meven tried to speak, this time to call out to his father. But he couldn't even open his mouth. There was nothing for a few moments. Then again, he heard a voice. Now he could tell it was coming from below.

"Meven! By all the gods, Meven!"

The voice was a little louder, still familiar and comforting, with a whisper wrapped around its edges.

Bishop DeNogaret! Meven wanted to holler back. The voice certainly sounded like the Bishop's.

The birds spun him about once more. He was so high up, the

air as cold as an icy stream. Dizzy from the height, from the birds tossing him about, from the pain that continued to race through his limbs. He began shivering uncontrollably. They seemed to grip him tighter.

"Play with the King," the small brown-black bird said. "Play, I tell you. Revel in his suffering! Drop him! Drop him now!"

He was falling again, face-first this time, the ground rushing up to meet him. The birds that had been swarming Gerald were racing toward him now, letting him get a good look at his fallen attendant, blood splattered on the patches of snow. He caught a glimpse of another figure, this one rushing away from the palace, past Gerald and standing directly under him.

It was Bishop DeNogaret!

Meven was suddenly grabbed again, a dozen feet above the ground, the birds' talons digging in harder than ever. In an instant, he was going higher once more. He felt blood spilling from his wounds, making his skin feel oddly warm in contrast to the cold, cold air.

"Bishop DeNogaret!" he tried hopelessly to call out. The Bishop was waving his arms, the cane he sometimes used in one hand, leaping and trying to swat at the lowest birds. Meven considered the Bishop's antics would be comical at another time, an old man swinging at birds so far above his head. The priest's movements were jerky and desperate and futile, and he called out to Meven until he was hoarse.

"Play with the King," the brown-black bird continued.

"The man below," a large crow prompted. "Shall we play with him, too?"

"No!" Meven finally found his voice. "Run, Bishop!" But his words were lost in the wind and the wings, and the spittle that flew from his mouth sprayed against his face.

"Yes, let us play with him, too!"

"Kill him. Kill him. Kill him," the largest crow droned.

"No. Not kill that man. But you can play with him, too," the brown-black bird agreed.

Meven saw a swath of black fly away from him, and registered that some of the birds had released him. The ones that retained their grip flapped their wings harder to stay aloft.

"No! Leave the Bishop alone!" Meven cried.

The young King watched as a small swarm of birds dropped toward Bishop DeNogaret. The priest remained intent on Meven, spread his arms wide, cane held high. The light from the stars and the snow showed that the priest was talking, his mouth moving quickly.

A prayer, perhaps, Meven thought, one that would do no good against the avian assassins. Then the birds were taking Meven lower, and he could hear the Bishop.

"Release King Meven!" Bishop DeNogaret ordered. "Vile creatures of the dark powers, release him, I say!" The Bishop repeated the demand, and the birds that had dove on him fluttered back out of the reach of his cane and began circling. "The gods give me strength!" the Bishop continued. "Strength against you! Release King Meven!"

There was a power in the words Meven had not felt before, as if the Bishop was putting all of his presence into his plea. Faintly, Meven heard one of the crows protest, heard another bird call "Flee? Should we flee?" An angry bird grabbed Meven's ear and pulled hard, that pain momentarily overshadowing everything else.

"Release the King!" Bishop DeNogaret was keeping one swarm at bay by swinging his cane. He thrust his free hand at the birds that held Meven. "In the name of my gods, I say free him now!"

"Free him," the brown-black bird said. "Free the King."

"We should flee," the biggest crow suggested.

"Flee. Flee. Flee," became a chorus.

Meven felt the talons dig in, then relax. Then he felt himself falling. This time the birds didn't catch him, and he plunged into a patch of snow. The impact knocked the breath from him, and he gasped, trying to suck air into his fiery, aching lungs. He tried to push himself up, but his arms wouldn't cooperate. Finally, he managed to roll over onto his back. The pain in his chest eased.

Bishop DeNogaret loomed above him, cane swatting at a mass of blackbirds. The cane connected with one of the birds, dropping it next to Meven. It was the small brown-black bird that had been directing the swarm.

"Flee!" a crow called. "Flee now!"

"Flee. Flee. Flee," the chorus continued. Then the words became whispers, as the cloud of black dispersed.

For Meven, there was only the cold and the pain, and the blessed visage of the old priest.

Bishop DeNogaret knelt at Meven's side and helped him to sit. His thin fingers danced over Meven's arms and legs, and his eyes narrowed as he took in all the wounds.

"Will I die?" Meven managed.

The Bishop shook his head. "No, no. No broken arms or legs. So many cuts, though. Blood all over. And your ribs, I fear you've broken a few. And your nose, broken too."

Meven struggled to reach a hand up to his face, his arms aching like they were on fire. He brushed his nose and cringed at the new pain. His fingers tentatively touched his ear, and he discovered the bird that bit him tore off his lobe.

"The guards are coming, Meven. We'll get you to your chamber."

"Gerald . . ."

"He's dead, Meven. The birds killed him, like they nearly killed you."

Meven craned his neck, seeing the broken brown-black bird. "Odd-looking bird," he managed. "Not a crow or a blackbird."

"It's a cowbird, Meven. Not from around here."

"Where?"

Bishop DeNogaret rose and stepped back as the guards approached. Four of them gently hefted Meven.

"Where is the cowbird from?"

Bishop DeNogaret ground his foot against the bird, making sure it was dead. "From the Old Forest in Nasim-Guri," he said, as he escorted the guards back to the palace. "Cowbirds are unique to that part of the world."

"Birds attacked me and Kalantha, the wedding party."

"Yes, yes. But that was two years ago. This attack . . ."

"We were going to Nasim-Guri," Meven said. "Two years ago."

The Bishop made a tsk-tsking sound. "Don't talk, King Meven. Save your strength."

Meven ignored him. "My cousin was going to marry the princess of Nasim-Guri. But the birds attacked us."

"Yes, yes, Meven. You need to rest."

"They killed Prince Edan and all of his attendants. Almost killed Kal and me." He paused as they passed by Gerald's body. "And now they killed Gerald. He was my favorite attendant, Bishop DeNogaret. He was a friend."

"I will preside at his funeral, Meven. We'll bury him on the palace grounds if you wish."

"They killed Gerald and Edan, all those people, the birds."

"Rest, Meven."

"Bishop DeNogaret?"

"Yes, Meven?"

"We're not safe because of those birds."

"I'll protect you, Meven. I promise I won't let . . ."

"You can't protect me from them. There's only one way I'll ever be safe."

"Rest, Meven."

"The birds come from Nasim-Guri. So I want to go to war against Nasim-Guri. I'll take the fight to them."

"But I thought you didn't want a war. I thought . . ."

"I've changed my mind, Bishop DeNogaret. I want to start planning this war right now."

The Bishop patted Meven's arm and guided the guards through the doorway into the palace.

"In the morning, King Meven. We'll start planning the war in the morning. Tonight, you need to rest."

19 · Lives in Shadows

> I find evil interesting. I do not like it, but it is, nevertheless, interesting. Evil is unfathomable, and it challenges the good people of Paard-Peran. Too, it presents obstacles for we Finest. Without evil, guiding the chosen among the Fallen Favorites would be too easy a task.
>
> ~Able Ironhooves, mentor to Steadfast

"And so you will have your war." Eyeswide was perched on the back of the chair that faced Bishop DeNogaret's desk.

The Bishop was standing, leaning on his cane. With his free hand he brushed at the dirt he'd gotten on his robes when he knelt by Meven. He noticed a spot of blood and scowled. "Ruined, this new robe is. Though perhaps one of the cleaning women can do something with this. If not, I'll add it to her rags."

The owl closed his eyes and waited for the Bishop to finish his fussing. He heard the heavy chair pull out, and the Bishop ease into it, the wood creaking. There was the soft clink of the cane being propped up against the desk.

"Yes, I will have my war," Bishop DeNogaret said. He was leaning over his desk, his chin reflecting on its shiny surface. After a moment, he steepled his fingers. "A lovely war."

The owl opened his eyes. "But at too great a cost."

The Bishop raised an eyebrow. "Soldiers will die, yes. But the lives of simple men . . ."

"I meant at too great a cost to me."

The Bishop spread his hands on the desk and straightened so his face was level with the owl's. "What do you mean, old friend? You lost only one member of your flock tonight. That's insignificant."

Eyeswide made a hissing sound. "The cowbird you killed. I favored him, DeNogaret. He had great promise. Intelligent, loyal, he was a creature I intended to shape further. I had plans for him."

"One bird. Insignificant," the Bishop repeated. He held a finger to his lips and cocked his head, hearing footsteps in the hall beyond his study. He continued when the sounds were gone. "One death, Eyeswide. The King lost someone, too. His attendant, Gerald. Meven fancied that man."

"You wanted the attendant dead. You said he was gaining influence with your hollow King."

"Yes, Gerald had to die."

"My cowbird presented no threat."

"The bird's death accomplished what we needed. It helped foment this war. That bird nudged Meven in the right direction."

The owl ruffled his feathers, the motion making him look much thicker. "Wouldn't it all have been easier, *old friend,* if you had simply exerted your control over Meven? Worked your *own* mind magic?"

The Bishop shook his head. "You well know that the longer someone is under your control, the more control you demand, the less useful they become. Their mind slips away. And I can't afford to have a drooling idiot on the throne. Like you, Eyeswide, I live in the shadows."

"Until your plans are fully realized."

"Yes, until that time. And so I must be careful with how I manipulate the King."

"I suppose," the owl returned. His eyes were unblinking. "And he owes you his life now . . . or at least so he believes."

The Bishop nodded. "And he believes his enemy is in Nasim-Guri."

"So he will war against the people there. What you wanted all along. But even though he goes along now, that doesn't assure you that he'll agree with fighting Uland next, then perhaps Vered. You might not have the control over him you need."

The Bishop laughed, the sound grating and condescending. "Neither do your ways of control guarantee things, *old friend*. Your Vision Pond, dominating your flock. No guarantee at all. Besides, I don't need that kind of control over Meven. I don't need to control his actions. I just need to control his choices."

"Choices?"

"If I can control the choices, I can control the outcome."

"I handpicked that cowbird," the owl said softly.

"No significant loss, I say again," the Bishop's voice had an edge to it now. "Not in my scheme of things." He rose and padded to the window and opened it wide, seemingly oblivious to the cold air that rushed in and set the curtains to dancing. "And don't you have a task to tend to, *old friend*? Kalantha Montoll."

"I will find the child, DeNogaret. And I will slay her for you." He pushed off the back of the chair and flew through the window, angling over the bloody patch of ground where the King's attendant had lain. "Slay her like you did the cowbird."

The owl's eyes were keen, and he spotted the crushed bird against a small patch of snow.

20 · The Famed Vershan Library

One of the men I shepherded in my early days on Paard-Peran was an "author," or so he called himself. He penned stories of people he met, elaborating quite considerably. I could have written better~had I fingers and thumbs. More of what he wrote was fiction than fact, though he touted it (and believed it to be) the latter. Nevertheless, I enjoyed reading over his shoulder. Would that he knew I could read . . . well, I'm certain that would have been his best tale.

~Hefty Thunderrun, Finest shepherd to Orlan Graman the Fourth

The library at the High Keep Temple in Galmier would have fit into one corner of this place—and until now Kalantha had considered the High Keep library terribly impressive.

When Ergoth escorted her here for the first time a little more than three months ago now, she practically collapsed in surprise. She hadn't imagined that so many books existed in the entire world. And though she had been coming here at least once a day since then, she was still in awe of it.

The ceiling was domed, its lower edges rising twenty feet above the floor, and the center reaching up twice as high. It had painted white-robed priests reading books, writing books, and dyeing and embossing leather covers decorating its surface. In pastels, all around the men, animals cavorted, minstrels sang, and warriors in armor fought—it was as if the tales from the books were coming to life. Several massive iron chandeliers hung from the ceiling, and these were embellished with thick, spiraled candles of multicolored wax.

The floor was equally ornamental. Made of dyed tile chips, it showed white-robed acolytes and priests praying, and in the background were horses racing, three-masted ships sailing, children playing with cats and rabbits, and women picking flowers and washing clothes. Each day Kalantha found something she hadn't noticed before in the tiles.

And last week she decided to be bothered by the images of the women.

She realized none of them were on the ceiling, and none were illustrated doing anything important. Priests, acolytes, and visitors to the library walked over the tile women every day. But not Kalantha—she was careful to pick her path so that she never stepped on a woman or a child.

Despite this, Kalantha loved this place. She was captivated by the books, and the silence, and by the musty wonderful smell hanging heavy in the air. The walls were lined with bookcases that reached up nearly twenty feet and had wheeled ladders attached to them so the books at the very top could be retrieved. Urns, clay gargoyles, and sculptures of wild animals were displayed on top of the shelves—and spiderwebs clung to them. There were also shelves cutting at sharp angles throughout the entire library, forming a maze she had yet to fully figure out—but that Ergoth assured her made sense by subject and author. Small tables were scattered amid the maze, and she was seated at one now, on a chair so high her feet couldn't touch the floor.

The book's leather binding felt smooth and good against her fingers, and she handled it reverently, like she handled everything here. It was a nature study of the north countries (all the books she'd perused the past few weeks were about animals).

This one focused on birds.

She was having trouble reading several of the passages. It was not because of the words, though some were quite long and she had to decipher their meaning from the words around them, but because the thought of birds made her relive the attack on the wedding party, where everyone died but her and Meven, relive a second attack in the Galmier Mountains, and a third on the palace grounds.

She knew she would never be able to chase those images out of her mind.

Was Meven all right? she wondered. Did he think of her?

Did he realize her birthday had been only days ago? That she was thirteen now?

And what was he doing . . . attending parties, certainly . . . meeting with important people, certainly . . . riding one of the prized noriker stallions, likely.

Thinking of her? Thinking of her *now?*

She shook her head, as if Meven were a cobweb she was trying to dislodge.

She returned her attention to the page.

She was reading about crows, and how some could be made to talk by slicing their tongues and reciting words and phrases until the birds repeated them. So far the book had made no mention of other dark birds talking. And these crows that had attacked her hadn't just *mimicked* speech, they were "talking."

She loosed a ribbon from her hair and carefully placed it in the book to mark her spot, then she returned it to the shelf, leaving it pulled out just a little so she would have an easier time of finding it tomorrow.

"Are you leaving?" The whisper came from around the corner.

"Reshara!" Kalantha spoke a little too loudly and instantly lowered her voice. "My eyes are sore from reading so much.

The letters are looking like fuzzy insects marching across the pages. I have to quit for the day." She poked her head around the corner and spotted her new friend.

Reshara was a few inches shorter than Kalantha, though at fifteen, she was two years older. Overly thin, she had a gaunt face, and her elbows looked unusually large because her skin seemed stretched too tight. When Kalantha met her a week ago, she thought the older girl ill. But now she knew that wasn't true. Reshara simply didn't eat much and rarely went outdoors, and she spent practically all her hours studying about history, religion, and the Vershan Order. And when she wasn't studying, she was usually praying.

"I was hoping to study with you." Reshara looked clearly disappointed.

Kalantha almost agreed to stay longer, but she hadn't seen Rue all day. "Tomorrow I'll study late with you."

"And maybe I can help you and Ergoth look for those bird books you've been talking about."

Kalantha smiled. "I've been finding lots and lots of bird books."

"Just not the right one," Reshara finished. She let out a paper-thin sigh and touched Kalantha's arm. "But I'll help. Together, we'll find just what you're looking for."

"Thanks."

Kalantha retraced her way through this section of the shelf-maze, and followed the hall that led from the library and to her small, sparse room. Her room was no different than those the acolytes lived in, as she'd been in Reshara's room and noted that. Most people here were treated all the same. And, like at the High Keep Temple, there were few frills. Simplicity made people look inward and to the gods, not to "things," she'd heard the priests say. She grabbed her wolfskin cloak, then after a few minutes ventured outside.

The Vershan Monastery was a castlelike structure. A low stone wall surrounded the place, which was built on a small hill.

Sentries were posted on crenellated towers so they could look down on the land and see any threats approaching. The walls were thick and the windows narrow everywhere. It was designed so arrows could be fired out far more easily than they could be fired in.

Ergoth said the priest-architects were a little concerned after the first two monasteries were destroyed, and they constructed this one with defense in mind.

"The archers can't do much if another earthquake happens," Kalantha had told him. "What good are the sentries then?"

Ergoth hadn't answered.

It was snowing this early evening, big fat flakes that drifted down and dared her to catch them. She tipped her face up and stuck out her tongue, and once again thought of Meven. They used to catch snow together when they were younger and played around the High Keep Temple.

The faint snow cover, coupled with a full moon, made the ground so bright she didn't need a lantern. Kalantha could smell the hay and the horses as she crunched toward the stables. She knew some of the acolytes found the odors strong, but she didn't mind them at all. She loved grooming and feeding the horses, and didn't object to cleaning out the stalls. It was what she did to "earn her keep." Everyone who lived at the monastery—from the chief prelates to elderly priests to the acolytes, even to visitors researching in the library—"earned their keep" by cooking, cleaning, and in general keeping the monastery shining.

Kalantha wasn't the only one who worked at the stables. The priests employed a handful of young men from the surrounding villages to take care of the horses and other livestock.

One young man in particular had caught her attention, and she often looked for him before she started her chores.

She loved working in the stables, and she was here every night and many afternoons. It gave her an excuse to talk to Rue. The Finest was kept toward the back of the largest barn, where the smells were the strongest, but where it was also the warmest because the hay was piled in bales against the back wall and helped to keep out the wind.

"We'll go for a ride tomorrow, Rue," she told him. "Haven't been for a few days, I know, but I've been reading so much in the library and meeting so many people. There's this girl, Reshara. She's only two years older than me and she's an acolyte already. Smart! She can read, though I don't think quite so well as I can. It always takes her so long to finish a single page. I don't say anything to her, though. I don't want to hurt her feelings. She tries so hard. She likes horses, I think. At least she says she knows how to ride. But I don't think she likes to be *in* the stables. She works in the kitchen to pay her way."

Kalantha brushed the Finest's mane. "I'm sorry we haven't been out for a few days. I've found quite a few books about birds, and I have to read them all. And Ergoth promised to help me all day tomorrow. Reshara's going to help, too."

She brushed his front legs now. "I'm . . . comfortable here, Rue. I miss Morgan and High Keep. And I miss Meven. But the priests and acolytes are very nice to me, and one of the older prelates thinks I should . . . hmmmm, how did he put it . . . 'pursue a religious life.' He says I'm too smart not to 'do something' with myself. I don't know, Rue. Maybe I'm suited to it. I like to read, and I suppose I don't mind praying, though the priests pray far too often here. They thank the gods every day for everything. You'd think the gods would get tired of all the thank-yous. But being an acolyte would be better than sewing all day, I think. I don't have a lot of choices, you know."

She brushed his back legs, too, thinking the activity good for her after sitting so long in the library. "Maybe I should be an acolyte. Maybe the prelate is right. It's what Bishop DeNogaret and Meven wanted me to do. Maybe they're all right and I shouldn't fight the notion. Besides, Reshara likes it. Maybe I should have paid attention to Meven and the Bishop."

Tell me about Reshara, Gallant-Stallion prodded. He was pleased she had a friend.

"She's from Po-San in Durosinni. That's a long way from here. At least I think it is. I never paid attention to maps before. She's fifteen, and her parents sent her here and said she had to study hard. They're farmers, her folks, and not doing too well because their crops failed last spring and the spring before. Said they wanted her to have a better life than them. Reshara told me she hadn't wanted to be an acolyte. She liked the farm. But now she says it's okay. She's been here two years, Rue. But I only met her two weeks ago. This is a big place. Maybe I should think about it."

Think about what, Kalantha? About staying here?

She brushed at his legs now, then his sides. "Do you like it here, Rue?"

Yes, Kalantha. This place is warm, and you seem happy here.

"But are you happy?"

Was he? Gallant-Stallion hadn't given that any thought. He didn't mind this place. It was indeed warm, compared to being outside, and he always had plenty to eat and drink. The company of the dozen horses kept here was . . . acceptable. However, he had to admit he was achingly tired of hearing Boots complain. It was cold or too warm, windy or too still. The dozen other horses stabled here were tired of it too, and often they were nickering at Boots to be quiet. Between Boots grumbling constantly and all the horses telling her to stop it, the stables were never peaceful. And he couldn't keep an eye on Kalantha from here. That bothered him, though not as much as when they were separated in villages or at the palace. He thought well of Ergoth, and of the other priests he'd noticed working in the stables.

He knew his charge was safe here.

What does it matter if I am happy? Gallant-Stallion posed instead.

She shrugged and scratched at a spot between his eyes. "You're my friend, Rue, and I want you to be happy."

I am treated very well here, Kalantha. And I have your company every day. What more could I want? Other than to know how you are important to Galmier and what I can do to help, he thought.

That answer seemed to mollify her. "So let's not wait until tomorrow for that ride." She led him from the stables, and climbed up on his back.

Moments later the Finest was galloping across the snowy pasture. It was fenced, and the horses were let out into it each day, but it wasn't large enough for a good run. Gallant-Stallion took the fence in an easy leap and sped into the Gray Woods. The course was familiar, and their favorite, though they'd never taken it at night.

When they headed back to the stables, they saw a magical sight: a doe and two fawns standing like statues against a cone-shaped balsam fir. Gallant-Stallion slowed to a trot so he wouldn't spook them and so he could take in the sweet aroma of the tree.

Gentle evening to you, mother, the Finest said.

And to you, the doe replied. *Good foraging.*

Kalantha couldn't tell the two were talking, but she stared at the fawns and wished Reshara could see them.

I live in the stables near the big building, Gallant-Stallion told her. *I've no need to forage. Men feed me.*

Her eyes looked sad. *I am sorry for you then. I live where I want.*

Gentle evening, he repeated, as he slowly trotted by.

The stables came into view moments later, and Kalantha led Gallant-Stallion back to his stall.

"Maybe I will stay here," she said, still thinking about a religious life. "But I have to find out about the birds first. I never told you, Rue, but one of those astrologers by that starry lake told me I was in danger. Somehow she knew I had . . . royal blood, she called it. Said you and I should leave this place, go south and buy our way on a ship, go to a small island. Maybe I should have told you before now. I've got too much to think about, Rue. Stay here? Go to an island? I don't know what to do. I suppose I'll have to choose soon, huh?"

She was quick to tidy up all the stalls, then she hurried out the door, closing it firmly behind her.

Good she shut it. Girl left the door open too far before, Boots complained. *It was cold while you were gone, big horse. Wind came in and bothered me. Cold. Cold. Rude of her and you to leave the door open. Rude to let a bird in. Birds do not care where they poop. In the oats, maybe. On me, maybe. Rude. Cold.*

Gallant-Stallion looked around the stable, his eyes searching into the dark corners and finally resting on a sparrow nested on a high bale of hay. He let out a sigh of relief and thrust Boots's frettings to the back of his mind.

Sparrows were of no concern.

Kalantha would be busy tomorrow in the library and likely

would not come to visit him until the evening again. He decided to visit the Finest Court for a few hours. Though he had nothing of interest to report, he knew it was past time to tell the court . . . something. He intended to tell them that his charge was happy, maturing perhaps because of her surroundings, and that he still didn't know why she mattered so much to Paard-Peran. Too, he wanted to describe the beautiful Lake of Stars. He appeared to fade from his stall, though a ghostlike image remained for a moment.

Had Gallant-Stallion stayed a little longer, he would have heard Boots complain to his fading ghost-image that the bird was a mean, black crow, not the little sparrow that was still at the back of the stable and for the most part beneath her notice.

This larger bird had not remained long; perhaps he was fearful that someone might come along and shut the door and lock him in. But while the crow was here he at first talked in the tongue of a man. Then he talked to Boots and the horses in their own language, asking about Kalantha and the punch.

Boots explained that she was more than happy to tell the crow every detail she could remember. It was nice to have a creature want to listen to her, one that did not tell her to be quiet all the time.

The bird promised he would come back with more friends, Boots finished, not knowing that Gallant-Stallion could not hear her. *Hope that is soon. I would like to talk to the big crow longer.*

21 · Warring Factions

The common folk of Paard-Peran seek to look up to great men, not knowing the truly great men toil tirelessly in the fields all around them. They should not be looking up, they should be looking eye to eye. The common folk seek to honor great kings. But too often they find~too late~that kings are not great. The common folk should be honoring their brethren instead.

~*The Old Mare, from the chronicles of her first visit*

The great owl was perched on the back of the chair, staring across the desk at Bishop DeNogaret. The owl trembled slightly, as the priest had been harshly berating him and making veiled references to the cowbird's fate.

"You anger me, Eyeswide. So very, very much."

The owl dipped his head. "I am sorry, Bishop. I mean only to please you."

"Would that your intentions matched your accomplishments."

"I came here with news, Bishop."

Bishop DeNogaret steepled his fingers and scowled at the surface of desk, seeing his reflection mirrored back perfectly. Looking at himself eased his ire somewhat . . . but not enough.

"News that you haven't killed Kalantha Montoll. That's the news you bring. News of your failure."

"The girl with the green eyes," the owl said. "Sister to the King."

The Bishop waggled his fingers, a signal he often used to dismiss the owl. But Eyeswide stayed, though he trembled more noticeably.

"One of my flock found her only two days past, Bishop."

The Bishop finally brightened, and he raised his gaze to meet the owl's. "But she is not yet dead, is she? You come to tell me of your failure . . . again . . . to kill one small girl."

The owl gave out a low *whoooot*, then shifted his weight from one talon to another, a human gesture he'd picked up from watching men. "Bishop DeNogaret, she spends most of her time in a place I cannot look into, a holy place that . . ."

"Your Vision Pond cannot spy inside." The Bishop made a huffing sound. "A temple, a monastery, the home of a priest. Something blessed and reeking of goodness." He smiled. "A priest who worships Peran-Morab and her ilk."

"Likely, Bishop. But my flock flies over the Gray Woods, and my trusted crows watch for her on the horse. They will bring me more information soon, and then when I see her again, I can strike."

Bishop DeNogaret drummed his fingers on his desk. "Well, at least that is . . . something. Better than your last report, Eyeswide."

The owl puffed out his chest a little and finally stopped trembling. "So I have not displeased you today, Bishop?"

"Not today, old friend." In a dozen steps he was at the window, tipping his face up to catch the warm rays of the early summer sun. "Return when you have even better news."

The owl pushed off from the chair back and vaulted out the window, the breeze from his wings fluttering the Bishop's robes.

Bishop DeNogaret watched the owl until it became a speck in the night sky. Then he closed the shutters and grinned widely. He had a small map of Paard-Peran hanging on the only piece of wall that was not taken up by a bookcase. It was not near the size of the one in Meven's war room, but it was just as detailed.

"I will have all of you," he told the map, stabbing a finger at the island continent. He was eye-level to Galmier. "In the shadows of the throne, I will have Galmier and Nasim-Guri, Uland and then Vered. All of it." He traced the borders of Galmier, then let his finger slide down to the Old Forest. "With the help of my feathery friends, I will have more power than any one man has ever had. With the blessings of Abandon and Iniquis."

He rocked his head back and breathed deep, finding a trace of the owl scent and the Old Forest in the room, holding the air in his lungs and then breathing again until his chest felt like it would burst. He released the breath slowly and returned his gaze to the map.

"And when my enemies have made attempts on the 'King,' I'll ferret them out and slay them. And when no one else who is alive threatens me, I'll . . . remove . . . dear Meven. I will have the power and the crown then. Of course, he will have ceded the power to the Temple first . . . in the event of his death. Meven is a wise enough King to do such. Perhaps I shall have him tend to that paperwork this day."

He returned to his desk, still grinning wildly, and he stared at his reflection.

NINÉON COMMANDED ONE HUNDRED ON WING, ALL OF THEM flying over the Gray Woods. She saw the trees differently now than in the before time, when all she did was hunt from their branches. Now she saw even hair-thin branches and noticed the curl of each oak leaf below her. Everything was so vivid and intense, and at times she had to force away the details lest she become so absorbed she couldn't concentrate on her mission. She could not afford to be overwhelmed just by looking at the landscape now. She had more important things to do.

The scents were more intense, too, especially wafting up from the firs. She missed that about the Gray Woods, particularly the balsams. The Old Woods didn't have as many pines, and everything there smelled fusty and decaying.

Her flock of one hundred were mostly crows, but there were also blackbirds and grackles, the latter of which she found annoying because of their chattering. She elected to leave the bats behind, not caring for their smell and not liking the look of some of their beady eyes (besides, it was early evening, and the bats preferred to go out when it was thoroughly dark; good of her not to have dallied so they could have joined her).

The flock arced down just inside the forest, following a merchant trail, then dividing. Ninéon and her half flew east, away from the Old Forest, and she directed the rest to the west. They would meet up when the last bit of twilight disappeared.

"Ninéon, there. There! There!" a grackle shouted.

She clacked her beak and looked behind her to scold the bird for being so noisy.

"There! There!" another grackle picked up the call.

"Men," a crow announced in a softer voice.

Ninéon saw them when the grackles increased the tempo of their annoying chorus. She swiftly silenced the birds with a steely glare.

"Another patrol to make a report about to Eyeswide," the lead crow said. "Eyeswide will be glad for news."

To report to Bishop DeNogaret, not Eyeswide, Ninéon thought. "Yes," she said. "One more patrol to report. Eyeswide will be pleased with our news."

"Too bad it is not a large patrol. I see only a few men. Summer, they should be walking in greater numbers. Too hot for them," the lead crow speculated.

"Yes, a small patrol." An idea blossomed. "And soon to be a dead one. The men of Nasim-Guri are enemies to . . . Eyeswide," Ninéon said. "We shall slay these . . . for Eyeswide."

"But I thought we only observed," the lead crow said.

"When the force is too large for us to handle," Ninéon corrected. Her heart pounded in her chest. She was anticipating the slaughter.

"Do we leave one alive? Like before?" This came from a young crow.

"You refer to my pet, Herbert the woodsman," Ninéon said as she dived toward the patrol.

"Yes, Herbert the woodsman," the crow answered.

Ninéon considered the notion for a moment. The more influence she exerted on Herbert, the more simple he became. "No," she said after a moment. "Herbert is not used up yet."

22 · Fade to Fall

Most Fallen Favorites have the attention span of a crack of lightning. For that brief instant they are utterly transfixed by something. Then their minds wander, the lightning forgotten. Fortunately, all of those I watched over had enough presence to concentrate throughout the storm.

~*Dappled Lockwood, shepherd to Doleful Smith of Uland*

The stablehand was raking scattered hay, but because he was paying more attention to Kalantha than to the work, he was merely moving the hay around.

"You take good care of that horse, Kal."

"Rue takes very good care of me, Dree." Kalantha was giving Gallant-Stallion fresh water and oats.

The young man likes you, Gallant-Stallion said.

"Maybe," Kalantha whispered. "Or maybe he just wants some company."

Then he wants company every time you come to visit.

She smiled and brushed his mane and tail.

"I'll be back tomorrow, Rue." Then she skipped to the front of the stable.

Dree leaned on the end of the rake. "Beautiful day, Kal. It's like this autumn is holding on to summer weather with both hands."

"Poetic, Dree."

"Surprised you're not taking that big horse for a ride, this weather being so nice."

She edged past him and went out the door, moving slow and waiting for him to follow.

"I have a lot to do today, Dree. I'm going to work in the garden this afternoon, and . . ."

"Why?"

She cocked her head and studied him.

Dree was a year older and a few inches taller. He had broad shoulders that strained the seams of his tunic, his arms thick with muscles from lifting things in the stable. His trousers were loose, held around his waist with a braided cord that looked like it came from a curtain. His hair was the color of wheat and hung to his shoulders. It was always clean, but always straggly, and as long as she'd known him, eight months now, she'd never seen him comb or trim it.

"Why what?"

"Why work in the garden when you don't have to?"

She laughed. "I love the garden, Dree. And I don't at all mind the work." Then she frowned, instantly thinking of her old friend Morgan from the High Keep Temple. He was the gardener there, and he taught her about all manner of plants, and about life. Suddenly she missed him terribly.

"What's wrong?" Dree propped the rake against the stable and ran his fingers through his hair. He put on a concerned look, but Kalantha wasn't sure if it was genuine. "Did I say something?"

"Nothing you said. I was just thinking about someone." She thrust her hands in her pockets and glanced back through the stable door. Rue was in the back, and she couldn't see him through the shadows. "Someone from a long while ago."

It was his turn to laugh. "You're thirteen, Kal. Nothing's 'a long while ago' for someone so young."

"And you're not so much older. How long have you been here, Dree? A year, you said. Right?"

"Year and a half. About that. I like it enough here to stay. For some time more, anyway."

"And before that? Where were you?"

"Worked odd jobs in a village to the south. Woodstone. I think I might've mentioned that to you before. Yeah, I think we talked about it once."

"For a year, right? Woodstone?"

A nod.

"And before that?"

"Alsdon, Guilford, Witdell Harbor. A couple of farms in between them. A fishing boat for a few months. And before that I lived with my uncle. I was a child then." He brushed his hair behind his ears. "But that was a long while ago, Kal."

"So you have 'a long while,' too."

He leaned his head back and watched a hawk fly south.

"Guess we've got some things in common, Kal." The hawk out of sight, he returned his gaze to her. "No family. Not anymore, neither of us. Just this place. You've never asked me about where I was before this temple . . . until now. Why you curious all of a sudden?"

Kalantha peered over the fence at the temple. "It's a good place, Dree. Don't you think?"

She didn't see him shrug. "Yeah. Sure. It's a good place. The work isn't too hard. A place to sleep, plenty of food. A warm place. Clothes, though they never fit just right. A coin every once in a while. Good enough. So why you want to know what I think about Vershan? You usually just want to talk about books and horses."

She waited, knowing he'd say something else if she didn't leave.

"This place is better then Guilford, for certain. And better than Witdell. Didn't have a bed, there, in either place." He paused: "And the people here are nice enough."

She thought he might say, "And you're nice enough, too." But he didn't.

"The people here are very nice," she said after a few moments. "And I like the gardeners." A pause: "More, I guess, I like the garden. We're going to thin out the Marybells and the Dusty Millers and pull out the marigolds that've died. There aren't any roses here. I miss the rose bushes of . . ."

"Of what? Where?" He stepped near her and nudged her shoulder with his finger. "Where did you come from, Kal? Huh? You started the questions."

Again she peered into the shadows of the stable, wondering if Rue could hear their conversation. For some reason, she didn't want the punch to catch her in a lie. "Dree, the last place I stayed was a little village at the edge of the Lake of Stars. I don't remember the name of it. And before that . . . Stilton." There, that wasn't a lie. It just wasn't the complete truth.

"And they had roses there?"

She slipped through the rails of the fence. "I have to help them thin the flowers, Dree. And we're going to take some into the greenhouse so they'll be ready for the spring. I'll see you later."

LATER WAS AT SUNSET, AFTER KALANTHA HAD FINISHED DINner and helped scrub the tables. She went to visit Gallant-Stallion. Dree was sitting on a fence post, eating raspberries from a wooden cup and watching her approach.

"You're missing the evening prayer session, Kal."

She stopped in front of him and brushed the hair out of her eyes. Her face was rosy from being out in the sun so many hours.

"I went this morning. And there were prayers at dinner. I usually don't go to the evening prayer session."

"All that praying, you'd think . . ."

"I *am* thinking," she cut him off. "I'm thinking about staying here. For good. In fact, I am going to stay. I'm going to be an acolyte." She was surprised she said it out loud, as she'd only been mulling it over for the past several months.

"Good for you, Kal. Vershan's a good enough place," Dree said. "And I'll stay, too, as long as it's good. As long as folks're good to me."

"So why aren't you in the temple, Dree? I've never seen you in the temple praying, or in the library studying. The library is amazing. It would take a dozen lifetimes to read everything in there. There are so many books, and they add more every month. I'll never find the book about birds that I've been looking for. Can you even read? Why aren't you an acolyte? You could be a priest! That would be more than good enough, I should think."

He gave an exaggerated shrug of his shoulders and stuffed his mouth with raspberries. Some of the juice ran over his bottom lip, and he wiped it off with his sleeve. After he finished eating, he shrugged again. "So much goes on in that head of yours, Kal. So much thinking for someone's who's only thirteen." He set the bowl on the railing and slipped off the post. "I'm not going to be a student here, if that's what you're getting at. I'm never going to be a priest, not even an acolyte. Don't call me lazy. I see that look on your face."

She thoughtfully chewed on her lower lip.

"I'm not lazy, Kal."

"Far from it," she said. "No one works so hard in the stable and fields as you. But don't you want something more?"

"Why?"

She opened her mouth to say something, but stopped herself. Why indeed?

"I'm content with what I do. Happy. Why change things when things are going good? Besides, studying . . . now *that* would be hard work."

GALLANT-STALLION WAS LISTENING TO THEM, FINDING HIM-self neither pleased nor displeased with Kalantha's decision to stay. He did feel a little relieved that she'd made a choice. Young people were so often torn between all the things they wanted to do. Making a decision was a good thing.

It will not be so bad, he said to Boots, *staying here. You have not been complaining, lately.*

The food is good and sweet, Boots replied. *And I am not rained on.*

It really is not a bad life, Gallant-Stallion continued. *Kalantha comes to visit at least once a day. Maybe this pastoral existence will be all right. Safe. Plenty to eat, and a roof over our heads. I am taken care of, even while I try to take care of her.*

The food is good and sweet, Boots repeated. *I am happy here.*

I will be happy, too, Gallant-Stallion returned.

"Rue!" Kal hurried into the stable and rubbed the blaze between his eyes. "At dinner tonight, when I was talking to Ergoth and his brother, I made a decision. I'm going to be an acolyte. I'm going to stay here."

She reached for the brush and started working on his mane. "I wonder what my brother and Bishop DeNogaret would think? Funny, isn't it? I ended up choosing the life they tried to choose for me?"

23 · Swordplay

A blade sings when it cuts through the air. It is a sharp, yet breathy sound that is pleasing until one considers what the song is about.

~Roan Wanderer, shepherd to the warrior prince Doyle Neben

The snow drifted down lazily from a morning sky as dull gray as the doves that gathered beneath the overhangs on the west palace wall. It wasn't so cold this early winter morning as it had been on the few previous ones, and for that Meven was grateful. He hadn't complained on this or the previous mornings, as all of this had been his idea—standing out on the snow-covered palace grounds, practicing while most of the townsfolk were just stirring from the beds and unlikely to catch sight of him. He'd been at this, on and off, for a few weeks. The men had been at it for a few months, all part of the army he'd been amassing since the assassin-birds tried to carry him away.

Meven didn't want his subjects to see him. He feared he looked gawky and awkward, and was not as proficient as the others on the field. However, once his skills were better, he'd make sure the people of Nadir saw him.

And even if some of the townsfolk happened by the road

that came around this side of the palace, he suspected they wouldn't recognize him. He was dressed the same as everyone else, and his helmet, though open, effectively concealed him.

Meven was dressed in a chain mail shirt, the links tight and all of it so heavy he felt as if a horse were sitting on his shoulders. He wore a blue tabard over this, the Bishop's colors. No, *his* colors now, he thought. All the soldiers wore the chain shirts, save the three commanders who wore something called lamellar, small plates that had been tied together with leather thongs, hanging to their knees but slitted up the sides so they could sit on horses.

Meven's soldiers mostly came from area lords, though some were the sons of Nadir merchants or townsfolk who came from money.

Soldiers were not poor men—in Meven's country or in the neighboring ones. It was the practice that they be able to buy their own mail, and have a sword, shield, bow, quiver and arrows. The commanders had the most money and had horses and better armor. They were usually older and more skilled, and Meven envied them of their ability to slash and parry with a variety of swords. Once in the King's employ, as all of these men on the grounds were, and many, many more stationed elsewhere, they were paid a monthly salary in coin and were given a place to stay in the royal barracks—unless they were patrolling the countryside. Though Meven suspected none of them were noble by birth, they were respected by both nobles and the common folk, and the most successful of them would be deeded land.

Meven knew there would be plenty of land to give them after Nasim-Guri fell. And if he decided to continue the war beyond that, land from Uland, and then Vered. The young King had no doubt his army would be victorious, as the soldiers had been training diligently, and more were being added to their ranks now each day.

When they weren't fighting, or rotating patrols, they were busy repairing and shining their armor and weapons, grooming themselves—the soldiers were fastidious and courteous, and were always bettering themselves by reading, writing poetry, or singing. They worked to stay above the general populace of Nadir, and Meven was proud of them for their efforts.

Some of the soldiers were a year or two younger than Meven (boys as young as ten were hand-picked by local lords to leave their families and train with the lord's fighting men).

Out of the corner of his eye, Meven watched one such boy now. He was a head shorter than Meven, but his shoulders were half again as broad, and his arms were thick. He darted in to his opponent's side and thwacked him with the flat of his blade. It clanged dully, and the opponent announced, "Point."

Meven copied the gesture with his paired opponent, a soldier twice his age, with a broad chest and short, bowed legs. But his opponent had been watching too, and he easily anticipated the move. He nimbly stepped aside and slapped Meven on the back with the flat of a short sword.

"Point," Meven conceded. The blow was pulled, but it hurt, and Meven grimaced and spun, dropping to a crouch and jabbing forward, touching the tip of his own sword to his opponent's stomach.

"Point!" the soldier said. "Well done, Sire."

Meven beamed and stood, and the soldier clapped a hand on his shoulder.

"Sire, you are doing much better today." His eyes sparkled with pride, as he'd been Meven's primary teacher. "You do me well, King Meven."

Meven was breathing quickly, the air coming in puffs away from his red face. "Then let's go at it again, Baylor. And this time do not go so easy on me."

The soldier grinned and nodded, spread his legs into a balanced fighting stance, and waited for Meven to come at him.

"HE DOES NOT INTEND TO GO TO WAR WITH THE SOLDIERS, Bishop. So why does he fight with them?" Ninéon watched the soldiers from the windowsill high in Bishop DeNogaret's study.

The Bishop stood behind the falcon, dressed this morning in a charcoal robe that was tied with a rich blue sash. The falcon relished the scent of the Bishop this morning, a mix of sandalwood soap and musk that was unfamiliar and therefore interesting.

Ninéon turned his head and looked up at the elderly priest. "Or does he intend to fight?"

The Bishop shook his head, his eyes on Meven now, able to pick him out of the dozens of men feinting and slashing and dodging and kicking up snow.

"No, he will not fight."

"Then why this? Why all of this work? Why sweat in the snow? Why risk injury for nothing?"

"Ninéon, Meven thinks it was his idea to learn swordplay."

"But it was yours."

A nod, eyes still on Meven. "He was bored, Ninéon, and I needed him focused on something. Besides, this is good for him. He'd not been active for some time, slouching in front of the fire, restless and doing little but reading and praying. He never cared for winter, save when he was playing with his sister. But this is giving him something to do."

"And it keeps him from getting underfoot."

"Perceptive, Ninéon."

"No doubt the soldiers benefit from his presence."

"Indeed you are very perceptive."

"Their morale higher because the King of Galmier is in their midst, an equal to them on the field, not better than them. They bruise him and best him. And they will fight much harder for him because of that. His presence inspires them, my friend, and it fosters their loyalty."

The Bishop finally dropped his gaze to Ninéon. "And what have you to report?"

The falcon gave a last look at the soldiers training, then flew to the chairback. She noticed the chair had either been repaired or replaced, as the marks from her and Eyeswide's claws were absent. She dug her talons in deep when she thought the Bishop wasn't looking.

"The patrols in Nasim-Guri are thin and spread out. It is a peaceful country, Bishop DeNogaret, with no thought that someone would make war against it. Apparently they have no clue you have assembled an army. However, they have scouts, and soon, I should think, they will notice the men moving south toward their border."

"How practiced are their patrols?"

The falcon ruffled her feathers. "The patrols are not trained soldiers like those who practice in your field. Some are skilled with swords. . . ."

"And you know of their skill because . . ." The Bishop turned away from the window and looked past Ninéon to the falconer standing in the middle of the room. The man had been serving as the falcon's escort to the palace.

Herbert was meticulous in his appearance, beard short and the gray hairs gone, obviously covered by some dye or coal dust. His hair was trimmed close to his face, which was still rugged-looking and lined like a walnut shell. He was wearing a woolen cloak and leather shirt and breeches, not the same deer-skin outfit as on the times before.

The Bishop considered asking the falcon how she managed to clothe her pet, but decided to press on the other matter. "How do you know only some of the men are trained?"

Ninéon stretched her neck and spread her tail feathers. "I have watched them, Bishop. My crows and I have seen the skirmishes they wage for practice and to ward off the cold. Some clearly are skilled. But most could very easily be defeated by King Meven."

The falcon was pleased that the explanation seemed to satisfy the Bishop. She had no intention of revealing that she'd been leading secret strikes against the smallest of patrols—to better the skills of her crows, *and because she liked to kill.* It was because of those strikes that the falcon knew some of the men were able fighters.

"Spread thin?" The Bishop was looking at Ninéon now.

The falcon made a bobbing motion with her head. "Sometimes I have trouble finding them. Not because they hide so well, but because there are so few of them. They walk the borders, mostly, and there is no rhythm to it that I could discern."

"And had there been a pattern, you would have noticed it."

"Of course."

"Perhaps the King of Nasim-Guri simply does not have as many soldiers."

"And neither does he send many of them out in the cold. Kind of him, wouldn't you agree? Good for us?"

The Bishop glided away from the window and sat at his desk opposite the falcon. He glanced briefly at his reflection in the desktop, and brushed a previously unnoticed crumb from his lower lip. Then he studied the falcon.

"The King of Nasim-Guri has half the number of men I do. His land's nobles—my sources tell me—have not ceded many to his army, as this is a time of peace. The King of Nasim-Guri has not been to war in his lifetime, and he is not expecting a war now."

He again looked at the falconer Herbert. The man had moved only a little since coming in with Ninéon on his arm, and that was just to shift the weight on his feet to be more comfortable. Herbert's eyes had looked clear when the Bishop saw him a few months past. This was the pair's thirteenth visit to this study, and each time Herbert looked increasingly tired. The skin was sagging beneath his eyes now, and those eyes were dull and filmy. A tiny spittle bubble rested at the corner of his mouth.

"My soldiers also are unaware they will strike at Nasim-Guri, as there's been no formal announcement," the Bishop said. "We've been letting most of them think we're doing this as a precaution, against Uland. Only the commanders, myself, and Meven are aware of what we truly plan."

"And Eyeswide."

"And you, Ninéon." He thrummed his fingertips on the very edge of the desk, careful not to smudge the polished surface. "Though I am confident that deep down the soldiers know a war is approaching. Else they would not be drilling so. I'll need to strike soon before the whispers of Uland and other speculations become too loud."

"Whispers you started."

The Bishop did not reply.

"So just when does this war against Nasim-Guri start, Bishop DeNogaret?"

In his mind the Bishop pictured the table-map in Meven's war room, with all the painted soldiers spread out throughout the marshy heart of Galmier.

"They are nearly in position now, most of them," the Bishop said finally. "I suspect you saw the troops when you flew here.

It is a game of strategy, Ninéon, moving playing pieces around on a big board. Except these pieces are alive, and the board is the cold, marshy heart of Galmier and the fertile forests of Nasim-Guri. It is a game I will win."

The falcon said nothing.

"The ones practicing on the palace grounds will leave tomorrow. And they will reinforce and replace the ones who fall at the border between our countries."

"The war starts then," Ninéon said. "Tomorrow."

The Bishop nodded. "Yes, the war starts tomorrow, on King Meven's sixteenth birthday. And Nasim-Guri should fall before spring's end."

He looked past Ninéon and up at the face of the falconer Herbert. The bubble of spittle had popped and a thin line of drool edged over the man's lower lip.

"SIRE, MUCH BETTER!"

Meven dropped to the ground and rolled, springing up a few feet from his soldier-instructor and crouching. His chest was heaving, as he'd been at this much longer today than the previous sessions. The burn he felt inside was a little uncomfortable, but also invigorating.

"Again!" Meven called. "Come at me again."

The soldier obliged, this time pulling no punches and striking for Meven's right side. Meven barely dodged the blow this time, and the sword caught at his tabard and ripped it. The material fluttered like a pennant and threatened to tangle his sword arm. Meven ripped the cloth free and in the same motion spun around behind his sparring partner, rushing at him from behind and thwacking him with the flat of the blade on his shoulder.

"Point!" the soldier conceded with surprise. Then he quickly retaliated and swung to face Meven, bringing his blade down quickly and smacking the King's thigh. The soldier's eyes narrowed, for fear he struck too hard, but Meven nodded and yelled, "Point," then started circling.

A ring of soldiers had formed around Meven and his partner, with half cheering on the soldier, and the other half the King.

"Give me your full measure," Meven told the soldier. "No reprisals, I swear."

The soldier hesitated a moment, then nodded and darted in, sweeping with the flat of his blade to his right, the metal singing in the winter wind. Both men were tiring, but Meven had youth on his side. He saw the move coming, as the soldier was slowing, and he pivoted out of the way.

Repeating a move the soldier had used on him a moment ago, Meven sprang forward and thumped the blade against his partner's thigh. Then he circled around and struck him on the back of the other leg. The soldiers who'd been championing the King cheered louder.

"Point and point," the soldier-instructor conceded. "Those were as good as death blows." His breathing was as ragged as Meven's now, and the air came from both of their mouths in uneven foggy puffs. "You grow stronger and faster every day, Sire."

Meven didn't answer, as he was putting all his efforts into staying one step ahead of the soldier.

"I'd welcome you into my unit," the soldier continued. "You're quick, Sire!"

"Aye!" hollered a commander who'd joined the audience. "I would take you to battle with me this day! You are good with a sword."

Meven allowed himself a wry smile. He knew the soldiers would be leaving tomorrow for Nasim-Guri. Part of him wished he could join them.

For the first time in some months he felt truly alive.

24 · Gods and Birds

I have shepherded priests on Paard-Peran~four of them, all men of different ages and of varying degrees of devoutness. I would like to meet the powers of this cherished world some day and see if the Fallen Favorites' images of them having two legs are true. Or if my perfect pictures of hooved divine beings is the closer match.

~Midnight Kabarden, veteran Finest

Kalantha was waiting outside the library when the morning caretaker came to open the door.

"Child, but you never stop reading!" he said as he gestured her inside. "Would all our acolytes devour books with as much enthusiasm as you hold in your young heart!"

Acolyte. Kalantha sort of enjoyed the sound of that. She was an acolyte now, having been welcomed into their ranks on the first day of winter. It had taken a few months of study to qualify, and there were "tests of faith" she had to pass. It was a good choice, she kept telling herself, even though a small part of her still thought about heading to a southern port and using the diamond the astrologer gave her to buy passage to an island filled with strangers.

She touched the stone hidden on the silvery chain beneath her tunic. She wore it every day, along with the knife Bartholomew had given her—not wanting to leave either gift alone in her room. She told herself it wasn't because she feared them being stolen, though that small part of her considered the possibility. A larger part believed she kept them close simply because they were gifts. However, she knew acolytes were not allowed to carry weapons, and she wondered what would happen if someone caught her with the knife. Would she be punished? Or would she be asked to leave? They preached peace and forgiveness here. Only the sentries who manned the towers were armed.

"What is it you're studying, Sister Kal?" the caretaker asked.

"Birds," she answered. "I still want to learn all about birds. It's been quite some weeks since I'd read about them. There were all those tests and such, you know."

He nodded and shuffled toward a counter laden with books he needed to reshelf. "I like birds," he said. "I think the common sparrow is my favorite."

"A sparrow?" Kalantha looked at him and scrunched her face. "But they are so plain . . . and they're everywhere, no matter the time of year. I think I like the summer hummingbirds the best. They're hard to find, and that makes them special."

The caretaker nodded. "I suppose. But I like the sparrow because it is so common and is 'everywhere, no matter the time of year.' You see, Sister Kal, whenever I want to watch a bird, I can always find a sparrow. The small creature obliges me."

The caretaker said something else, but Kalantha didn't hear him. She was scooting toward the eastern wall, where she'd left a book with her ribbon marking her place. It took her several minutes to find it, as she got herself turned around in the maze. Despite all the months she'd been here, she still hadn't figured out the pattern to this place.

She selected a chair at a small table and started reading. She wasn't reading every word now, as she realized she'd be an old woman by the time she managed to work her way through all these nature books. Neither did she have as much time as she used to for her search. As an acolyte, she had a daily work, prayer, and study routine. There wasn't much time for herself. But today, for a change, was all hers.

She was skimming the pages now, running her finger over the words and feeling the raised letters where the ink was thick in places. After an hour, she considered herself done with this one. She tied the ribbon in her hair, replaced the book, and looked to the next one.

"Good morning, Kal." It was Ergoth. Despite dragging his left leg, he'd moved up so silently he startled her. "Sorry. I try to be quiet in this place." He had a stack of books in his arms, and he put them on his side of the table.

"You're going to help me today? On your free day? Thanks." Kal tugged out a book titled *Birds of the Old Forest*. She doubted it would be of much use, as the birds she was interested in had been in Galmier, not Nasim-Guri. But she intended to give it a brisk skimming. She settled herself opposite him.

"Well, yes, I'm going to help you. But I have a little reading of my own, first."

She gave him a disappointed look.

"Won't take me long. I also promised to help my brother with a little research on our family."

"Why?"

"Well, as you know, many of my relatives are acolytes and priests. And we have a cousin joining the Order come the first of summer. My brother and I thought we'd put together a family tree of sorts for him, so he can see which ancestors were priests, too."

"Nice," she said. But her tone was terse. Kalantha considered her task far more important and thought about telling him so. Instead, she carefully opened her book and started skimming. This book smelled particularly fusty, and she noticed that along the bottom the pages were wavy, as if they'd been wet. A few flecks of what she suspected was mold were near the spine. "Ewww."

An hour later she was more than halfway through the book. She hadn't found anything particularly interesting in it and was about ready to give up and find another. She spotted Reshara shuffling down the aisle.

Reshara waved a greeting. "May I join you?" she whispered. Kalantha had to strain to hear her.

"Of course," Ergoth replied. He leaned over and pulled out a chair, grimacing when the legs made a screeching sound against the tile. "I was just about ready to take a break from my project and help Kal."

"That's why I'm here, too," Reshara said. "Kal, what would you have us research first? Kal . . ."

Kalantha wasn't looking at Reshara anymore. She was staring across the table to the book in front of Ergoth.

"Kal, what?" Reshara said. "What are you . . ."

Kalantha was up in an instant, sliding around the table and standing next to Ergoth, thrusting her finger at the sketch of a man that filled the right-hand page of his open book. The man was tall and thin, the illustration capturing a presence about him. His dark eyes stared out from the page.

"That's Bishop DeNogaret," she said. Not realizing she was being rude, Kalantha turned the book away from Ergoth so she could see it better. "Only the line underneath it says it's 'High Cleric Noggaret,' and it says he lived more than a hundred years ago. Can't be. It's Bishop DeNogaret. Sort of."

She continued to stare slack-jawed at the sketch.

Ergoth gently moved the book back squarely in front of him. He pointed to a section of text opposite the picture, careful not to touch the ink.

"Who's Bishop DeNogaret?" This came from Reshara, who looked concerned that Kalantha had become so agitated.

"He's a very important man," Ergoth whispered. "I've never met him, but I hope one day to attend a service of his. He's the advisor to the King of Galmier, and he presides over the temple in Nadir."

"Very important, then," Reshara hushed.

"That's him," Kalantha repeated. "That picture is of Bishop DeNogaret. Though he looks a little younger there. Has more hair. But those eyes. I know the eyes."

Ergoth shook his head. "Can't be, Kal. Noggaret, admittedly sounding similar, is a different family. And this man is not the kind and wise Bishop in Nadir. This man is said to have worked with the followers of Abandon and Iniquis to bring down a Vershan Temple dedicated to Peran-Morab, sister of the creator-god. That temple predates the monastery."

"The first monastery I came to? The one the earthquake took down?"

"By about seventy or so years, Kal. See, not the same man." He closed the book. "Noggaret was known for being greedy and warlike, and he was driven from the Vershan Order after he was linked to the destruction of the temple."

"That wouldn't be Bishop DeNogaret, then," she conceded. "He's a very good man . . . even if he does want me to be at Dea Fortress. He wouldn't hurt anyone, Ergoth. He's kind and wise, and he's taking good care of my brother. I'm sure of that."

"But maybe there is some family tie somewhere to Bishop DeNogaret, if you say they look the same. A distant relative." He put the book on the top of his stack. "So you've seen this Bishop DeNogaret in person?" Ergoth seemed impressed.

Kalantha nodded. "He raised me," she said after a few moments passed. She was an acolyte now, and it was probably time she told these priests who she was . . . at least she should tell Ergoth, she decided.

Ergoth's raised eyebrows begged her to continue.

"My name is Kalantha Montoll, not Kal Morgan. Meven, my brother, is the King of Galmier. Bishop DeNogaret raised both of us after our parents died."

Ergoth bolted up, so surprised he knocked his chair over. It clunked loudly against the tile floor, and he quickly righted it.

"You're of royal blood!" Still his voice was a whisper. He was a trusting soul, and it was clear he believed her.

She blushed, wondering if she should have kept it secret. "Yes, Ergoth, but . . ."

"Then why aren't you a princess or something?" Reshara's eyes were wide with wonder. "My goodness! Why aren't you at the palace wearing fancy clothes and . . ."

Kalantha dropped back into her chair, let out a great sigh, and told them of her life at the High Keep Temple, of the attacks of the assassin-birds—part of which she'd already told to Ergoth in Stilton—and about how the old King of Galmier died. She left out what she considered the tedious parts.

"So my brother went from being Prince of Galmier to King in a few weeks. And he and Bishop DeNogaret insisted I be sent to Dea Fortress."

Ergoth drew his lips tight and shook his head. "A strict Order, Dea is. More work than study, and I suspect you'd not like the place. So many rules and so much discipline. Very devout, the people there are. But they are little else."

"You've been there?" Kalantha had been curious about the place.

"Austere and cold, very traditional. I found it a place for great introspection, and I almost joined the Order, because at the time I needed direction. But I decided to follow my brother into the Vershan Monastery instead. There's much more freedom here. But if you are to be at Dea Fortress . . . why are you here?"

She explained about running away, narrowly making it from the palace grounds because of the birds. "I like it here," Kalantha admitted.

"And I'm glad you're staying," Reshara said. She stretched across the table, nearly upsetting Ergoth's stack of books, and she grabbed Kalantha's hands and gave them a squeeze. "I'm so happy for you . . . for us!"

Kalantha looked to Ergoth. He had an almost vacant look on his face, and his eyes were fixed on the shelf behind Kalantha, though he seemed to be looking at something far beyond this room.

"Ergoth . . . aren't you happy that we've royal blood in our Order?" Reshara was perplexed at his expression. "I think it's wonderful. Don't you think . . ."

"Elated," Ergoth said, still managing to hold his voice to a whisper. "Royal blood, Kalantha. I had no idea." He blinked and his face brightened, then he smiled warmly at Kal. "I'll go tell the chief prelate. He should know. You should have told him months ago."

He got up and hurried down the aisle before Kalantha could protest. "I—I—I guess I should have told everyone. I just didn't think it was necessary."

Reshara was grinning. "It'll be nice to have someone around related to a King. Why, maybe he'll come to visit."

"I don't want Meven here, Shar. I ran away!" Kalantha's voice rose a little and from somewhere a few aisles away came a harsh "Shhhhhh!"

Kalantha made a huffing sound.

"So what can I do to help with this project of yours?"

Kalantha reminded her about the assassin-birds, and Reshara saw the space on the shelf where Kalantha had removed a bird book. Reshara took the next one in line and started reading.

"So this is like a calling for you, Kal? Finding out about the birds?"

"It's something I have to do, Shar."

Kalantha watched her friend for a moment, then reached to the top of Ergoth's stack of books, taking the one he'd last looked at that had the illustration of Noggaret. It took her a few minutes to find the right page, then she backtracked a few pages to the beginning of the section and started reading. She hadn't quite gotten to the part about Noggaret when she swallowed hard.

"Meven needs to see this," she whispered.

"What did you say, Kal?" Reshara hadn't quite heard her.

"I'll be back in a little while," Kalantha lied. She tucked the book under her arm and threaded her way through the maze of shelves, getting turned around and lost once, but eventually finding her way toward the center and the way out. She waited around a corner until the caretaker took a stack of books and disappeared into the other side of the maze. Then she slipped out of the library and headed to her room.

She moved quickly, not wanting anyone to see her take a book from the library. Only the most senior priests and prelates could remove books, the Order was so protective of all its manuscripts. Kalantha could read all of it in the library without getting in trouble, but there were always people there, and she wanted to read this book alone. She felt bad about lying to Reshara about coming right back, but she suspected her friend wouldn't mind.

Kalantha shut the door behind her. There were no locks here, but everyone respected a closed door. She sat on her cot under a slit of a window and started reading from the beginning. From time to time she heard footsteps outside her room. None of them stopped, so they were probably acolytes going to and from their own rooms.

She didn't skim anything this time, wanting to catch each word. And by the time the sun went down and she had to light a lantern to continue, she'd only made it half of the way through. It contained a little information about Ergoth's family, and that family—and several others mentioned—had nothing to do with what Kalantha considered the heart of the text.

"If Meven were here, he'd understand all of this better," she said. "Always with his nose in a book, always reading or praying. He'd know better than I. He's smarter." She yawned, and her head bobbed. She was having trouble keeping her eyes open. She hadn't heard anyone passing by her door lately, meaning people were busy with chores or were praying. Most of them were probably going to bed, as everyone seemed to get up so early here.

Kalantha bit her lip hard, the pain keeping her awake. She turned the lantern wick higher and added more oil. Then she kept going. Her stomach rumbled; she'd been so engrossed in the book that she'd forgotten to go for dinner. Reshara and Ergoth might have missed her. But there were so many priests, acolytes, sentries and other workers here that they ate at different times. Likely no one noticed her absence.

"But they'll know I haven't helped clean the stables yet today. Dree will be asking about me." She let out a sigh that ruffled the curls that hung down her forehead. "Just a few more pages." Then she'd talk to Rue and go to the kitchen for some bread and cheese. There was always bread and cheese there, and sometimes slices of meat that were left over from dinner.

But a few more pages first. She chewed on her lip again, put the book on the cot, stood up and leaned over it. She knew she wouldn't fall asleep if she were standing.

"Five more pages," she decided, arbitrarily picking a number. But after the first five she read a second set of five, and a third. The sky was so dark now she knew it must be very late. She rubbed at her eyes and yawned again and again. "Five more."

And another five.

Her eyes grew wide.

Opposite the page she was reading was an illustration of a glass window. The panes formed the image of a bird with its wings outspread. On a small table beneath it was a statue of another dark bird. She kept reading, returning to look at the picture. "I have to show Meven and Bishop DeNogaret," she said.

She made sure the knife Bartholomew had given her was still in the sheath on her belt, touched the diamond beneath her tunic. Then she put on her wolfskin cloak, wrapped the book in a blanket and tucked it under one arm and grabbed up her bag of trinkets. Then she hurried from her room and to the stables.

"Rue . . . Rue!" The stables were dark, and she didn't want to light a lantern. "Rue."

The Finest left his stall and approached.

It is late, Kalantha. Why are you here so . . .

"We're leaving, Rue. Now. We've got to go to the High Keep Temple and find my friend Morgan. He'll get this book to Meven. I can't go back to the palace, Rue. The Bishop might see me, and I can't risk that. But Morgan can take the book to Meven."

Book?

"This book." She nodded to the blanketed bundle. "It talks about some bad people, Rue. They worship the dark gods, not the good ones. Oh, it talks about good priests who fought them. But it says the bad ones, a long time ago, trained birds. So I think someone very bad trained those birds to attack Meven and me, and made them kill Edan and the wedding party. I don't know why, yet. But Meven will figure it out. I've got to get this book to Morgan at High Keep Temple. He'll get it to Meven. He'll want to know that someone was behind those horrible birds. And he'll want to find out just who it is. My brother's the King of Galmier, a powerful man. He'll be able to stop whoever's behind those horrible, horrible birds. Then Meven and me will be safe."

She led him through the stable door, coming face to face with Dree.

"Kal! Where have you been. We've been looking for you!"

"We've?"

"Reshara and me. When you didn't come out here tonight, I worried that you might be sick. Been awfully cold, you know. So I found Reshara. Said you weren't at dinner, and she was going to your room, getting Ergoth and some of the other priests."

"No!" Kalantha paled. She couldn't afford to have the priests looking for her. She was an acolyte now, not just a visitor, and she was certain they'd pursue her, thinking something wrong and trying to help. "I can't have them look for me!"

She heard Boots making a snuffling sound, but was unaware the plow horse was complaining about the cold and about being woken up—and about being kept awake by Kal and the punch and Dree.

Then Kalantha was walking with Gallant-Stallion down a trail that led from the stables and to the winding road that would soon hook up to the merchants' trail. Dree followed her.

"Where are you going, Kal? You can't just leave Vershan in the middle of the night. Where are you going?" Then he touched her shoulder and pointed to the monastery. Candles and lamps were being lit, and the once-dark building was coming to life. "Everyone's going to be looking for you."

She sucked in her lower lip and defiantly shook her head. "I'll come back, Dree. After my brother reads this book." Everything looked black and white to Kalantha now—the snow bright white even this late because so many stars were out, the sky black as ink, the trees dark slashes. No other colors intruded on the path ahead. Despite the starkness, Kalantha thought it beautiful.

"I have to hurry. Good-bye, Dree."

"Kal, they'll stop you. You're one of them, now."

"I can't let them stop me."

"They'll know you've taken your big horse and . . ." He scratched at his head. "Maybe they won't. You hurry, Kal. To wherever it is you're going."

He turned away from her and rushed into the stables. Suddenly the horses were nickering and stomping, and he was leading some of them out, swatting them on the rumps and shooing them onto the grounds.

As she started down the path, she looked over her shoulder and saw him lead another few horses out, one of which he was quickly saddling. Then she concentrated on the way ahead. "Hurry, Rue. Dree's distracting the priests. They might not know for a while that you and me are gone."

Neither Kalantha nor Rue saw a dark shape against the roof of the stables. Black against black, it would have been difficult to spot even if they were looking directly at it.

When Kalantha and Rue were out of sight of the stable, the shape spread its wings and flew north. The crow was every bit as in a rush as Kalantha and the Finest.

25 · A Turn in the Weather

There is beauty in constant things, and in knowing you will always
have a cool and clean stream to drink from, a patch of long and sweet
grass to graze on, and a delightful and soothing breeze to ruffle your
mane. If the Fallen Favorites were more perfect, I think their land
would be too. They would never be too hot or too cold, they would
never want for food or drink, and they would not need clothes to keep
the play of the wind away from their skin.

~Dancing-In-The-Paddock, Finest pony,
on her reflections of Paard-Peran

The astrologer told me to go south, Rue—if I wanted to be
safe. She even gave me a diamond to pay for passage for us.
This diamond would buy us a lot more than passage. Clothes,
food, many, many, many nights in one of those warm inns with
soft beds and pillows. Pieces of cake for dessert." Kalantha
was leaning against Rue's neck, trusting him to find the way
north. "I'm going to have to pay her back someday. And I'm
going to have to find that street in Nadir where I . . . borrowed . . . some clothes. Pay that family back, too. And the
people in Stilton. They gave me more clothes, this wonderful
cloak. Fed me and were kind. I owe people, Rue. How am I going to pay them all back?"

"Pay who back?" Dree kneed the sides of the dappled gray
horse, catching up to Kal and the punch. "Lost track of you
sometime in the night. Found you by luck. Now . . . pay who
back? And what diamond? I thought I heard you mention a di-

amond. Who do you know who has a diamond? And why did you leave Vershan? I'm the one who usually does the leaving." Dree looked haggard from lack of sleep and worry. Still, he straightened his shoulders and put on a strong front.

"Why'd you come after me, Dree?"

"I don't know. I guess I figured you might need some help. All those priests and such were certainly trying to find you last night. And then there were all those loose horses to gather up. Reshara was terribly worried about you. Ergoth, too, it looked like. Pay who back?"

"People who've been kind to me." Kalantha stretched forward and patted the punch's neck. "I have to get a book to my brother, Dree, or rather, get it to my old friend Morgan, who will take it to him. Then after my brother reads it, he can figure out some things. Then I'll bring the book back to Vershan. It should stay in their library. It's theirs, after all. I'll come back to Vershan with the book. It's a nice, safe life I've chose for myself there."

"Be a lot easier just to have your brother come to the library, wouldn't it? Then you wouldn't have to make that ugly horse tromp through the snow, and you wouldn't have to risk frostbite."

She didn't answer, but she realized it indeed would have been easier, provided Meven would have left the palace and come south. And if he had, the Vershan priests wouldn't be worrying over her now. She pictured Reshara and Ergoth, her closest friends there, searching the grounds. She should have told them she was leaving and trusted that they wouldn't object.

It had started snowing, and that plus her being so tired was making it difficult for her to see. She huddled into her wolfskin cloak, the edges of it draping down to cover Gallant-Stallion's sides.

The Finest appreciated the warmth from the cloak and from Kalantha on his back.

Will we really be returning to the monastery, Kal?

She shrugged, the gesture lost on the Finest.

Kal?

"Of course I'll be going back to Vershan." She was talking to Rue, though she couched her words so they could have been meant for Dree. "It is safe there, and I like being safe. Once I thought I didn't want to be an acolyte . . . but I think that was because Bishop DeNogaret and my brother told me I had to be an acolyte. I don't like being told what I have to do. But I like that monastery. I like being safe." She glanced over her shoulder. There was no trace of the path that led to the monastery, the snow having blanketed everything. "I like the library, and my friends Reshara and Ergoth. I like you, Dree. So we'll go back." She leaned closer and spoke into the punch's ear. "But only if you like it there, too. Do you like it, Rue?"

Again, she'd asked the question. Gallant-Stallion didn't answer at first, as he did not want to influence her choice.

The Fallen Favorites had free will. They needed help sometimes, but Gallant-Stallion wasn't ready to nudge her one way or another. Not on this matter. The stable was pleasant enough. He was cared for while he looked after her. But it wasn't near the Sprawling River, which he cherished and thought of often. And he'd not encountered another Finest there. He truly missed his own kind.

You enjoy the monastery, Kal, and I enjoy your happiness. I believe when spring planting time comes, I will enjoy the monastery more. Boots likely will be returned to Stilton, as she should have been returned last spring, he thought.

"So we will go back together," she decided. "But first we've something terribly important to do. We have to get this book to my friend Morgan, the gardener at the High Keep Temple. It will be good to see him, Rue. I don't know if it's right, but I think I miss Morgan more than I miss my brother. A lot more.

Still, we'll have to be careful when we get there . . . just in case Bishop DeNogaret is at High Keep for a visit. I can't have him send me to Dea Fortress."

She straightened, then nudged his neck. "But maybe the Bishop and my brother would give their blessings to me studying at the Vershan Monastery. It's a religious life, just what they wanted for me."

After another few moments: "Decisions are so hard for me, Rue. I'm never sure anymore if I'm doing the right thing. Maybe we shouldn't be going to the High Keep Temple, Rue. Maybe we should go straight to the Bishop and Meven now with this book. To the capital—Nadir." The book was still wrapped in a blanket and held close to her chest with her left arm. The fingers of her right hand were holding Gallant-Stallion's mane. "It needs to get to them anyway, this special book. Meven and the Bishop will be able to figure out who taught those assassin-birds to attack us. They'll be happy I've brought them this book. So happy they'll give their blessings to my staying at the monastery!"

I thought you were afraid of confronting your brother and the Bishop directly.

Something about the plan didn't sit right with the Finest, but he couldn't figure out what bothered him about it. Though Kalantha was a child, and prone to change her mind, as children do, her plan had merits. King Meven might indeed be able to puzzle out who was behind the birds.

"I am afraid of my brother and the Bishop. Running away isn't always the answer, is it?" She was talking louder now, so caught up in her ruminations she'd momentarily forgotten about Dree.

He rode only a few feet behind her, listening intently.

"You don't run away from things, Rue."

No trace of the evil birds since we left the palace, Kalantha,

Gallant-Stallion offered. Their threat may have passed. *This trip could be for nothing. Birds might never trouble us again.*

"Maybe," she said. "But I want Meven and the Bishop to see this book. Now. I don't want to wait until the spring when the weather is more agreeable."

The Finest had learned that children were impetuous. They didn't want to wait for anything.

"I just hadn't counted on this bad weather," she continued. "This is the end of winter, Rue. But it's snowing harder than it has for weeks. It's getting so I can hardly see." She paused. "Maybe we should have waited until tomorrow or the next day."

It is not too late to turn back and go another day, Kal.

"No. The library caretaker might have noticed this book missing." She slumped to his neck again. "There are so very, very many books in that library he might not notice if a hundred are missing. But Ergoth was looking *at* this book. And now Ergoth might be looking *for* this book."

Gallant-Stallion could tell she was angry at herself for being so rash to jump at this notion.

"Oh, Rue, why don't I think things through sometimes? Why can't I be more like my brother, smart and . . . and . . . and. Oh, Rue." She didn't say anything else, though her mind was warring with words.

Dree's head was cast at a curious tilt. And when it appeared Kalantha was done talking, he spoke: "Are you talking to your horse? You are talking to your horse, aren't you. Just like he can understand you. Kal, you're touched."

Kalantha just urged the punch faster.

They stopped for a few minutes an hour later, and Dree slipped off the dappled horse. "Kal . . . I'm following you 'cause . . . well, I don't want you to be alone. And you can at least tell me what this is all about. I just left the best place I've ever lived to follow a girl who talks more to her horse than she does to me. And you say you're going back to the monastery. Eventually. But I don't think you will. I think you're like me. Moving all the time. But I don't talk to animals like they're people."

She jumped off the punch's back, landing in a small drift. She shook her cloak, knocking the snow from it. "I said I'm going back to Vershan. But there's this book." She reached up and took it from the punch's back, hunching over it as she unwrapped it, not wanting the snow to get on it and cause the ink to run. "Come look."

Dree feigned interest at first. "It's a book."

"You really can't read, can you?"

He shook his head. "But I don't need to. Reading never helped me plant a field or rake hay." Suddenly he brightened. "Kal, this is an old book, and look at the edges, all the way around."

"Gold," she said. "A lot of old books have pages brushed with gold."

"There's gold on the cover, too. This embossing. Kal, this book is worth a lot."

"All books are valuable, Dree."

"No, Kal, this book is worth coins. We should take it south and sell it, we could live well for a few years. Just on this one book. Think of it. Nice inns and warm meals. Not having to work for anyone. And just for one book. Maybe you should have taken more than one from that library."

She looked at the book closely now, at the fine leather binding and the gold leaf. The gold brushing was still thick and shiny on the pages.

"It is worth a lot," she admitted.

"I know places where we could sell it. And these horses. Buy passage on a ship and sail far away. Oh, Kal, what a life that would buy us for a while." He closed his eyes and a serene expression settled on his face. "C'mon, I know a city where there would be a few buyers for this."

"It would be nice," she whispered, "Having a good life for a while. Inns with soft, soft pillows. But I'd never sell Rue."

"Well, at least let's get rid of that book. Imagine the coins!" He made a move away from her, then stopped when he saw her grimace.

"That would be easy, Dree. Too easy. I can't do that. I can't even think about doing that. I've got to get this book to Meven. Then it has to come back to the monastery where it belongs."

He took a step toward her again, his hands reaching out as if to take the book.

"Don't," she warned.

He balled his fists and set them on his hips. "Don't give up an easy life, Kal. Don't you do it. I won't let you do it."

She wrapped the book and put it up on Gallant-Stallion's back.

"I helped you leave Vershan, Kal. I created a diversion. I let the horses out so the priests would have to deal with them. Bet it took them all night to figure out that your ugly horse was gone . . . and you with him. I helped you."

"So you think I owe you?"

He ground the ball of his foot into the snow. "Well, no. You didn't ask for my help. Nobody owes me anything. It's just that you can't let an easy life slip away from you."

She reached inside her tunic and brought out the diamond the astrologer had given her. Unhooking the clasp, she gave the necklace to Dree. "This'll buy you that easy life, Dree. Probably bring you more coins than the book would."

He stared at it, then at her. "Diamond. You have a diamond."

"Had."

"I can't, Kal. I . . ." For a moment it looked like he was going to give it back. But in the end he took it, putting it around his own neck and climbing onto the back of the dappled horse. Then without a word, he headed south.

Gallant-Stallion nuzzled her.

"I know," Kal answered. "He made his choice a long time ago. I've only recently made mine . . . wherever it leads me."

26 · The Harshest Winter

When I need to realize just how beautiful the lands of the Finest Court are, I visit Paard-Peran.

~Surefoot, Finest mountain pony

An hour later, Kalantha nudged Gallant-Stallion again. He'd slowed, as the snow was deeper, perhaps because they'd wandered well off the trail.

"Rue, that astrologer told me that to be safe, we should go south and get passage on a boat. Dree's going south, for certain. But that astrologer also said that sometimes being safe isn't the 'safe' answer. I think maybe she was trying to tell me that if I run away from something, I'll just have to keep running and running. So maybe I'm doing the right thing by leaving the Vershan Monastery and getting this book to my brother. It should go straight to him, Rue. I should do it, not Morgan. And I'll make Bishop DeNogaret and Meven see that they're right—a religious life would be good for me. But at the Vershan Monastery, not at Dea Fortress. Then Meven can come south and visit me. Can you see it . . . the King of Galmier and maybe Bishop DeNogaret, and probably some soldiers for escort . . . all visiting me at the monastery? It's safe and warm there, Rue."

She fell silent again and Gallant-Stallion continued to plod north. The Finest was hoping everything would work out just the way she said. And that somewhere in the book she carried against his neck Meven could manage to learn something about the evil birds, and thereby figure out just who might have sent them against Kalantha and Meven.

Then Kalantha truly would be safe, and Gallant-Stallion would breathe easier as he shepherded her.

Perhaps, he mused, this girl on his back was to make her mark on the world by preaching the tenets revered by the monastery. Maybe that was why he was to shepherd her. Maybe some divine force had led them to the monastery.

He stopped his wonderings several minutes later when the late winter snowstorm turned into a blizzard. The Finest had been in the Galmier Mountains in the winter. It was colder there than here, but the snow had never seemed so spiteful, coming at him fast and biting, stinging his eyes and pelting his hide and causing Kalantha to huddle closer and shiver. The wind had never whipped so shrilly around him, sounding like a hundred hungry wolves and flapping his mane so that it lashed at his face and made it even harder to see where he was going. Was it the harshest winter this land had ever felt?

The blizzard was a vile creature as far as Gallant-Stallion was concerned. It breathed—the wind—and it stalked them as if it were a starving predator circling and circling, coming closer then darting away. Teasing them mercilessly and wearing them down.

From time to time the Finest thought he saw the beast's eyes. But he guessed those were just distant fires from some village, or perhaps his mind playing tricks. He could smell the creature-storm, too. The snow had a crisp and pleasing odor that reminded him of early spring rains. But it also carried the scents of rotting wood that lay beneath the snow, and animals that had died to predators or the weather. But those scents were not as strong, and so Gallant-Stallion concentrated only on the storm smell and worked to find his way through it.

The weather let up a little the following day, the snow still falling heavily and covering up dropped branches and other obstacles. Gallant-Stallion had to travel slowly on those times when he alternately found the merchant trail, and then lost it and wandered trying to find it again.

Kalantha twice mentioned going back to the monastery, but dismissed the notion both times. She worried the weather might be worse behind them. Then she settled on finding Stilton.

"Just to stay for a day, Rue. Get something warm to eat. I'm so hungry. Aren't you? If I was smart like my brother Meven, I would have snuck into the monastery kitchen and . . . borrowed . . . food for us."

Gallant-Stallion had managed to forage on young evergreens, and he knew the girl must be hungry. She'd been eating snow to quench her thirst. But there was so much snow that it covered up anything she might be tempted to eat. Yesterday she'd tried some of the evergreens the Finest was nibbling on. But she spit them out.

"Stilton can't be too far, can it?" She tried to remember how many days it had taken her to travel from Stilton to the Vershan Monastery. "Too many. Too far. Rue!" she was exasperated. "Wait! The old monastery!" She was thinking of the one that had caught fire. It would provide shelter from the storm.

She explained her plan to the Finest, and he was quick to agree with her. Now, if only he could find his way.

Steadfast, he implored. He hadn't tried to contact the spirit of his mentor in many days. *Steadfast, I fear I am lost. Steadfast!*

There was no change in the wind or hint of Steadfast's presence. So Gallant-Stallion called to him again and again, as he trudged through the deepening snow in the direction he thought the burned monastery lay.

Another night was coming, and they hadn't found the ruins. Neither had he heard from Steadfast. Kalantha had slept on and off, though it wasn't enough. And though her wolfskin cloak was warm, it wasn't enough either. The Finest worried his charge was going to starve or die of exposure before he found the ruins or Stilton or anyplace safe from the foe the raging winter storm had become.

No book is worth this, Gallant-Stallion said. He was talking in hidden speak, and knew Kalantha could hear him. But she didn't reply. *Nothing in a book is worth your life, child. Paper and ink are not so valuable as you.*

Perhaps she was sleeping again, he thought. Or perhaps she hadn't the strength to talk with him.

Kalantha! The Finest stopped and tried to pick through the howling wind. *Kalantha, listen to me!* He heard something—other than the storm—and with the wind competing he was having difficulty determining just what the noise was. Something was not right, he knew. *Kalantha, wake up!*

She stirred a little and mumbled something about Dree that he didn't catch. Then he swore he heard someone else talking. He turned back the way they'd come, noticing that his hoofprints were already getting difficult to spot with the snow filling them up. His ears pointed forward; nostrils quivering, he begged the wind to tell him what it knew.

Cold. Cold. Cold. Never been colder. Never been more tired. Never been more hungry. Hungry. Hungry.

It was Boots, Gallant-Stallion realized, and he whinnied to the plow horse, so she could find him.

Man on my back is too heavy. Too cold. Too hungry. Hate you, punch, Boots said as she caught sight of the Finest through the driving snow. *This man follows you. Hate you. Hate you. Too cold. Too hungry.*

"Kalantha!" Ergoth threw his hood off and waved frantically.

"Kal!" This came from Reshara, who was riding a stocky pony and who was thumping her feet into its sides in an effort to get it to hurry. "Kal!"

Kalantha pulled back her hood, returned the wave, and waited for them to reach her. She drew her face forward until it looked pinched in an effort to keep the snow out of her eyes. "What are you two doing out here? You could die in this weather!"

"*We* could die?" Reshara looked worried. "*You* could die. Kal, you're so white!" The thin girl was trembling from the cold, but she seemed more concerned about her friend.

"Why did you follow me, Shar? You shouldn't be risking yourself for me!" Kalantha glared at Ergoth. "And I don't need a caretaker, priest. I've managed on my own. You know that. This was foolish, you coming after me."

Somehow Ergoth managed the faintest of smiles. "I know you can take care of yourself, Kal, under normal circumstances. But things aren't normal any longer."

"It's a storm, Ergoth. There are storms in the winter."

"No, Kal, worse than that. There's a war."

War. She mouthed the word and instantly pictured the woman astrologer on the edge of the Lake of Stars. The woman had mentioned a war, and that royal blood was involved.

"I learned it from the Chief Prelate. After I left you in the library I went to talk to him, about you being of royal blood. I was excited. I couldn't get in to see him for hours . . . then I found out why he was so busy. Galmier has declared war on Nasim-Guri, Kal. And we're in Nasim-Guri right now. We've got to get back over the border into Vered, go back to the monastery where it's safe."

Kalantha stared at the priest in disbelief. *My brother wouldn't start a war,* she mouthed. *Never ever.*

"Kal, we have to go back." Ergoth was insistent. "Girl, I wish you had bit and bridle for that big horse of yours. There's nothing for me to grab on to." It was clear he wanted to grab some reins and pull her back to the monastery with him.

"Sometimes being safe isn't the safest course," she whispered. Louder, practically shouting as the wind gusted stronger: "So that's why you came after me, Ergoth. To save me from the war."

The thin girl shivered in her wool cloak. "I'm the one who followed you, Kal. Two days, but I couldn't quite catch up. Lost sight of you a couple of times. And then I got lost."

"But I found her," Ergoth supplied. He was talking loudly now, as the wind was howling like a hundred maddened ghosts. "And I told her about the fighting, and how this country isn't safe. And now we found you." He waved his arm to the east. "And now we better find a place to wait this storm out. Then we're going home to Vershan."

He took the lead, Boots complaining without letting up, Gallant-Stallion making sure Reshara and her pony was between him and Boots. And just when night was the deepest, and they thought they couldn't go on any longer, they managed to reach the monastery ruins. Moments later, all of them were safely inside the entry hall.

The wind raged all around them, and snow blew in through broken upstairs windows. They were cold, but it was a cold they could tolerate now.

Cold. Tired. Hungry. Angry. Hate you, punch. I want to be home. Cold and tired and hungry and cold. I want a barn around me.

Quiet, Boots, Gallant-Stallion said. *Be quiet. Be quiet. In the name of everything, be quiet.*

For once, the plow horse stopped talking.

Reshara found a few chairs upstairs that had not burned in the fire, and these she broke up and put in the fireplace in the kitchen. Ergoth managed to get a blaze going, and he, Kalantha, and Reshara huddled around it. He'd brought some bread and cheese with him, and they ate the last of it while they warmed their hands.

"What happened to cause the war?" Kalantha stared at the flames, not wanting Ergoth and Reshara to see she was almost crying at the notion. "My brother wouldn't have started it. Nasim-Guri must have. That King must have done something horrible."

She didn't see Ergoth shake his head.

"My brother is peaceful. He reads and prays. He wouldn't start a war. Never ever. Never."

"No, Kal. From what the Chief Prelate said, Galmier attacked without warning, sent a wave of soldiers at the northern border of Nasim-Guri and wiped out all the sentries stationed at the bridges. Then another wave went deeper into the country. The Prelate said two of the smallest villages just inside the border were completely overrun, and even the women and children were killed. No one was left alive. As I said, we're going back to the monastery, where it's safe." He paused. "At least where it's safe for now."

Kalantha backed away from the fire and paced behind the two. "The King of Nasim-Guri started it, I just know it."

"I really don't think so, Kal. I think your brother did." Ergoth was watching her, his back to the fire, hands behind him, still warming them. "The Chief Prelate says it looks like Galmier wants to swallow Nasim-Guri up. The Prelate thinks Vered will be next, or Uland to the far north, and so he's calling his priests back to the monastery and meeting soon with the King of Vered. I suspect Vered will be marshaling its forces in case Nasim-Guri falls quickly and Galmier presses farther south." He glanced at Reshara, who was sitting cross-legged in front of the cookfire, listening to them, but politely staying out of it. "There hasn't been a war for a long time, Kal. No one was expecting this. And so Nasim-Guri is going to fall. It's not a matter of if, it's a matter of when. It's just a matter of how quickly."

Kalantha paced faster and went to the doorway, looking out into the large entry room and seeing Gallant-Stallion watching her.

"No," she said. A tear crept down her cheek and she brushed at it. "Nasim-Guri isn't going to fall."

"They don't have the soldiers Galmier does," Ergoth argued. "They weren't prepared. They . . ."

"You don't understand." Her tone was terse and her green eyes shone with ire. "If my brother started a war, like you claim, I'm going to make him stop it. I'm going to Nadir first thing in the morning, and I'm going to make him stop all of this."

"That would be too dangerous," Ergoth protested.

"Sometimes the safe way isn't the best way."

Gallant-Stallion was listening closely.

Kalantha was at a crossroads, like he was.

He knew the stables at Vershan were safe and comfortable, and he'd accepted them. Vershan had been safe and comfortable for her, too. It was easy to be comfortable. He understood Kalantha now, better than he had before. She was deciding between safety and uncertainty, between contentment and risk.

"My choice is not to be safe," she told Ergoth. "I have to do something about the war and my brother. I just have to."

Ergoth stared, at an uncustomary loss for words.

"There's one slice more of this bread." Reshara finally broke the uncomfortable silence. "Let's share it. I think we'll all be getting a little thinner before we get to Stilton or Cobston . . . on our way to Nadir." She licked her fingers. "Should've brought more with me, but I didn't know the snow would keep coming down. Or just how far away Nadir is. Slow going in all of this. I hope we don't have to kill one of the horses for food."

"That'll never ever happen." Kalantha sat next to Reshara and brushed the hair away from her eyes. "Why did you follow me, Shar? Why did you have to follow me and put yourself in danger?" Kalantha wagged her finger in a gentle scolding. "It's not that I don't appreciate you being worried about me and all, but . . ."

"I wasn't worried, Kal. I guess I should have been, but I wasn't. Well, now I know for certain I should've been, worried. With all this snow and the war. I just thought that going after you would be . . . exciting."

Kalantha drew her lips into a thin line and tapped her fingers on the tile floor.

"Kal, I just knew somehow that you were going to see your brother, the King of Galmier. I saw you take that book from the library, and I heard you say something about showing it to him. I just wanted to go with you. I've never met a King before. I've never been to a palace or seen anything rich. I didn't think the priests at the monastery would mind if I went away for just a little while."

"She didn't ask them," Ergoth cut in. "About leaving or about borrowing a pony."

"And I didn't know about the war when I left, Ergoth. I was just following Kal. And I'm not going back to the monastery yet. I'm going with Kal." She draped an arm around Kalantha's shoulders. "I'll help you stop this war. Least I can do, I figure, since you're my friend."

Kalantha smiled. "If the storm ever stops and we get out of

here, Shar. And if we make it to Nadir, I'll introduce you to my brother."

Reshara beamed.

IT WAS LATE MORNING THE FOLLOWING DAY WHEN THE weather broke.

The sky was a sheet of gray that still threatened snow. It seemed to hang low above the treetops. The wind had let up only a little, sounding mournful as it cut across the drifts.

Kalantha worried that if they waited for better weather, they might be waiting a long time.

"I wish you'd go back to Vershan, Ergoth, and tell the Chief Prelate that Reshara and I are going to Nadir. He should know that I'm going to make my brother stop this war."

Ergoth was riding next to her. "Kal, you amaze me, so young and determined. But, you're a child. A girl. One small girl is not going to stop a war . . . even if you are the King's sister. I should pluck you up and carry you back to the monastery. That's what I should do."

"But you won't."

"No. But only the gods know why."

"Then why are you coming with me and Shar?"

He shrugged. "I wouldn't be a very good priest if I let two young girls ride off to the palace on their own, would I?"

She gave him a smile that reached her eyes. "Ergoth, you're the first priest I've well and truly liked."

"What about me?" Reshara kneed her pony so it would come up on Kalantha's other side.

"I like you too, Shar."

The thin girl returned her smile and shivered. "I hope it's not too far to Nadir. It's so cold out here."

Cold. Cold. Cold, Boots echoed.

Gallant-Stallion cut the plow horse a warning stare.

"Well, I'm not very cold today," Kalantha lied. She tugged her wolfskin cloak off and passed it to Reshara. "How about we trade for a while?"

Reshara hesitated for the briefest of moments, then she passed her wool cloak to Kalantha in exchange. "Thanks, Kal." Softer: "And I don't care what Ergoth says. I think you can talk your brother into stopping all the fighting. I think you can talk anyone into anything."

Kalantha brightened and tipped her head up, hoping to see the sun poking through. She checked again throughout the rest of the morning and the afternoon, finding a few paler spots in the sky where the clouds were thin. But they were never thin enough to let the sun wholly through. When she looked again at about the time she guessed was sunset judging by the darkening sky and her rumbling stomach, she saw a large bird circling overhead.

Birds always made her nervous, but this wasn't a dark one. And when it dropped a little lower, she could see that it was an owl.

"I thought they only flew at night," she said to herself, watching the bird and sensing no threat in it. Mildly curious, she pointed it out to Ergoth and Reshara.

The thin acolyte was looking to the sky, too, though at a point more distant than where the owl flew. "I hear you," Reshara said.

Kalantha mistakenly thought Reshara was talking to her.

"Owls are nocturnal," Ergoth said. "But sometimes they get spooked into flying, something disturbing their tree. Or sometimes, like us, they're just hungry. Looks like he has company."

"I hear you," Reshara repeated softly.

Kalantha watched as a flock of blackbirds joined the owl. "No!" she hollered. Then she was slamming her heels against the Finest's sides and holding tight to his mane. "Run!" she hollered to a surprised and confused Ergoth. "The assassin-birds I told you about. Just run!"

Gallant-Stallion's hooves churned through the snow, kicking it up all around him and trusting that the merchant trail they were on was free of fallen limbs and ruts. He heard Boots behind him, but not the pony, so he whipped his head around and saw the pony a hundred yards back on the trail, Reshara standing on the ground next to it. He spun around and Kalantha saw the girl, too.

"Rue, hurry! Go back! We have to save Shar!"

He galloped toward the fallen acolyte, passing by a stunned Ergoth and stopping just short of Reshara. Kalantha slipped from his back and hurried to Reshara, looking up once to see more birds circling and dropping.

"Shar! Get up on your pony, Shar!"

Kalantha tugged at the girl's arms and was taken by surprise when Reshara tugged back and pushed Kalantha to the ground. In the same motion, the girl reached for the long knife in the sheath at Kalantha's side. She yanked it free, raised it above her head, and brought it down hard. Reshara would have skewered Kalantha, had she not rolled under the pony.

"Shar! What are you doing?"

Gallant-Stallion was also taken by surprise, but he was quick to act. He drove forward, knocking Reshara over, but careful not to trample her. He didn't want to hurt the girl until he knew what was going on.

Kalantha sprung up on the other side of the spooked pony, just as Ergoth had managed to turn around and join them.

"Kal? Reshara?" His eyes widened and his mouth dropped

open when he saw the knife in Reshara's hand. "Wh—what's going on?"

Before either girl could answer, a piercing cry cut through the air. They all looked up, just in time to see a cloud of black descending, led by a large owl with outstretched talons.

27 · Spilling Royal Blood

Visiting Finest say my little village is sleepy and uninteresting. That is because they are only passing through. This village, my home, is peaceful and happy. The people are friendly, most of them, and therefore they are interesting to me. I prefer peace to excitement. And if other Finest creations did more than pass through, they would prefer peace to excitement, too.

~Mara, shepherd to the village Bitternut

Reshara clutched the long knife tighter. "You have to die, Kalantha. My mistress wills it."

Who? Mistress who? Kalantha mouthed as she rushed toward Rue. "Shar! What are you doing?"

Ergoth had managed to climb off Boots's back. Dragging his left leg, he shuffled toward Reshara, arms out and palms toward her. "It's the snow," he said. "Made you a little crazy, Reshara. Put the knife down. Put the knife . . ."

At that instant the cloud of birds descended, the owl—its sharp talons outstretched—went straight for Reshara. The young acolyte had been so intent on skewering Kalantha that she'd been oblivious to the approaching owl.

It slammed into her, talons reaching into the hooded recesses of her cloak and finding her narrow throat. The owl clawed furiously, wings beating maniacally to keep it aloft while it rended its prey.

Ergoth was lumbering toward Reshara, now bent on getting the owl off of her. He wasn't worried about the knife; Reshara dropped it and was flailing at the bird with her slender hands.

"Help!" Reshara pleaded.

Ergoth reached out, and his own fingers closed on feathers. But he was pushed away from the girl and the owl by a swarm of cowbirds, grackles, and crows that had joined the fight.

Kalantha was waging her own battle. Rue was at her side, rising up on his hind legs and kicking at the cloud of birds around him. Kalantha was pummeling the birds with her fists, her anger making her faster and stronger. She had managed to drop a few of the smaller birds, and stomped them into the drifts. But there were so many, and they were scratching at her face and arms and ripping the thin wool cloak she was wearing. The cloak became a hindrance, as it was tangling around her legs. So Kalantha shrugged it off and swung her fists wildly now.

Kal! It was Gallant-Stallion calling to her through the cloud of black. *Stay next to me! Close, Kal.*

She was trying to do just that, but it was so hard to see with the flutter of dark wings all around her. The noise was becoming deafening, from the wings and the birds' cries, from the mournful wind and from Reshara screaming.

The Finest cursed himself. There'd been no hint of the birds, and he'd thought them no longer a threat. He'd even said as much to Kalantha, in a half-hearted attempt to discourage her from pursuing the book about birds.

What a fool I have been, he thought. *The girl, somehow, knew the birds had not left her behind. The Fallen Favorite recognized a danger when I could not. Steadfast! Steadfast, help me save her!*

But Gallant-Stallion knew that the spirit of his mentor, even if he were here, could not help him. The birds were a tangible, horrible peril. And though he'd faced more of them in the past, the danger was greater here. The snow was deep and made it more difficult for him to move. He couldn't run to safety with Kalantha, not with the troubled Reshara and the priest Ergoth also in jeopardy. Kalantha would not leave her friends. And Gallant-Stallion did not want to leave them either.

He caught a glimpse of Ergoth through the sheet of feathers and beaks. The priest was barely able to stand, the flock spinning around him and clawing at him. Still, he was flailing away at them, while at the same time trying to reach Reshara.

The girl was whimpering, and her hands were only feebly trying to push the owl away. She dropped to her knees and shuddered.

Stay with me, Kalantha! Gallant-Stallion called. He pressed forward, trying to reach the fallen acolyte. At the same time he tried to puzzle out why the girl would have attacked Kalantha. Was it as Ergoth said, the snow had made her mad? *Stay with me. We need to help your friends.*

Kalantha moved forward, the snow up to her knees in places. Her shoulder was against the Finest's side, as if she could keep track of him that way. Her eyes were closed tightly against the birds that continued to scratch at her face.

"Why now, Rue? Why would they attack us now? What have I ever done to anyone?"

"Die Kalantha! Die!"

The voice stopped Kalantha and the Finest for the merest of heartbeats. The voice didn't belong to Reshara or Ergoth. It was throaty, a hush wrapped around its edges.

"The owl!" Kalantha said. "That's the owl talking!"

He thinks Reshara is you, Gallant-Stallion supplied.

"My wolfskin cloak," Kalantha breathed.

Instantly the Finest knew what she meant. Kalantha had loaned Reshara the wolfskin cloak . . . the cloak Kalantha had been wearing since the village of Stilton. The owl thought he was attacking Kalantha.

"Die, Kalantha! For my master, Die!"

"Kill the girl," a big crow shrieked. "Help Eyeswide kill the girl."

"Killherkillherkillherkillher," a chant began.

"I will not fail him again!" This from the owl, who had Reshara in a deep drift now, only her legs and arms sticking out. He clawed furiously at her face and throat, his talons and his stomach feathers solid red from her blood.

Gallant-Stallion fought his way through the cloud of birds, smashing several of them beneath his hooves, biting at them and catching one in his teeth, clamping down hard until he felt its bones break, then tossing it away.

He reared up above the owl, just as it managed to pull back Reshara's hood.

"Who?" the owl asked. It sounded more like *whoooo* in its throaty voice. "Who is this? Not the girl I need. Not the girl I was to slay. Not the girl with the green eyes."

Then the owl was flying up and at Gallant-Stallion.

"Finest!" Eyeswide hissed. "I will have you! Then I will have the deceitful girl. Both of you to be certain. I will not fail again." The owl's eyes flashed and spotted Kalantha at the Finest's side. "She is the one! Her!"

The owl narrowly dodged Gallant-Stallion's hooves and shot toward Kalantha. But Kal dropped in a crouch, the owl flying over her head and up, then banking back to come at her again.

The crows and cowbirds were swarming Reshara, and more were still swarming Ergoth. The priest was using his arms like clubs, and he was striking at least one bird with each swing. His hands were a mass of cuts, and blood ran in rivulets down his cheeks.

You will not have Kalantha! Gallant-Stallion shouted

through the chorus of birds and the flapping wings. With a fury born of anger and frustration he spun and slashed out at the approaching owl and sent it back into a drift. *You will never have her while I live!*

Then the Finest was biting at more of the birds and slamming as many into the ground as he could. The snow was red all around him. Kalantha was contributing to the carnage. She'd managed to retrieve her long knife that Reshara had dropped, and she was swinging it like a scythe. The blade was sharp, just as Bartholomew had told her, and it sliced through the belly of one crow, then slashed off the wing of a cowbird.

The owl dove toward Kalantha, then he changed his mind and shot skyward. "Follow me!" he called to his malevolent flock. He intended for them to regroup away from the slashing hooves of the Finest. He wanted to survey the scene from a safe vantage point. "Follow me, all of you! We have them!"

The crows, cowbirds, and grackles were quick to fly away from the big punch.

"Killed her!" a crow cried. "We killed the girl like Eyeswide wanted."

"Killedherkilledherkilledher."

The owl fumed, but did not correct his flock. From fifty yards overhead he gazed down at the bloody patch of ground. A girl was down, dead, but not the one he'd intended. The girl with green eyes tricked us," he sneered. "Hid in another girl's clothes."

Eyeswide didn't know who the slain girl was, but she'd been wearing Kalantha's wolfskin cloak. The owl had been scrying on Kalantha since she'd left the monastery with the Finest. He gathered a reasonable number of birds and went in pursuit. Where the man and the dead girl came from, Eyeswide could only guess. And why had Kalantha hid by giving the other girl the wolf cloak?

"Hated horse," Eyeswide cursed. "Hated horse. Hated girl."

Below, Kalantha was at Reshara's side. She crushed snow in her hand to melt it, and used that to wipe the blood off her friend's face.

"Dead, Rue. Shar's dead."

Ergoth was leaning on Boots, pale with pain and anguish. He looked between Kalantha and Shar, then glanced overhead, to where the birds circled. Shar's pony had run off, and with snow swirling all around, he couldn't see it.

Boots had fared well, only suffering a few scratches. The birds had not been after her. Gallant-Stallion, however, was laced with slashes everywhere, and his blood continued to drip onto the snow. He was looking at the birds overhead, dozens of questions dancing in his head.

Kalantha, we must leave this place, he told her. He cast a quick look at the ground. Dozens of broken bird bodies littered the bloody snow.

"And go where?" she said. "Where is safe from those evil, evil birds?"

Ergoth thought she was speaking to him. "Back to the monastery, Kal. We'll have to take Shar back. Bury her properly. The Chief Prelate . . . we'll have to tell him about the birds. Let's leave now. Before those birds decide to come back." He paused and shuddered when he saw the owl swoop closer, then climb again. "Those are the birds you told me about? That I only deep down half-believed you about, Kal? How could such things exist?"

"No place safe, Rue. No place will ever be safe." She glanced behind her, several yards away was the book wrapped in the blanket. She had dropped it. "But maybe my brother Meven can figure it all out."

She struggled to her feet, wincing. "I'm hurt bad, Rue. Though I don't look near so bad as you."

Ergoth finally realized she was talking to the punch. He stared at the big horse, seeing just how injured it was. "By the gods," he hushed. "Poor horse." Then he looked back at Kalantha. "We need to move, girl. Now. There are a lot of birds up there, and they're watching us. You can't ride that horse of yours, but you can ride Boots. We'll go south, find Shar's pony. We'll have to . . . leave Shar here. Until we can get help, and then we'll . . ."

"We're not leaving her here. The birds will eat at her. I know. It's what crows do. And I will walk with Rue out of here. I'm not leaving my beautiful horse, either."

Then Kalantha was looking skyward again, her eyes following the circling owl and trying to count just how many blackbirds and crows were up there. More than were dead on the ground, she thought.

"Oh, Shar. What were you doing? Why did you come after me? Did those birds somehow . . ."

Kalantha. Look!

"What, Rue?" Kalantha followed his gaze. To the south, higher in the sky, another swarm of birds approached. "By all that's holy. We can't stand against all of them."

28 · Eyeswide's Stand

Men struggle for power and wealth and to gain a piece of ground. Animals struggle only to survive. I think that animals, with their limited wisdom and intellect, are actually the more sagacious of the two.

~Dunlegs of the Misty Pasture, once shepherd to a Dolour King

What have you done?" The cry came from Ninéon, who was leading the second wave of birds. She flew straight at Eyeswide, and the owl stopped his dive on the people below. "What in the name of Iniquis and Abandon have you done, stupid, stupid, stupid owl?"

"Done?" Eyeswide stared angrily at his lieutenant. "Ninéon, I am working to kill Kalantha Montoll and her friends. I had called for you to join me . . . and you are late!"

Ninéon's eyes were blackest black as they bored into Eyeswide's golden ones. "Fool of a fowl, Eyeswide! You killed the wrong girl. Reshara, the one dead below, was my puppet. I took her mind only days ago, to learn about Kalantha, to be able to follow them. Reshara would have killed Kalantha for you, fool of a fowl! Look at the dead down there, Eyeswide. More dead birds! You could have spared them had you waited for me, and had you waited for Reshara to do your bloody work for you!"

Eyeswide darted toward Ninéon, claws outstretched. He slashed at the falcon, like one man might slap another. "You dare call me a fool? I killed your puppet? I did not give you the right to take any puppets! Only I can subjugate a man. It is not your right, Ninéon. Only I can do this!"

The falcon's eyes narrowed. "I can do as I please, owl." There was disrespect in the tone, and in the fact that Ninéon called Eyeswide "owl" instead of by his name. "I am powerful, owl. You made me that way. And I think I am more powerful than you."

"No!" Eyeswide spat. "No creature is more powerful than I. Not stronger, not smarter, not . . ."

Eyeswide didn't get a chance to finish his rant, as Ninéon slipped beneath him, then angled up behind him and slashed with her talons. She drove her beak into the back of his neck, then pulled free and slipped around to face him.

She narrowly managed to avoid his talons, then she darted in, leading with her beak and slamming into his chest. "With me!" she hollered to her band of crows.

To Eyeswide's horror, the birds who had been following Ninéon now flew at him and his assassins.

BELOW, KALANTHA AND ERGOTH LOOKED UP IN DISBELIEF.

"I . . . I . . . what's happening?" Ergoth had a bleeding hand cupped over his eyes, trying to discover what was transpiring in the deadly aerial dance overhead.

Kalantha shook her head and glanced at Rue. "So hurt, you are, my magic horse," she whispered. Her lower lip quivered. "At least they fight each other now. We can use that." She stared skyward again. "Ergoth, we can leave while they fight. I need to get to my brother, and that means going to Nadir. But we can't go all the way with Rue like this."

Ergoth didn't reply, he was still caught up in the carnage overhead.

"Priest!" Kalantha shouted. "Priest!"

He dropped his gaze for a moment, then looked up again.

"That burned monastery is the closest place. I'm taking Rue there. You can help put Reshara on Rue's back. I'll not leave her here for whatever birds are left. Priest!"

Ergoth hobbled to Reshara and pulled the wolfskin hood over her head. The girl's face and throat were so torn he couldn't bear to look at them. He and Kalantha managed to wrap the cloak around Reshara like a shroud, then hoist her onto Gallant-Stallion's back.

"So much blood," Ergoth hushed. "I've never seen so much blood."

"I have." Kalantha's voice was even. "When the birds came before and killed my cousin and his soldiers." Then she was leading Rue back toward the burned monastery. "Maybe the birds can't get us there. Maybe."

Ergoth climbed onto Boots and followed her, trusting the plow horse to keep right behind Kalantha and the punch. He looked up, not taking his eyes off the battle in the sky until they were near the monastery and the birds were out of sight.

"OWL . . . YOU KILLED MY PUPPET. FOOL, YOU ARE! FOOL, I call you! You dared to kill my new pet! Now you die for that! For that and more!" Ninéon was faster than Eyeswide, a fact the falcon had hidden until now. More agile because of her form, and perhaps because of her scant years, she dipped away from him only to come back, talons and beak driving into him.

Her crows helped. Most of them fought with Eyeswide's flock, in particular going after the cowbirds and grackles. The crows hesitated in killing their own kind. Likewise Eyeswide's crows held back, uncertain and bewildered, and looking for direction from the owl.

But Eyeswide had thrown all his efforts into surviving, and so he didn't call to his flock.

Feathers and blood fell with the snow, then one cowbird fell, and then another.

"Stop this!" Eyeswide shouted at Ninéon with as much strength as his throaty voice could muster. Despite everything, the owl didn't want to kill his lieutenant, as he'd put much effort into the bird. But when Ninéon didn't stop the assault, Eyeswide redoubled his efforts, clawing savagely at the falcon, finally finding his way beneath the feathers on her body and drawing blood.

At the same time, Ninéon attacked him, driving her beak into his throat again and again, like a man might wield a dagger. Fury drove her on, and she shouted her anger at Eyeswide for slaying her pet.

"Reshara would have killed the girl with the green eyes. Bishop DeNogaret would have been pleased!"

The owl's eyes grew impossibly wide. Had he mentioned the Bishop to Ninéon? He thought not. He'd only told Fala, his former lieutenant, about Bishop DeNogaret after the hawk had been with him for a few years. How had Ninéon learned about the Bishop?

Distracted with the questions that tumbled through his mind, Eyeswide didn't anticipate Ninéon breaking away and climbing. In the next instant she was diving down on him, head stretched forward as if she would impale him on her beak. The owl cursed and plummeted, rising a few feet above the ground and turning on the falcon.

Only to discover she wasn't there.

"Where?" he screamed. "Where in all of this forest are you?"

Feathers and blood rained down on him, as the battle above continued. Was she there? In the midst of all of that?

"Doesn't matter," he cursed. "I will stop this. I will not lose another bird."

Yet four more cowbirds fell dead before the owl was halfway to the fight.

"Stop this!" he called to all of them. And for a moment part of the force—those loyal to him—did stop. It was to prove their undoing. Ninéon's crows took advantage of the pause and pecked and clawed and buffeted their brothers. "I order all of you to . . ."

Eyeswide felt a brief jolt of pain the likes of which he'd not experienced ever before. Icy and fiery at the same time, starting at the back of his neck and then radiating out to the end of each feather.

For more years than any man or creature living walked Paard-Peran, Eyeswide had lived. Easily twice the years of Bishop DeNogaret. Older than a Finest. Wiser than anyone, Eyeswide thought. Wise and bright and filled with purpose.

The Bishop and Ninéon thought they were smarter, the owl mused, smarter than he and smarter than each other. But both were shortsighted, he realized, their goals small. The owl knew he'd had his wide eyes set on the true prize his entire life. And now all his wisdom and cunning would be lost from this world.

Such pain he felt! Then he felt nothing. There was no more pain, no sense of the cold wind about him. The snowflakes landing in his eyes did not register as wet.

There was nothing but the cacophony of birds fighting birds and the sound of the wind whipping around him, his heart hammering and his feathers fluttering. And Ninéon.

She'd been behind him, somewhere, keeping out of sight while he tried to rejoin the flock above. And she'd come at him when he wasn't expecting her, ramming her beak into the back of his neck, severing his spine.

That one brief stab of excruciating pain. Then nothing.

Eyeswide tried to flap his wings to stay aloft, but his body wouldn't respond. He couldn't even turn his head to see the falcon that he knew was behind him.

"You blessed me," Ninéon said as he fell. "You awoke me from a simple existence."

Eyeswide hit the ground, blood-red snow showering up from the impact.

"You taught me," Ninéon said, hovering, looking at the great owl's corpse. "And now the student surpassed the teacher."

Then the falcon was rejoining the flock, demanding those once loyal to Eyeswide swear fealty to her. The fight raged for many long minutes more, until more cowbirds and grackles fell. And until Eyeswide's crows pledged their loyalty to a new master.

KALANTHA TUGGED RESHARA'S BODY INTO WHAT HAD BEEN the dining room of the burned monastery, stretching it out in front of a fireplace that hadn't been used for years.

"You intend to burn her?" Ergoth stood in the doorway, looking between Kalantha and the plow horse and punch.

"Too cold to dig up the ground and bury her," Kalantha said. "And I've no shovel." She rolled the body into the fireplace. "There's some furniture upstairs I can use. I know how to start a fire. My friend Morgan taught me."

"She should be buried. It's the way of our Order."

Kalantha slid past him and started up the stairs. "I'm not in your Order, Ergoth, not any longer. And I'm not about to leave her for the crows or leave her to rot. And she's not in your Order any longer either. She's dead. Dead because the birds took her over." Kalantha was certain of it. "I don't know how the birds managed it, but they did. That's the only explanation for why my friend would try to kill me."

Less than an hour later plenty of wood—chair legs, bedposts, table legs, most of which already showed fire damage from the blaze that had ruined this place—was piled over Reshara.

"I'll start the fire when we leave in the morning. I've heard that burning bodies stink bad. And I don't want to smell my friend burning."

Ergoth continued to watch her. "You're only a child," he said. "You shouldn't be tending to these things."

She went to the punch and inspected his wounds again. Then she went outside and gathered as much snow in her borrowed woolen cloak as she could carry. She returned and started rubbing handfuls on the cuts.

"Thirteen," she said. "I'm thirteen. But I'll be fourteen in the spring, and the spring's not far off. Besides, someone has to 'tend to these things.'"

Ergoth helped her rub the snow on the punch's wounds. "I doubt this will help him much."

"But it won't hurt him," she countered. "And it will wash some of the blood away. There's just too much blood. Besides, my Rue heals fast. Maybe he'll feel good enough to travel come tomorrow morning."

"And that would be to Nadir?"

"Yes. To find my brother. There's a book . . . ." She pointed to the blanket-wrapped book propped up by the doorway. "I want him and Bishop DeNogaret to see it. Maybe they can figure out who taught those horrid birds to be so mean." She ran her fingers through Gallant-Stallion's mane, which seemed hopelessly tangled. "And if there is a war, like your Chief Prelate claims, I'll get my brother to stop it."

SHE SLEPT ONLY A LITTLE THAT NIGHT, BY A FRONT WINDOW on the second floor. Mostly she looked out to see if there were birds circling.

29 · Reunion

The smell of blood is perhaps the foulest of all things I have noted in my few years on Paard-Peran. I prefer the scent of the Sprawling River, which stretches through the heart of Galmier, where I currently travel with my charge. The river twists and turns, rages, and at times it moves so slow it looks like a piece of slate. It overflows its banks, but it gives the land back in dry times. It always smells different, depending on the season. And therefore it always smells the same. It washes away all the spilled blood. And it leads my charge home to Nadir.

~Gallant-Stallion, shepherd to Kalantha Montoll
of the royal house of Galmier

They'd stopped in Stilton for food, and Kalantha spent all the trinkets Bartholomew the merchant gave her to buy wolf-skin cloaks for Ergoth and herself and to pay for Boots.

There were fewer men in the stilt village, as some of them had been conscripted by a local lord to join Galmier's army.

Kalantha and Ergoth had noticed too many signs of the war as they traveled from the burned Vershan Monastery to the older one that had been destroyed by the earthquake—where Calvert still lived—to Cobston, then Stilton. There were mass graves along the way, and places where small trees had been cut down for firewood and shelters. The snow was dotted with pink blossoms of blood all along the merchant trail.

The air had been too cold for the snow to melt, and so the traces of blood remained.

There were a few broken weapons and pieces of blue tabards.

And there were reports from the villagers in Cobston and Stilton. The news was the same.

The war was going well for Galmier, and Nasim-Guri was crumbling.

"Two days and we'll be in Nadir," Kalantha said as they left Stilton. "Sooner, save for Boots. Plow horses are supposed to be steady walkers. Some of the ladies around High Keep Temple rode them, saying they were more surefooted than a riding horse."

"But Boots . . ." Ergoth laughed. It was the first time he'd laughed in many days, and the sound surprised both of them. "Thank you for her, Kal Montoll. I hadn't the wealth to buy a horse."

"I didn't have much choice, did I? Not if you were coming with me to the palace. Rue is strong, but I don't think he'd like the both of us riding him. Would you, Rue?" She leaned forward and patted the punch's neck. "All healed, aren't you? Or getting there, at least? Wish I could get rid of my wounds so fast."

There was a long scar on her arm, as thick as the ropy one on her neck. The other cuts would melt after a time. Ergoth had his share of cuts and bruises, too, and coupled with his missing fingers and bad leg, he looked like he was a victim of the war.

You worry about returning to the palace, Gallant-Stallion said. *You want to see your brother, and yet you still fear him.*

"I have to see Meven to put an end to the war." She was careful to talk to the punch as if she were speaking to Ergoth. For some reason, she didn't want the priest to know she had a "magic horse." "I want Meven and Bishop DeNogaret to look at this book. I want to know who trained those evil birds." She straightened and squared her shoulders. "And I don't want them to send me to Dea Fortress."

Ergoth cleared his throat. "Which is why I'm along, eh, Kal?"

She hadn't admitted that, but it was true. Ergoth was an adult and a priest, and therefore a measure of protection.

"Am I with you to keep them from sending you to Dea Fortress?" Ergoth was scrutinizing her. "Despite the way things work in this world, you want to be responsible for yourself."

"I am responsible," she said.

"You are also only thirteen years old, Kal Montoll."

"But soon I will be fourteen."

Cold, Boots grumbled. The plow horse hadn't spoken much during the trip, except for when they were in Stilton and she brightened at the prospect of being next to the horses and goats in the pen for warmth. *Cold and tired. Hooves are sore. Man on my back is heavy. Hate all the snow. Hate all the cold. Hungry and cold. I want a barn wrapped around me.*

Boots, Gallant-Stallion began. *Soon you will be in a fine stable in Nadir. There will be plenty of oats and . . .* The Finest stiffened and his nostrils flared. He thrust his ears forward and searched through the light woods in front of them. He thought he smelled something. Unusual, yet familiar, something that set the hair along his back to stand up. He stopped, and Kalantha nudged him in the sides.

"What is it, Rue? Do you hear something?"

Hear? No. I smell something, Kalantha. I smell trouble. He looked this way and that, and she started looking, too.

Ergoth pulled on his reins and got Boots to stop.

Cold, the plow horse continued to complain. *Cold and hungry.*

Hungry! This came from farther ahead.

We are hungry! And from the side. *Hungry so! Our bellies burn.*

Wolves! Gallant-Stallion told Kalantha. Then he charged north and east, angling away from where he heard them.

"Hurry, Ergoth. Wolves! Hurry! Hurry!"

"Move, Boots!"

The plow horse galloped faster than Ergoth had believed possible. Snow churned up behind Boots and Gallant-Stallion. The Finest was heading toward a small hillock he'd noticed the first time he'd passed through this part of the country. He knew the wolves were quicker than Boots, and so he needed a defensible position.

Getting Kalantha to safety was his priority. But he knew she wouldn't go along with leaving the priest and his plow horse behind.

Hungry! the wolves barked in a chorus. *We hunger. We hunger. We hunger.*

It is the big horse! another howled. *The big horse from before. The one who talks and kills.*

Leave us be! Gallant-Stallion shouted in the wolf-tongue. Out of the corner of his eye he caught sight of the pack. It moved like gray lightning along the ground, a blur of fog color across the top of the snow, weaving in and out of thin river birch trunks. He recognized a few of the wolves from the distinctive markings around their heads. This was the same pack that had hunted them near Stilton last year. But it was a smaller pack, perhaps splintered, or perhaps cut by the cold and hunters.

We hunger! We hunger, talking horse!

Leave us be! Gallant-Stallion shouted.

We will leave your bones for the carrion birds. This came from the lead wolf, one larger than the others. It was cutting to the east, legs speeding over the snow. Its body far lighter weight than Gallant-Stallion's, it did not sink into the drifts.

In a heartbeat the pack was nipping at the Finest's hooves. The lead wolf howled in triumph, as his brothers and sisters circled the punch and the plow horse, then darted in.

Fear! Boots whinnied. *I fear. Help, punch. Help me.*

Gallant-Stallion was trying to help all of them. He bucked and brought his front hooves down on a small dark gray wolf. There was no remorse this time when he felt its back break under him. He stomped the wolf once more to be sure it was dead, then turned his attention to another.

Kalantha had pulled her long knife free. She wrapped her left hand in Gallant-Stallion's mane and leaned as far to her right as she dared. She slashed at the wolves leaping for her, stabbing one in the throat and another in the front leg.

Ergoth had no weapons, and so he tried to use his fists to bat them away. This only resulted in him getting bitten. He cried out in pain and started kicking. At the same time Boots tried to copy Gallant-Stallion, rising on her rear legs and flailing out with her front hooves. When that proved unsuccessful, she jumped forward on her front legs and kicked out with the back, smacking the lead wolf in the head and sending it reeling backwards.

"Good girl!" Ergoth told the plow horse. "Oh, good girl!"

The plow horse bucked again and again, striking another wolf. Ergoth continued to kick out at the ones jumping at him, screaming when a skinny pale gray wolf avoided his foot and clamped its teeth down hard on his leg. The wolf dropped and let its weight pull Ergoth from the saddle.

"Ergoth!" Kalantha watched him fall, and she slashed even faster at the wolves all around her. "Ergoth! Get up!"

The priest tried, but the skinny wolf was on his chest. Another joined this wolf, as did another. Ergoth's screams were short-lived, and the wolf trio began to feast on him.

Fear! Boots wuffled. *I fear! Help me!*

She continued to kick backwards, crushing the skull of one wolf, but presenting an opening for two more. A large black wolf with silvery gray markings on its face—a new one to this pack, Gallant-Stallion thought—raced in and lunged for Boots's belly. A second followed it, and they tore at the plow horse.

"Rue! Help them!" Kalantha shouted, though she knew the punch was doing everything he could just to keep her and himself alive.

Gallant-Stallion continued to strike one wolf after another. He'd killed six of them, but there were another twenty in the pack. Half of these were now feasting on the plow horse and the priest. But the other half were concentrating on the punch and Kalantha.

"Get us out of here, Rue!" Kalantha was sobbing, still swinging away with her knife, cutting into the hide of a young female wolf, but not stopping the creature. She was crying for Ergoth and Boots, crying that she'd asked the punch to take her away.

Kalantha was so tired of running away from things.

"Rue! Run!"

He did just that, slamming another wolf into the ground, then vaulting over the wolf carcasses in front of him. He threw everything into running, trusting that Kalantha would hold on. If she slipped off, the wolves would have her, and he wouldn't be able to save her this time. His lungs burned, despite the cold, and his legs protested each length he managed. His legs were torn from the wolves' teeth and claws. His sides were slashed. The wounds from the assassin-birds had been bad enough, and he'd only started to heal from those.

It was pain upon pain, and his mind and heart pounded. It would be so easy to stop and give up, to let his spirit drift with Steadfast's. But there was Kalantha to think about. One fist was gripped tightly in his mane, the other still held the long knife. She was pressed forward against the back of his neck, the book between her and him.

"Run! Run!" she continued to call.

And he continued to do just that. He pulled great gulps of

the wintry air into his lungs, and he flew over fallen trees and low-spreading evergreens. He angled to the west now, where the merchant trail continued to wind north paralleling the Sprawling River. In moments he was on it, his hooves pounding even faster against the level ground.

The wolves were baying behind him, and he could hear the clacking of their jaws and the cries of their hunger. But after a moment more, and then another, their howls were softer. He risked a glance behind him, seeing them slow, then concede. Then they were speeding south over the trail, giving up on him and returning to join the pack feasting on the plow horse and the priest.

Still, Gallant-Stallion didn't slow. If anything, he reached deep inside himself and managed a little more speed. He ran for an hour, he guessed, perhaps more. He ran until his legs gave out and he tumbled forward, spilling Kalantha and her precious book.

She hovered over him, until he picked himself up a few minutes later.

"Lame," she said, feeling his front leg. "You're lame, Rue!"

They slowly walked the rest of the way to Nadir, stopping often, and avoiding soldiers marching south. The city looked different, grayer and sad. And the cemetery on the southwest side looked fuller, with recent mounds covered by snow. Someone had found a way to dig through the frozen ground to bury their fellows.

It wasn't difficult to slip onto the palace grounds this time. Kalantha led Rue through a side gate, one a thin stream of ragged-looking soldiers were going through. The men didn't pay her the slightest attention, and only a few of them watched her head to the royal stables.

"I'll make Meven stop this war," Kalantha told Rue. "And

after that, when everything's peaceful again, I'll get him to read this book. Then he and Bishop DeNogaret can . . ."

"Can what, Kalantha?" The Bishop was standing just inside the stables. Cloaked in dark gray, arms crossed in front of him, long sleeves hanging down.

He looked like a statue, except that his face was white, paler than she'd remembered, and his eyes were moving, narrowing. He fixed her with a withering stare that sent a shiver down her back.

"Bishop DeNogaret can . . . what?" He tapped his foot, and she dropped her book.

"B—Bishop DeNogaret!" Kalantha was at once relieved and frightened. "I need to talk to you. This war, it has to stop. And the birds. I've discovered something that . . ."

"That you'll tell no one about, Kalantha. The war will not stop, and you'll not worry about the birds. Ever, ever again."

She nervously looked around him, seeing no stablehands. Odd, she thought. There was always an attendant in the stables.

"I should have dealt with you myself a while ago," he purred. He unfolded his arms, his hands looking like bird claws to her. He took one step forward, then another, his eyes holding her in place.

Kalantha tried to move, tried to drop her hand to the long knife at her side. She tried to holler for a stablehand or for anyone. But her throat had gone instantly dry, her tongue thick and unwieldy. Her feet were rooted to the ground just inside the stable doorway. It was those eyes. He always could hold her in place with just a look.

"I should not have relied on others. But that was my mistake." He moved closer still, a smile playing on his lips now. "It will be quick, Kalantha. It will not hurt . . . much."

Another step, and his shadow covered her. His hands moved

toward her throat. Then he was falling backward, driven to the stable floor by Gallant-Stallion.

The Finest drove his front hooves against the Bishop's chest, fire shooting up the punch's lame leg. The Finest came down on the Bishop again, this time on a hip, and he felt the man's bones break.

Gallant-Stallion reared once more.

"No, Rue! Stop!"

The Finest came down, hooves inches from the Bishop's head.

Bishop DeNogaret's eyes were closed. His chest rose and fell faintly and steadily.

"He's unconscious, Rue. Don't kill him. No more killing." There were bloodstains on the Bishop's robes, and she stared at them. "Too much blood everywhere."

She shuffled close to the Bishop and looked down at him. "Oh, Rue, I don't understand. First Reshara tried to kill me. I think maybe the Bishop was going to kill me, too. What have I done? Did the birds control him, too? What did I do to make them want to kill me?"

Something, was all Gallant-Stallion could say. *You did something. Somehow you pose a threat . . . to someone. Maybe to the Bishop.*

"It hurts to think about this." She slammed the palm of her hand against the side of her head. "All the blood and killing. Reshara and Ergoth and Boots. The birds and . . ." She stopped when she heard a repeated shrill whistle.

It was followed by the pounding of footsteps across the grounds. She looked out the stable doors and saw a quartet of palace guards churning through the snow. Meven was behind them.

She hardly recognized him, broad-shouldered and thick around the chest, his hair so terribly short and his face red from the cold and the exertion of running.

"Kal!"

A minute more and he brushed by Gallant-Stallion and was at her side, hugging her fiercely, then looking down, horrified, at Bishop DeNogaret's prone form.

"It was the horse," one of the guards said. "I saw him strike the Bishop."

"We'll have to kill the horse," another said.

"No! Don't let them, Meven. Don't you dare let them kill Rue." Words tumbled from her lips, about the Bishop coming at her, about the wolves, about the birds. She talked so fast little of it made sense, but enough seemed to get through.

"Carry the Bishop into his bedchamber," Meven ordered. He was still hugging Kalantha. "And have someone tend to him. Leave the horse be. For now. This is my sister's horse."

Kalantha smiled at that. Tears streamed down her face, happy tears for the first time ever in her young life. "Rue saved me again," she said. "Rue always saves me."

Meven finally released her and watched three of the guards carry the Bishop. The fourth remained to watch over the King.

Meven's eyes were glassy, and he was rubbing at them as he continued to watch the guards and the Bishop grow smaller as they neared the palace. Then he was shaking his head, as if he were knocking something loose inside.

"Kal, so many, many things have been happening."

"I know. This war. You started a war, Meven. How could you possibly do . . ."

He was still shaking his head. "I don't know. I don't know." He met her gaze. His expression made him appear hopeless and lost. "I don't know. It was the birds. They're from Nasim-Guri. That country's a threat. I have to put an end to that threat, Kal."

"Then why are you using soldiers to kill Nasim-Guri's men, when the birds are the ones you're after?"

Meven stared blankly. "I—I—I don't know." He rubbed harder at his eyes. "Things are so foggy, Kal. I'm not sure what I should do."

"I have some ideas," she answered. "And the first one is to call an end to this nasty, nasty war. No more blood, Meven."

Several moments of silence passed before he nodded. "All right, Kal. I guess. Yes, I guess I can stop the war."

"Then I want you to read this book."

He took her hand, and they walked toward the palace. "All right, Kal. I'll read your book."

"And stop the war."

"Yes, stop the war. I haven't been myself lately."

She looked over her shoulder at Rue.

"And we're going to get someone to tend to my beautiful horse. My very, very beautiful horse."

"Hateful horse." The words were too soft for any of them to hear. They came from high overhead, from a fog-gray falcon that circled the royal stables and that glared at the King and his sister. "Hateful horse."

The bird banked away to the south, streaking in a line for a spot where the Gray Woods met the Old Forest. "No more blood, Kalantha Montoll? I don't think so."

Jean Rabe's epic fantasy trilogy continues in

Finest Challenge, **coming soon in Tor hardcover.**

Here's a preview. . . .

Prologue

In the company of cobs, trotters, and warmbloods I discovered that joy is gained not from wanting something, but from treasuring something already possessed. If only all of my Finest sisters and brothers— and all of the Fallen Favorites—could learn such wisdom at a wise horse's hooves.

~*The Old Mare*

The sparrow had a black spot in the middle of its breast and a red-brown crown, with not a single dark feather on its head. No bigger than a man's palm, it had a loud, clear voice, chirping merrily on a beam above the prized norikers as it built a nest. Its sweet song ended in a low warble when it paused to gather straw and strands of horsehair. It wove quietly for a few minutes, then it began to sing again.

Gallant-Stallion would have enjoyed the sparrow's presence were he not in so much pain. He was severely lame, two days past striking a hoof on a sharp rock while fleeing a pack of wolves with his charge, Kalantha. Reaching the royal stables and walking into this stall were quite possibly the most onerous feats he'd attempted since coming to Paard-Peran.

He tried to think about Kalantha, safe with her brother somewhere on the palace grounds. That notion pleased him, but not enough to keep his mind away from the ache that pulsed up his leg and settled in his chest. His hoof had become so sore he could no longer put any weight on it. The groom's ministrations weren't helping—yet—though he appreciated the care and the time the man spent.

Gallant-Stallion watched the sparrow while the groom gently applied a poultice. The smell of the herbs was overly pungent and wholly unidentifiable. It chased away the comforting musty scents of the stable and made his nostrils flare in protest.

"This will draw the soreness out. I took some dried devil's claw from the cabinet. Not enough so the stable master'd miss it—he'd be furious if he discovered I'd used it on a big punch like you. Ground some white willow bark and mixed in ginseng and some other things. Put some ginseng in your feed, though not so much it'll turn your stomach. Should make you feel better."

Gallant-Stallion listened to the explanation, suspecting that the man was simply talking to himself and did not believe that any of the horses in this stable were capable of understanding. The groom was certainly oblivious that the punch only had the form of a horse, and was another creature entirely.

"And this will take down some of the fever."

The groom dipped a cloth in salted water and wrapped it around Gallant-Stallion's leg, just above the poultice that covered the hoof. "The gods know why I'm going to all of this trouble. You'll probably go lame again. Happens once, a horse is prone to it, I say. Sell you for meat then the next time. Break that girl's heart, I 'spect. But maybe it won't happen for a while."

Finished, the groom washed his hands in the salted water, then stroked Gallant-Stallion's muzzle. "A pretty horse you definitely are not," he pronounced. "But at least you've pretty eyes." He stretched a rope across the end of the stall, then stepped back and studied his handiwork. "I'll come back before the noon meal to see how you're faring."

The groom trundled toward the front of the stable, chattering to the King of Galmier's prized norikers as he went. The sparrow continued singing, and Gallant-Stallion was disappointed that other noises now intruded on the tune. The Finest heard the creak of hinges as the groom closed the wide door behind him and set a latch. There was the muted scratching of mice in the farthest corner, the wind suddenly picking up and whistling outside. He heard the clacking of small branches from the trees just beyond the wall behind him. A shrill whinny of a horse on the palace grounds was followed by the staccato orders a soldier shouted. Softest of all came the baying of a hound, probably down by the stream. The persistent nickerings of a pair of jutlands in the stalls directly across from Gallant-Stallion was the most annoying. They were heavy-bodied draft horses the color of honey, used for pulling large wagons. They'd been quiet with the groom present. But now one of them pawed at something it had found interesting in the hay, the scraping finally drawing the sparrow's curiosity and ending its song.

The jutlands and Gallant-Stallion were relegated to the rear of the royal stables and couldn't easily be seen by someone looking in the door. The Finest knew that was on purpose, as the norikers that took up the rest of the stalls were among the most magnificent horses in this part of Paard-Peran. No doubt the grooms and King Meven wanted them to be seen.

Gallant-Stallion wanted a stall near the door—not so he would be put on display, but so he could better hear what went on outside and could better listen for Kalantha. He also wanted the terrible pain in his hoof to ease and the smell from the poultice to go away. He wanted the sparrow to start singing again, even louder this time, and the jutlands to stop nickering, the big one to stop pawing. He wanted . . .

My friend.

Steadfast! Gallant-Stallion had been so engrossed in his misery he hadn't immediately registered the air turning chill or the feathering of his breath. The arrival of his mentor's spirit startled him.

It is good your charge is safe. The misty outline of an impressive steed hovered in the space between Gallant-Stallion and the jutlands. The image was so faint, the Finest wondered if he was imagining it.

Steadfast, so much has happened! The wolves . . .

There will be time to speak of that later.

And Bishop DeNogaret.

The ghost-image pricked up its ears.

Bishop DeNogaret meant to kill Kalantha! Just yesterday at the entrance to this very stable! But I stopped him. I hurt him, maybe killed him.

And saved your charge. Admirable, Gallant-Stallion.

The norikers and jutlands could not hear the mental conversation Gallant-Stallion shared with Steadfast's spirit.

The Finest were using what they called hidden speak.

The sparrow was unmindful, too. It gave up on watching the pawing jutland and wove a long strand from a noriker's mane into the side of its nest. Pleased with its handiwork, it chirped piercingly.

Kalantha is safe, yes, Steadfast. She is with her brother, the King of Galmier.

The one called Meven Montoll.

A nod.

That is good. But it is not good that you are hurt.

Gallant-Stallion snorted. *Lame, the groom called it. I would not call this pain such a simple, pleasant-sounding word. That the horses of this world suffer such a condition! And worse that I complain about it. Some are killed because of it, Steadfast. I heard the grooms talk of such. Butchered for meat.*

Steadfast wuffled sympathetically. *You should return to the Finest Court, Gallant-Stallion. In the lands of the Court you will heal quickly. Whole, you can better serve your Fallen Favorite.*

Gallant-Stallion brightened, but he remained cautious. *I hurt, yes, terribly, but I do not want to leave Kalantha just yet. There is so much to do and . . .*

You suffer needlessly, Gallant-Stallion.

Perhaps you are right. I am overdue reporting to the Finest Court. I should tell them about the Bishop, that Kalantha is safe. I should take time to heal and seek the advice of Patience and . . .

The air grew slightly warmer, and Gallant-Stallion knew that Steadfast's spirit was gone.

1 · War Torn

A proper king's feet should be deeply rooted in his country. His heart should beat with concern for his people. His head should be filled with plans for a better future. And his eyes should always observe the rest of the world.

~Sorrel Wintermane, shepherd to Bernd Sameter,
first king of Nasim-Guri

The large tent had been intended for summer festivals, when long tables spread with desserts and fruits would be arrayed inside for the dining pleasure of noble guests. But the dirt and bloodstains marked the tent's new and grim purpose this early spring.

A guard bowed and held the flap open. "Sire."

"Are you sure you want to see this, Kal?" Meven squared his shoulders and looked down into his sister's wide green eyes. "It's cold out here. It smells pretty awful in there and . . ."

"You know I've seen wounded men before, Meven." A pause: "And plenty of dead ones." She pulled her cloak tight around her. "Besides, I'd rather be with you than in that old palace of yours. I don't like the looks some of your servants give me. Your palace is . . ."

"Our palace."

"Is too big. I could get lost in it." She brushed past him, then threw her hand over her mouth and gagged. Kalantha instantly felt weak.

The cloying odor of diseased and rotting flesh was the strongest, and under that the coppery scent of blood. Cots stretched end to end in rows from the front to the back of the tent, and not a single one sat empty. The most grievously injured rested the farthest away, which was where Kalantha headed. The people tending the wounded huddled back there, clustered near a single cot and talking so their words sounded like the buzz of an insect swarm.

She passed men with bandaged arms, some splinted with what looked like chair legs. A few had woolen strips wrapped around their heads. One man's eyes were thickly bandaged; his cheeks were pink with a fever, and his hands alternately clenched and released the blanket. She stopped and stared, wondering if she should say something to comfort him.

"Why don't you go back to the palace? I'll see you there in a bit." Meven moved up next to her.

She drew her chin against her neck. "No."

"Kal . . ."

"I want to see this."

Meven put a hand on her shoulder, the gesture somehow giving her strength. She straightened and stepped back from the feverish man, nearly backing into the cot behind her.

"I want to see what the war has done."

"What I have done, you mean." Meven sucked in a breath. "This is all my fault. By the gods, all of this is because of me."

She spun and looked up. Though only two years older, he was more than a head taller. "It's not your fault, Meven. It's not your war. Bishop DeNogaret . . ."

"Wanted the war with Nasim-Guri, sure. But I was weak enough to let him talk me into it. I think a part of me wanted Nasim-Guri, and maybe a part of me still does. More land.

More subjects and more power. But I don't want this." He gestured at the cots. "I honestly never wanted any of this."

He dug the ball of his foot into the ground and opened his mouth to say something else. Kalantha took a last look at the feverish man with the bandaged eyes, then went to the back of the tent.

"They're all so young, Meven. Why did you want to come out here this morning to look at them?"

He followed her without answering, then lengthened his stride and passed her by. He nodded to a young knight he'd sparred with once, but the man was unconscious.

"Theron, are these the men brought in late last night?" Meven directed this to the tallest officer in the huddle.

The man separated from the group and stopped at attention in front of Meven. "Aye, Sire. These men fought just across the border, against fifty Nasim-Guri soldiers. They drove the enemy back beyond the river, and killed more than a few of them. About a dozen of our men were wounded in the process. The worst we brought here, the rest were patched up and sent back out to fight. The villages farther south already were full with wounded, no room for these men. Not sure if any of them will make it, after us carrying them so far. Should have stayed with them in the field until the end, then buried them."

Steeling himself, Meven took a deep breath and edged forward.

The men who were gathered around the cot parted.

Theron whispered: "His name is Weldon Smithson, Sire. His father is a prominent wheelwright in Nadir and head of the guild. That's the reason we brought him, his father being in the city. Else we would have left him somewhere along the road and buried him in a field. We're all surprised he's still with us."

Meven knelt next to the cot and took Weldon's hand. The young man offered the King a weak smile.

"Has his father been summoned?"

"Not yet, Sire. We . . ."

Meven's eyes narrowed as he looked up at Theron and the others. "He should have been summoned last night when you arrived. Doesn't matter how late the time."

"We were tending to everyone, sorting things out, Sire, and . . ."

"Summon the elder Smithson now. Right now. His wife . . ."

"She died some years ago, Weldon told us."

"Brothers? Sisters?"

"One brother, Sire, and he's fighting north of Duriam."

"Summon the elder Smithson now," Meven repeated. "Now. Have it done, Theron. Do it yourself."

The tall man gave a nod and whirled on his booted feet, nearly bumping into Kalantha, who'd crept nearer.

Meven returned his attention to Weldon. "Your father will be here soon."

Weldon shook his head, and a line of blood spilled out of his mouth. "Don't want him to see me like this, Sire. I . . ."

"He'll see you now, and later when you're well. I'll have you and him brought to the palace for dinner. Next week, in fact."

Weldon's eyes were fixed, and his hand went limp in the King's grip. His breathing grew shallow.

"Weldon?"

The young man coughed, pinkish bubbles trailing down his chin. Meven raised Weldon's head.

"It will be a fine dinner," Meven continued. "Roast goose, I think. Brushed with butter and stuffed with rice and some of those tiny onions from the fall harvest that the cooks saved in the pantry. They say onions are the food of poor people, but I like them well enough. We'll have soup, of course. The cooks make soup every night. I get tired of it. Dessert. They always make dessert, too. I never tire of that. Have you a favorite cake?"

Sweat beads covered Weldon's face, and his skin had gone

paler in the few moments Meven held him. The young man was practically as white as parchment.

"Spice cake is my favorite, I think. My sister, Kalantha, she's right here behind me . . . she likes any kind of cake. The cooks put the frosting on thick for special occasions. And if we've raisins imported from the south, they use some of those, too. Do you think you'd like spice cake, Weldon?"

"He's dead, Sire."

One of the soldiers pulled the blanket up and waited for Meven to move.

"A dagger to the stomach, they said. Truly surprised he lived as long as he did, considering it took days to get here. We were certain he wouldn't make it through the night. I think he held on just because we told him you were coming by to visit everyone this morning. Said he'd never seen the King up close."

Meven pulled his arm free and released the dead man's hand. He stood shakily, his eyes locked on the corpse's fixed gaze.

The soldier tugged the blanket over Weldon's head. Behind Meven, a soldier covered another corpse.

"You'll clean him up before his father comes?" This came from Kalantha. "And take him outside this tent? No need for the elder Smithson to come into this horrid, smelly place."

The soldier looked to the King.

"Yes, clean him up," Meven said. "Put him in something not so bloody. He's about my size, so you can ask the steward for one of my tunics. Lay him in the palace entry hall if you'd like. Kal's right. His father . . . none of these men's families should see them in this place."

Meven stared at the blanket-draped form until Kalantha tugged on his arm. "We should go, Meven, and let these men tend the wounded. They're not working with you here."

Meven numbly concurred and let her lead him from the tent.

Kalantha breathed deep once the soldier closed the flap behind them. "Smells better out here. Will smell even better the farther we get from the tent. I think . . ." She spotted two more tents, smaller than this one and closer to the wall. She realized more wounded were in them. Between the tents was a tarp covering a mound of something.

"Bodies," Meven said, following her gaze. "They put the dead outside and cover them up until the families arrange for burial. And if there are no families, or if they can't tell who the dead are, they bury them in a mass grave near the cliff."

Kalantha continued to stare. "How many?" she asked finally. When he didn't immediately answer, she asked again. "How many soldiers have died?"

"Knights and soldiers," Meven said. "And some villagers who joined up along the way." His voice was flat. He glanced down at his hands and saw they were covered with Weldon's blood. The front of his richly embroidered tunic was blood soaked, too. "I don't know how many. A lot, I'd guess. Not near so many as Nasim-Guri has lost, the soldiers tell me. Too many, though. There are more dead and wounded in the villages between here and the Nasim-Guri border. Too many."

They didn't move and didn't speak for several minutes. The wind fluttered the edge of the tarp, revealing the bare feet of several corpses. A dog barked in the distance. Closer, a knight drilled a gathering of soldiers preparing to march to Nasim-Guri. They looked young and clumsy.

"How could I have wanted all of this blood, Kal?" He still looked at his hands. "How could I have wanted all this death?"

"Bishop DeNogaret . . ."

"He encouraged me to make war, Kal. But he didn't force me. He couldn't have forced me to do something I didn't truly want to do."

She vehemently shook her head and opened her mouth to argue. But she stopped herself.

"I wanted a bigger country, Kal. Maybe I still do, a part of me wants it. But I don't need a bigger country. Galmier is more than enough for me to rule." He let out a clipped laugh. "Too big for me to rule. Prince Edan should be alive and King. The crown falling to me is an accident." He finally raised his head and looked toward the palace. "I needed the Bishop's help to manage all of this . . . the estate, the city, the country, and the war. We're very close to winning, my advisors tell me. Nasim-Guri could be ours in a week or two, the capital falling. The Bishop—"

"Now you have me."

Meven smiled, honest emotion behind it. "I *will* need your help, Kal."

"Bishop DeNogaret, is he going to live?"

Meven pointed to a tower with an elaborately crenelated top. "He's high in the north wing, and I've a few servants tending him." He shrugged. "They think he'll live. But they think he'll be crippled. Rue crushed his legs and broke his ribs."

"A horrid man."

"Bishop DeNogaret raised you and me, Kal. I just can't imagine why he'd try to kill you. Maybe he went mad. Happens to people, you know."

"Have you seen him?"

Meven shook his head.

Kalantha closed her eyes and remembered their arrival yesterday. Rue was moving slowly because of his lame leg. She took him to the stables and was looking for a groom to see to him when Bishop DeNogaret appeared. He had a knife, and he tried to kill her with it, all the while raving that he should have done the deed himself in the first place rather than relying on his bird lackeys. She would have died, but Rue attacked the Bishop and slammed his hooves into the man's chest. Rue would have finished it, but she and Meven pulled the punch back. The Bishop was carried to the palace. She wondered if she should have let Rue kill him.

"I'm certain Bishop DeNogaret had something to do with the assassin-birds, the ones that tried to kill us . . . and tried to kill me on the way here. That book I brought from the Vershan Monastery, it has a picture in it of someone who looks just like Bishop DeNogaret. There are birds mentioned in the book, smart evil ones. You promised you'd look at the book, Meven. I think Bishop DeNogaret is far more powerful than we realized. He caused the war, I know it."

Meven watched the knight drill the young soldiers. "Not right now, Kal."

"I think the book could be important. You promised."

"What's important is you going back to the palace."

"No. I'm going to stay with you and—"

"Go back to the palace and pack a few changes of clothes. We're leaving today for Duriam in Nasim-Guri."

Her eyes widened in surprise.

Meven faced the tarp-covered mound of bodies. "We're going to see King Hunter Silverwood in Duriam. I'm going to put an end to this war, Kal. No more killing. No more mounds of bodies waiting to be put in the ground. I have to summon my commanders, tell them the war ends this minute. Then I'm going to make amends to King Silverwood. Somehow patch all of this up. I could win in a week or two, have a lot more land and subjects, but—"

"You're right to stop it now." Kalantha's smile reached her eyes. "I'll start packing right away, Meven. But the book. I really think you need to look at it, at least the part with—"

"We'll leave this afternoon, Kal, after the noon meal and before sunset, after I've met with the commanders. I'll send them out along the fields to help spread the news. Then there will be no more blood spilled because of me. Never again because of me."

"The book, Meven. You have to—"

"I'll read it later, I promise. A book is not nearly so important as putting an end to this war." He made a huffing sound, his breath fluttering the hair that hung down over his forehead. "I promise I'll look at the book when we get back from Nasim-Guri. After the war is done."

Kalantha decided it was an argument she couldn't win and headed toward the palace. Neither she nor Meven saw a thin crow hovering above the largest tent-infirmary. It flew toward the palace, reaching it long before Kalantha. Perching on the north crenelated tower, it cawed to a dozen blackbirds, which were quick to join it.

"Ninéon," the crow said. "I must find Ninéon and tell her of King Meven's intentions."

"Tentions?" a big cowbird asked.

"Intentions, plans," one of the blackbirds corrected. "What plans, Arlee?" Not all of the blackbirds were capable of speech, but this one was and the crow knew her to be overly curious. "What plans does the man-king have? Are they interesting plans?"

Two blackbirds with small red patches on their wings moved close to the crow, their dark eyes wide and shining. One bobbed its head and made a sound that approximated "what?"

"What, what?" repeated the blackbirds who could speak. "Arlee, what?"

The largest edged near the crow and met its gaze. "Interesting plans, Arlee, else you would not want to find Ninéon. Share what you know!"

The thin crow drew itself up to its full height and fluffed its feathers before it divulged its precious news. "It is about King Meven."

"The man-king," one of the blackbirds cut in. "The one who glitters like a peacock."

Arlee narrowed his eyes to needle-fine slits. "King Meven says he will end the precious war."

The blackbirds squawked, and the nearest shook its head. "Bad plan. Most unfortunate."

The crow clacked its beak. "Ninéon will be angry."

"Yes! Bad angry, Arlee," the nearest blackbird agreed. "Bad, bad angry."

"But Ninéon will not let it happen," Arlee continued. "Ninéon will come here, and she will find the Bishop."

"Bishop DeNogaret," one of the blackbirds supplied, pleased with himself that he'd recalled the old priest's name.

"Yes, DeNogaret. Ninéon will talk to the Bishop. The Bishop will dominate King Meven again, manipulate him like the soft mud of the riverbank. Then the man-king will make the war go on. On and on and on."

"On and on!" The smallest blackbird spread its wings. "We will find Ninéon for you, Arlee, and she will make certain the blood continues to flow."